RACK & RUIN

THIRDS BOOK 3

CHARLIE COCHET

Rack & Ruin

http://charliecochet.com

http://reesedante.com

Proofing by Susi Selva

RACK & RUIN

New York City's streets are more dangerous than ever with the leaderless Order of Adrasteia and the Ikelos Coalition, a newly immerged Therian group, at war. Innocent civilians are caught in the crossfire and although the THIRDS round up more and more members of the Order in the hopes of keeping the volatile group from reorganizing, the members of the Coalition continue to escape and wreak havoc in the name of vigilante justice.

Worse yet, someone inside the THIRDS has been feeding the Coalition information. It's up to Destructive Delta to draw out the mole and put an end to the war before anyone else gets hurt. But to get the job done, the team will have to work through the aftereffects of the Therian Youth Center bombing. A skirmish with Coalition members leads Agent Dexter J. Daley to a shocking discovery and suddenly it becomes clear that the random violence isn't so random. There's more going on than Dex and Sloane originally believed, and their fiery partnership is put to the test. As the case takes an explosive turn, Dex and Sloane are in danger of losing more than their relationship.

ONE

"He's gonna run."

Dex took his partner's tac vest from him and handed it to his brother in the BearCat. "You think?" He peered out one of the BearCat's ballistic windows but couldn't see jack this time of night, especially since their little friend was well camouflaged among the Central Park greenery. It didn't help that Hobbs had somehow managed to park their black tactical vehicle in a thicket of trees shrouded in enough darkness to make Dex feel as if a black hole had sucked him up. He had to give his Therian teammate credit. Hobbs could park the BearCat up a freakin' flagpole if he had to. Maybe being a huge-ass Therian made it easy for him to maneuver huge-ass vehicles. Parks and Recreation was going to be so pissed if they found out they'd been driving off the roads.

"He always runs." Sloane removed his thigh rig next and handed it over. Dex promptly passed it off to Cael. His brother huffed but took it without question, undoubtedly knowing Dex was doing it to annoy him. Ah, the perks of working with family. Rosa sat on the bench, looking on in amusement and checking her Post-shift Trauma Care (PSTC) kit, while Hobbs sat in the driver's seat inside the front cabin bugging his spiky blond-haired partner. Calvin was in the passenger seat being a grump as he cleaned the scope of his sniper tranq rifle.

Dex had no idea what had Calvin sporting the pouty face. He wouldn't be surprised if it had something to do with his best bud sitting across from him. Either Hobbs was oblivious to Calvin's mood, or he was purposefully ignoring it. Considering he was sitting inches away from the nozzle of his partner's tranq gun, it would probably be in Hobbs's best interest to play nice. Dex had walked in on the pair sucking face back at the hospital after Hobbs had been hurt in the Therian Youth Center bombing. It had been one hell of a surprise and explained the pair's off behavior leading up to the incident. Things quickly returned to normal between the two afterward. Somewhat. If Dex were a betting man, he'd say that was the problem. Hobbs was carrying on as if nothing had happened, and Calvin had been hoping something had changed. He'd confided as much to Dex back at the hospital. Whatever was going on, Dex hoped the two managed to work it out soon.

Letty was checking the magazines of her various guns. And Ash... Dex didn't know where the hell Ash was. Just another shift for Destructive Delta.

Sloane pulled off his boots, and when he stood to remove his uniform shirt, Dex couldn't help but try again. "As much as we all love seeing you get nekkid, partner, I wish you'd at least reconsider—"

"Nope."

"Dude, the rest of your shit is heavy enough," Dex whined, lifting his arms to show the various pieces of tactical equipment hanging off them, the heaviest being the PSTC kit he carried to aid his partner post-shift.

"I'm not getting rid of my sneakers."

Dex let his arms fall back to his sides. "They're not even government issued!"

Sloane shrugged. "Don't care."

"You've had to replace two pairs in the last four months."

Sloane paused in the middle of unbuttoning his shirt to arch an eyebrow at him. "And whose fault is that?"

"It was an accident." Dex blinked innocently. The look on Sloane's face told him his partner wasn't buying it. Damn it. One would think being the team leader's secret boyfriend at the very least would earn him the right to get away with things others couldn't. But in Dex's case, it meant he got away with less because Sloane knew him far better than anyone—with the exception of his family—and loved to burst his bubble.

"As in you accidentally dropped my sneakers off the Brooklyn Bridge?"

Dex did his best to look affronted. "What are you suggesting? It was a windy day."

"Funny how nothing else got blown away," Sloane grumbled, pulling off his shirt and tossing it over Dex's head. He felt like a coatrack. The rest of the team didn't help at all with their snickering. A loud *thunk* sounded at his feet, and Dex pulled the shirt off his head to swipe up a boot.

"Size fourteen, man!" Dex waved Sloane's huge black boot at him. "Somewhere on the Hudson, a duck's using your sneaker as a flotation device."

"Ducks already float."

"Yeah, but their little legs must get tired of moving them

about." Dex wiggled his index and middle fingers to simulate duck feet. His half-naked, sexy-as-sin boyfriend held a hand up to stop any further protest. Dex wished the truck were empty so he could do some of his own pouncing on his jaguar Therian partner.

"Do you mind if I pause this incongruous exchange on waterfowl to catch our guy?"

Dex held back a smile. "Ooh, someone's been playing online Scrabble with Cael again. How many points did *incongruous* get you?"

When Sloane didn't reply, Dex turned to his brother.

"Fourteen," Cael offered cheerfully, earning himself a scowl from Sloane.

Dex shook his head. "Could have gotten twenty on Words With Friends."

"How—"

Rosa cut Sloane off, motioning to the large console's surveillance monitor, which had been keeping an eye out for their target via infrared video. "Looks like Sloane's right. *Cabrón's* in his Therian form."

"Striptease is over," Sloane informed them, hitting the large button on the BearCat's side panel, causing the screen to drop from the truck's roof so he could finish undressing and shift in private. Without his favorite peepshow, Dex turned to his brother who was looking somewhat spaced out. It had started a few weeks ago, and it was beginning to worry Dex.

"What kind of Therian is our friend?" Dex asked. When his brother didn't reply, Dex gave him a nudge. "You okay?"

"Yeah, I'm fine. Austen Payne is a cheetah Therian."

So his brother had heard him? And what? Chose to ignore him? "Cael—"

Cael shook his head, his stern expression telling Dex his brother wasn't in a sharing mood. Dex had considered pushing the matter but conceded now was not the time. Something was up with Cael and had been since he'd been in the hospital along with Hobbs after the bombing. Whatever was going on, it had to do with Ash. The guy had called in sick this morning, which was apparently like the second time he'd done so in the twenty-something years since joining the THIRDS. Lately Cael was easily distracted, his head elsewhere, which was dangerous not only for him but the rest of the team. Yeah, Dex would definitely be having a talk with his little brother. For now, he turned his attention to Rosa.

"So tell me something about this Austen guy."

"He's a slippery little shit," Rosa said, though she was smiling affectionately when she said it. "Fast as fuck too."

"Is that your professional opinion?" Dex teased, receiving a couple of loving expletives in Spanish. "How the hell is Sloane going to catch him?" If a cheetah Therian didn't want to get caught, he didn't get caught. Unless he made a stupid mistake. Rosa was right about how fast they were, whether in their Human or Therian forms. Dex remembered all the times he'd attempted to outrun his brother when they were kids. He never even came close to catching up with him despite being older and having longer legs—at least in his Human form. The only problem for cheetah Therians was the distance. They could only handle high speeds in short bursts. If Austen ran, Sloane could still catch up once the guy tired out. 'Course, who the hell knew where he'd run to by then.

"Sloane's not going to chase him," Rosa said, a wicked gleam in her eye. "He's going to hunt him. No one stalks like our team leader."

"Tell me about it," Dex muttered. The guy had a bad habit of walking into a room and scaring the ever-living fuck out of Dex. It wasn't right that a guy of Sloane's size made no sound when he walked in his Human form. He was like a sexy ninja.

Speaking of his sexy ninja partner, the screen rose, and Dex crouched down in front of the huge black jaguar, talking quietly. "You be careful." Sloane's glowing amber eyes stared at him, and Dex eyed him warily. He was familiar with that look. "Don't do it. Don't—" A broad, sandpaper tongue licked him from his chin to his ear. "Damn it! Right in the ear! Every freakin' time." One would think he'd have learned after the first few dozen times his partner had licked him to annoy him. "That was—as usual—extremely unpleasant. Thank you. I appreciate it."

Dex stood and wiped at his face and ear with his sleeve, ignoring his teammates chortling behind him. Letty opened one of the BearCat's backdoors, but Sloane had to quickly rub up against Dex's legs to leave his mark—as if it wasn't all over Dex already—before leaping out of the truck. That done, Dex went to the console where his brother was tracking Sloane. He watched his Therian partner pad silently toward some bushes before he disappeared into the shadows. Dex could have sworn there had been something stuck on his partner's back paw. Well, there was no way to know until Sloane returned. "You sure Sloane will be able to catch him?"

"Always does," Cael murmured.

"So why does Austen run?"

Cael shrugged. "I think he likes it."

"What do you mean 'he likes it'?"

His brother's cheeks flushed. Uh-oh. Dex knew that look. Cael worried his bottom lip and Dex waited while his brother racked his sweet little brain trying to figure out whether he should spill or not. "Austen's got a crush on Sloane."

Dex eyed his brother, a silent conversation going on between them in which Cael gave him a shrug and an apologetic smile. Interesting. Dex pursed his lips but said nothing. He sidled up to the bench before squeezing himself in between Rosa and Letty. There wasn't much to do now other than wait and tease a little information out of his teammates.

"Is this Austen guy reliable?" Dex asked. "And how come this is the first I'm hearing of him?"

Letty looped her arm around Dex's, and he smiled. He could always count on Rosa and Letty to bring him down to earth. They were both brutally honest and straightforward but always with the best intentions at heart. Sometimes it felt like they were the only two with functioning relationships. Rosa was happily attached to her long-time girlfriend, and Letty was happily attached to whichever hottie made her toes curl that month. This month it was a firefighter from Brooklyn with dimples in all the right places.

"Austen's good," Letty offered. "Practically grew up working for us thanks to Sloane. He found the guy years ago when he was just a kid, got him a job. I don't remember the story, but I'm sure Sloane'll tell you if you ask. Austen's a THIRDS SSA—Squadron Specialist agent. You haven't heard of him because, technically, he doesn't exist. Those guys don't work out of the office. You have to have high-level clearance just to access a file with his name on it. Every squad has their own specialist agent. Since they also function as confidential informants, they have to keep a low profile. Austen's been off on some job for Lieutenant

Sparks. He's got mad skills. If you see him or talk to him, it's because he wants you to."

"Sloane's coming back. And he's got Austen," Cael called out over his shoulder.

"That was quick." Dex sprang to his feet and decided he'd meet his partner outside in case Austen decided he didn't fancy getting in the truck. Having had no experience with the agent, Dex had no clue how Austen would react. Sometimes Therians were cooperative until they neared the big, scary black vehicle. The idea of being caged didn't appeal, and Dex couldn't blame them.

Dex jumped down and started for his partner when he noticed Sloane was walking funny. It was only when Sloane got close that Dex could see the reason why.

"Oh shit!" Dex doubled over laughing as Sloane hobbled over like he was drunk, the ferocity of having Austen in his jaws offset by the sheer hilarity of his partner trying to shake a black sock off his back paw. "Oh my God, I can't breathe," Dex wheezed, tears in his eyes.

Sloane huffed and continued to shake at his back paw, at one point skipping on his other three. Dex thought he was going to need Rosa to bring him oxygen. He'd been right. There had been something stuck on his partner's paw when he'd left the truck. How Sloane had missed a sock was beyond him, but it was the funniest shit Dex had ever seen. "Hold up!" Dex managed to get himself together long enough to jog after his partner who stopped and stuck his back leg out. With a grin, Dex tugged the sock off. "Okay." He received a huff in thanks.

Dex couldn't help but feel somewhat bad for the cheetah Therian dangling from Sloane's lethal jaws. The cheetah reminded him too much of Cael. Austen was small, lean, and clearly used to being dragged away by Sloane, judging by the way he hung in there looking almost bored by the whole thing. He didn't attempt to get away even once. His front paws were crossed as if he were chilling. It became obvious to Dex that Austen trusted Sloane. Any other Therian would be shitting himself.

As soon as his partner reached the truck, he released Austen and hissed. Austen chirped and pushed his nose against Sloane's, which made his partner's ears flatten against his head before he let out a roar. Not surprising, it startled Austen so bad had he been a cartoon, his spots would have fallen off. A bristled Austen promptly jumped up into the BearCat with Sloane on his tail. Dex followed and closed the doors behind them. The privacy screen dropped, and Austen shifted first while Sloane sat patiently beside Dex, waiting his turn. Since Rosa had experience working with cheetah Therians—considering her partner was one—she provided Austen with Post-shift Trauma Care, along with a THIRDS supplied disposable set of clothes, which she handed to him once he was strong enough to stick an arm out from behind the screen. A low grumble later, and Rosa disappeared behind the screen.

While Rosa helped their SSA regain Human functionality, Dex took a seat on the small single bench beside the weapons cage. Sloane immediately dropped his head on Dex's lap, looking for an ear scratch, and Dex obliged, smiling when he heard the deep chainsaw-like purr and felt it vibrating against his leg.

"At least when he sheds all over you, you can't see it." Calvin cast his tiger Therian partner an accusing glare. Hobbs sat up with a frown. He reached over and gave Calvin's blond hair a light tug. "I don't shed," Calvin protested. Hobbs nodded. Clearly, he disagreed. Dex watched the two in amusement as they argued, despite

Calvin being the only vocal one. It was amazing how much Hobbs could say with his expressions and hand movements alone.

A slender, sinewy young Therian who seemed to be in his midtwenties stepped out from behind the screen with a fierce yawn. He ruffled his dark hair and strutted over to the bench where he dropped down beside Letty with a wide grin. The guy looked like he'd just rolled out of bed after performing at some rock gig, despite the out-of-place outfit he sported.

Dex didn't have time to further study the agent before Sloane disappeared behind the screen. By now no one thought twice about Dex following his partner in. They figured after nearly a year of working closely together, Sloane no longer cared if his partner saw him naked post-shift. Of course, they had no idea Dex and Sloane did a lot more than work together, and seeing his partner naked usually led to naughtier things in private.

As soon as Sloane had shifted, Dex began the Post-shift Trauma Care. He hoped whatever information Sloane was looking to get from Austen, he'd be able to get it quickly. Sloane needed to eat a hefty meal filled with meat and carbs if he was going to regain his full strength. With the power bars and Gatorade finished, Dex helped Sloane back into his uniform. Not long after, Sloane was on his feet. He gave Dex a wink and a playful smack on the ass before hitting the button for the screen.

"Why did you run, Austen?" Sloane asked as he took the seat Dex had vacated earlier. "Again."

Across from him, Austen blinked at Sloane. "What do you mean, *why*? Because you guys are fucking scary, that's why. I never know who's gonna come after me. There are all these big dudes with guns running around these days and even bigger Therians with sharp teeth that could crush my tiny bones. Also, we cheetah Therians are skittish by nature, you know." He looked up at Cael and held his fist out for a bump. "Am I right, bro?"

Cael scowled at him.

"Dude," Austen whispered hoarsely. "You're gonna leave me hanging in front of the fit jaguar Therian? Not cool."

With a grunt, Cael bumped his fist against Austen's, drawing a big grin from him.

"We small Felids gotta stick together."

"You done socializing?" Sloane asked.

"Yep. What can I do for you, Agent Broody?"

Dex bit his bottom lip to keep himself from laughing at the nickname. Sounded like something he would come up with. It certainly described his sexy partner to a T.

"Don't suppose you're going to reconsider my offer for a private workout session?"

Cael hadn't been kidding. Austen did have a crush on Sloane. Dex was still trying to get a read on the guy. Part of him wanted to like the cheeky cheetah; the other part wanted to dislike him for the sheer fact he wanted to get his grubby little paws on Sloane. The guy made no attempt to hide his attraction to the larger Felid. Then again, Austen wasn't the first to have a crush on Destructive Delta's team leader. Dex had heard plenty of talk around the office from both male and female agents attracted to his partner, though no one ever approached Sloane. Hell, if Dex hadn't been partnered with him, he would have chalked Sloane up as being out of his league. There was also something about his sexy partner that screamed, "Approach with caution."

Austen turned toward Dex, seeming to notice him for the first time. He opened his mouth to say something, then paused before leaning in Dex's direction. "Damn. Look at those baby blues. Aren't you going to introduce me to your new pouty-lipped partner, Broody Bear?"

"That's Agent Daley. I told you if you called me that again I was going to kick your ass. You wanna pay attention even a little?" It was as if Sloane hadn't even spoken.

"Well hello, Agent Daley. You are one lucky dude. Destructive Delta has fine agents." He lolled his head back to grin widely at Hobbs. "And I do mean *fine*."

My God, it was like the guy was in heat. Hobbs smiled shyly before noticing his partner's subtle glare, prompting him to drop his gaze to his tac pants and brush off some dust Dex doubted was even there.

Sloane sat back and laced his fingers over his stomach. He stretched his long legs out in front of him and crossed them at the ankles. "Am I going to have to get you neutered?"

Austen gave such a start that he nearly fell off the bench. "That ain't funny, man. You shouldn't joke about shit like that."

A wicked grin came onto Sloane's face. "Who said I was joking?"

"I see. It's business as usual, then. Fine. It's getting ugly out there. I've got no sympathy for those bastards from the Order, but it's pretty messed up the way the Coalition's dealing with them. These dudes don't fuck around. I mean, they hunt the Humans down, catch them, beat the tar out of them, then leave them somewhere visible to warn the others. That's usually when someone calls you guys."

"Any luck tracking the Coalition?" Sloane asked.

Austen shook his head. "I haven't been able to get close enough. These guys aren't like the Order. They've got training. Not official government training, but like they've been shown the basics by someone who's trained. They know how to stay hidden. Wherever they go, they have two members in their Therian forms to sniff out anyone who might be stupid enough to follow them. And before you ask, it's never the same two Therians. So cross-referencing their classification through your fancy computer will probably give you a hit on every Therian agent in your organization."

"Great."

"Sorry. I know it's a big load of nada. *But* I can confirm you do have a traitor in your midst."

Crap. Not that they hadn't known but having someone else confirm it made it doubly fucked up. "How do you know?" Dex asked.

"Like I said. These guys haven't been officially trained. They've been shown the ropes by someone who has. An agent. There are two male Therians leading the Coalition. One of them communicates with someone several times a day and usually gives orders based on whatever he's been told. I've seen him answer his phone several times and, right after, tell his team to retreat. Seconds later, THIRDS agents show up."

Sloane nodded his acknowledgment. "Are you able to identify any of them?"

"No. They wear black masks that cover their heads and necks. The kind tactical teams wear under their helmets. Makes it so you can't see any distinctive features. The main guy I've seen only once. Well, all I saw was his figure. He's fucking huge. He was wearing one of those black masks, a black long-sleeved shirt with a bulletproof vest, and black-and-gray camouflage pants. It's no wonder the press keeps thinking they're THIRDS agents the way they're geared up. For all we know, your rat might be in there, but there's no way to tell. They don't let their guard down for a moment. I get the feeling they don't reveal their identities to anyone, not even each other."

"What about names?" Dex asked. "They have to call each other something, don't they?"

Austen's frown didn't bode well. "They use numbered codes, like one-eleven and twenty-three twenty-six. Have fun trying to figure out what the hell they represent."

Sloane nodded to Cael who added the numbers to the notes he was taking on his tablet. Cael would undoubtedly be adding an algorithm to Themis to find out what the numbers could pertain to. They'd be looking into that later, though Austen had a point. The possibilities were staggering.

"Any idea how many there are?"

Again, Austen shook his head in response to Sloane's question. "I can't imagine there are many. Whenever I've seen them, they've been in groups of five or six at most. Couldn't say how many groups there are, but maybe if you cross-reference incident times with locations across the boroughs, you might get a rough idea. Can't be two places at once, right?" Sloane gave Austen a nod of approval, which made Austen grin widely. "See. I'm not just a pretty face."

"All right," Sloane replied with a smirk before continuing with his questioning. "Anything on the Order?"

"I've thrown a few hooks out on that one. I'll let you know if anyone bites."

Sloane stood and held his hand out to Austen. "Good work. Contact me if you get anything."

"You bet."

"And next time," Sloane warned, though there was a hint of teasing in his voice, "try not to run."

Austen strode over to the end of the BearCat and turned to give Sloane a wink. "Now why would I give up the chance to be chased by a hot agent?" He saluted Sloane before opening up one of the doors and hopping out. He disappeared into the trees before Dex blinked. Rosa wasn't kidding. The guy was fast, even in Human form.

"All right, team. It's been a long day. Let's head back to HQ. Hobbs, get us out of here and stop by a drive-thru on the way. I'm starving." Sloane took a seat on the bench next to Rosa, and Dex dropped down beside him. They buckled up as Hobbs drove them out of the park.

Dex noticed his partner lean back against the truck's padded wall, then abruptly sit forward. Rosa and Letty didn't notice as they were chatting away, and Cael was secured behind the console, though he was staring off into space. Now that Dex thought about it, he never saw Sloane sit back against the wall like everyone else did. Dex leaned into his partner, his voice low.

"Hey, you okay?"

Sloane's smile went straight to Dex's groin. "Yeah, why?"

"The way you pulled away from the wall all of a sudden."

"You noticed that, huh?"

"Yep." There wasn't much Dex didn't notice about his partner, whether on the job or off. They might not have been officially dating for long, but they'd been seeing each other for nearly eight months. In that time they'd been through a hell of a lot together.

Sloane seemed to think about Dex's observation before answering. "It makes me feel sick."

"Motion sickness?" That couldn't be right. Surely if his partner felt motion sickness, Dex would have figured it out long before now.

Sloane shook his head and leaned into Dex. "It feels too

much like that chair."

Chair? What chair would make Sloane feel sick? An image flashed through Dex's mind, and he winced. Right. *That* chair. For years Sloane had been strapped down into a padded chair at the First Gen Research Facility while scientists did God only knew what to him and countless other Therian children in order to learn more about Therians. Dex could only imagine what the government had put Sloane through, and he saw enough pain in his partner's eyes to know it had been horrifying.

Dex's own experience with that damnable chair had come only recently, and although he was certain it couldn't compare to what Sloane had suffered, Dex was still finding it difficult to forget. His ankles, wrists, and head had been strapped down to the padded medical chair. It was the last thing he remembered from that day at the facility before Isaac Pearce plunged a needle into his neck and pulled his strings like a puppet, with Dex eager to please.

Instinctively, Dex rubbed the small, newly healed scar on his leg. If Sloane hadn't shot him and taken him down, Dex would have done exactly what that bastard Isaac had asked him to do. He would have killed an innocent man and then himself. Months later he still couldn't remember anything no matter how hard he tried. All he knew was what Sloane had told him. It frustrated the hell out of Dex.

"Dex?"

Dex snapped out of it to find Sloane watching him worriedly. "Are *you* okay?"

"Sorry. Just thinking. My next dentist appointment should prove interesting."

Sloane's expression softened, and he gave Dex's leg a pat, allowing his hand to linger a few seconds longer than necessary. "It'll get easier."

"Thanks."

Five minutes later they'd pulled up at a fast-food drive-thru, and Dex said a silent thanks to Austen for forcing Sloane to shift. The only time his partner indulged in anything remotely unhealthy was post-shift when his Therian body demanded meat and lots of calories. Hobbs waited patiently while Dex sat on his lap, facing the drive-thru speaker, and put in the team's order. This particular fast-food chain offered post-shift meals that had enough double quarter pounders to send a Human heart screaming for the hills. Dex put in everyone else's orders, then turned to Hobbs.

"What do you want, big guy?"

Hobbs pointed to the Therian specials and a meal with an Angus beef burger that looked like it was the size of Dex's head.

"You got it. Cal?"

"I'm not hungry," Calvin muttered. Dex twisted to look at Calvin who was staring moodily out his window. Turning back to Hobbs, Dex arched an eyebrow at him, and Hobbs shook his head. He pointed to the regular Human-sized menu and held up four fingers.

"Number four it is." Dex put in the order, Calvin protesting behind him.

"Damn it, Ethan. I said I wasn't hungry."

From the corner of his eye, Dex saw Hobbs give Calvin a pointed, no-nonsense look. Come to think of it, Dex couldn't remember Calvin having had anything when they'd stopped for lunch earlier that day. They'd been called out on a Coalition sighting, but as Austen had remarked, by the time they'd gotten there the group was long gone.

"Fine," Calvin grumbled, then pulled out his iPhone

from one of his pockets along with his headphones and stuck them in his ears. Dex got off Hobbs so the guy could drive up to the next window.

"What's eating him?" Dex asked Hobbs, his voice lowered. "You two still haven't worked things out?"

Hobbs shook his head, his expression troubled but he didn't "say" anything else. He simply pointed forward to let Dex know the line was moving. He clearly wasn't ready to share.

"Okay, but if you want someone to talk to, you just come find me." "Talk" being a relative term where Hobbs was concerned, though by now Dex had learned Hobbs could communicate just as easily with little to no words than most people did with whole conversations. Dex enjoyed Hobbs's company. The silence was never uncomfortable, and although Dex knew he fell into the category of people who talked too much, he appreciated Hobbs's sedate nature.

After they picked up their food, Hobbs parked the BearCat across a row of empty parking spaces, and they all got busy eating. Dex noticed how Hobbs reached over and plucked the closest ear bud out of Calvin's ear. That earned him a scowl, but Hobbs smiled widely. It was a sort of crooked schoolboy smile that was hard to stay mad at. Dex was glad Calvin wasn't immune either, and the blond agent's frown faltered before he laughed. He affectionately called his friend an asshole before stealing some of his fries.

"So how long has your brother had pre-birthday-party parties?" Sloane asked Cael.

"Since he was a kid."

"And Maddock went with it?"

"This is Dex we're talking about. It's better to surrender and go along for the ride than try and fight him on something he wants. Am I wrong?" Cael gave him a knowing smile.

Sloane hung his head as if in shame. "You're not wrong."

"You're so screwed," Rosa said, letting out an evil cackle.

"Thank you, Rosa. I appreciate that."

"Welcome to my world," Cael added.

Dex waved a hand at them. "You guys realize I'm sitting right here. Still, I enjoy listening to how fabulous you all think I am."

"More like what a pain in the ass you are," Cael said with a snort.

"But I'm a cute pain in the ass. Admit it. Look at these dimples." Dex pointed to his cheeks and grinned.

Sloane laughed before catching himself. "Crap. I *am* screwed."

Rosa, Cael, and Letty laughed over Dex's antics, and Dex leaned over Sloane to defend his honor when he felt Sloane's hand slip under his ass cheek and squeeze. Dex gave a start and blinked at his partner. With a wicked grin, Sloane leaned over to whisper at him.

"I might be screwed, but tonight you're going to be fucked."

Dex sat back and did his best to fight the hard-on Sloane's growly threat was giving him. The bastard. He knew they still had to get back to HQ, shower, and change before heading home. It would be at least another couple of hours before Sloane could make good on his threat. Dex told himself that was okay. He'd have two hours to devise a way to get back at his lover. The thought alone had Dex grinning. Yep, Sloane was most certainly screwed.

TWO

"Oh yeah. That's it, baby." Dex shimmied over to Sloane, bumping him with his hip. "Dude, come on."

Sloane shook his head, smiling as he took a sip of his beer. "Nope." He had to admire his partner's tenacity. Whether on the job or off, when Dexter J. Daley wanted something, he went after it until he got it, and he used whatever means necessary. If someone had pointed to Dex that first day they'd met and told Sloane they were going to end up together, Sloane would have ordered an immediate psych eval on them. Now, it was hard to imagine his life without that crooked boyish grin or infectious laugh.

"Can't or won't?" Dex pulled some funky disco moves Sloane was certain would make any other guy look like a giant douche, but not his boyfriend. *Boyfriend.* There's a word he was still getting used to. His boyfriend was the only guy he knew who had pre-birthday-party parties. Dex leaned into Sloane, talking low. "Come on, man. Everyone's drunk off their asses. No one's going to care if we dance together. I've danced with half the Defense Department. Even Hobbs danced with me."

Sloane cringed at the memory. "I'm pretty sure your horrifying attempt to teach him the Running Man does not qualify as dancing. Besides, Ash isn't drunk." Sloane made sure no one was watching before subtly squeezing Dex's side, making him squirm with a husky laugh that went straight to Sloane's dick. Then again, there wasn't much about the sexy blond that didn't get Sloane hard. Usually all it took was that disarming smile. That smile was dangerous. Coupled with those pale-blue eyes and those plump soft lips... Sloane really needed to get a hold of himself.

"That's because Ash's blood is made of acid or something equally toxic." Dex took Sloane's beer from him, his eyes on Sloane as he put the bottle to his lips and took a couple of gulps, exposing his neck. The little bastard. He knew exactly what he was doing.

"Damn it, Dex." Sloane forced himself to look away. The last thing he needed was to walk around with a hard-on in an apartment filled with fellow agents.

"Dance with me."

"I don't dance." *Why are you even trying? You know he's going to get his way. He always gets his way.* Sloane figured he should at least make it look like he'd tried. He started by swiping his beer back from his sexy partner.

"Ash is busy threatening people with imminent death if they puke on his floor. I still can't believe he volunteered to have my pre-birthday-party party at his place." Dex narrowed his eyes in suspicion, and Sloane tried not to laugh. His partner hadn't stopped questioning Ash's motives since their gruff friend offered to have the party at his apartment. Ash was a neat freak and hated having his stuff touched.

"He said there'd be more space." And there was. But it was still Ash's space.

Like most lion Therians, Ash didn't take kindly to having his space invaded by outsiders. Sloane tried to think of an instance where anyone who wasn't part of their team had been extended an invitation to the large, modern-style apartment. The place was spacious and open with cream-colored walls, except for the wall on the far end. That one was brick with two huge windows extending from the dark wood staircase up to the ceiling that overlooked the city. At the top of the simplistic staircase was Ash's office with a hallway that led to a bathroom and his bedroom.

Downstairs, the living room consisted of dark browns and reds. It was beside the open kitchen, which continued the brown color pattern with its dark cabinets. The appliances were all stainless steel along with the island counter chairs and cabinet door handles. The floors were wood, and there were several potted plants around the room. The apartment was minimalistic but bold, much like its owner.

Sloane was as curious as Dex was regarding the reasons behind Ash's kind gesture. Of course, there had been some rules. Ash put Cael in charge of the music, which meant no Billy Ocean, no Hall & Oates, and certainly no Journey. Dex had pretend-fainted over the news, and Sloane had soothed his partner while doing some pretending of his own—as in pretending it was a shame Cael had rejected the pre-1989 playlist. In the end, it had cost Sloane. Dex's pouting usually did, and a few minutes later Sloane found himself agreeing to let Dex program his favorite eighties station, *Retro Radio*, into the Impala's stereo. His partner had also somehow managed to make it the default station, which meant whether Dex was in the car with him or not, it was the first thing he heard when he turned on his car's stereo each and every time.

Dex clapped his hands to the beat of something that

sounded suspiciously like an eighties song before singing about friends not dancing and leaving them behind. Dex grinned knowingly. "He let me have one."

"And this is the one you picked?"

"I thought it appropriate."

"Still no."

"Fine," Dex said with a sigh. "Guess I'll have to dance with Taylor."

Sloane couldn't help his low growl. "Really? That's your game plan?"

"I can only say no to him so many times. Besides, it'll give me an excuse to punch him if he grabs my ass again."

"He grabbed your ass?" That sleazy asshole.

Dex grinned slyly. "Has anyone told you how cute your jealous boyfriend face is?"

Sloane grabbed Dex's wrist and led him to the center of the living room where everyone was pressed up against each other, dancing and grinding in a drunken orgy of frivolity. The majority of their teammates were so far gone by now and squished together, it was unlikely anyone would even be able to tell who Sloane was dancing with. He doubted they'd remember come morning. Sloane turned and pulled Dex close, letting his hand rest on Dex's hip. Dex lip-synched along with the catchy Daft Punk song as he moved, wriggling his eyebrows when it came to the part about getting lucky.

Sloane loved watching Dex dance. He loved the easy way he moved, the way his body responded to the music, like it was a natural-born instinct. One that couldn't be helped. Sloane found himself smiling as he watched Dex's body, studying his movements, the fluidity in which he adapted to the beat changes. Dex pulled some more disco moves that fit with the song and Sloane laughed.

"How long have you been dancing?" Sloane asked, aware of Dex inching closer.

"Since I was a kid. My mom used to dance with me around the kitchen when she was baking. On weekends, my dad would put on his records, and we used to jump around the living room until we were so tired we'd collapse from exhaustion. Then mom would bring us lemonade. They were both great dancers. Totally part of the swinging sixties crowd."

"Even your dad?"

"You kidding? He rocked the British Invasion. The Beatles, the Rolling Stones, the Kinks, Dusty Springfield, the Who. I've seen pictures of him and my mom. You should have seen him in his black turtleneck and mop top." Dex chuckled, shaking his head, but Sloane could see how much the loss still pained him. His partner adored Tony and Cael—his adoptive dad and adoptive brother—but that didn't make the death of his biological family any easier.

Sloane gave Dex a playful poke in his belly. "They'd have been proud of you."

"Thanks." Dex beamed, his smile disappearing the moment Taylor's arm landed around his shoulders. The guy never quit. He was always gravitating toward Dex, despite Sloane's obvious displeasure or the fact Sloane had already warned the guy once about trying anything funny. Agent Ellis Taylor was a good team leader, but he made it no secret he enjoyed a "fuck 'em and leave 'em" lifestyle. He slept around with teammates, indifferent to the consequences. As long as it didn't have an adverse effect on his own career, it didn't matter what happened to anyone else.

Taylor threw his arms up, drawing attention to himself as usual. "Holy shit, someone call the fucking press. Sloane Brodie's dancing."

There was a collective drunken cheer, and Sloane gave them a smirk before flipping them off.

"How'd you manage that, Daley?" Taylor threw his arm back around Dex only to have it swiftly removed.

"I have my ways."

"I bet you do." Taylor brazenly raked his gaze over Dex. "I bet you're full of surprises. Maybe Brodie will let me borrow you for a dance."

Unbelievable. "Maybe Taylor will remember our little conversation in the locker room not long ago," Sloane replied through his teeth.

Taylor squinted as he tried to recall. "Refresh my memory?"

Sloane flashed his teeth, feeling his inner Felid wanting to come out and play. "I'd love to." He grabbed a fistful of Taylor's shirt ready to oblige when Dex pushed himself between them. He turned Taylor around and sent him moving. The guy started to protest when something shiny, or who knew what, got his attention, and he disappeared into the crowd. Sloane braced himself, even managed a pleasant smile when Dex turned back to him with an arched eyebrow.

"So, what exactly had that conversation been about? You look just as pissed now as you did then."

There was no point in trying to hide it. "It was about you. I didn't appreciate the way he was talking about you."

Dex gave a snort. "That dude's a sexual harassment lawsuit waiting to happen." A slow smile crept onto his face as he started dancing again. "I was right, then."

"About what?"

"When I said you didn't want other dudes checking out my ass."

Sloane held back a smile as he tried to think up an excuse. In the end he gave up. "I got nothing."

"Aw, you were all jealous then too," Dex said quietly, shimmying closer to Sloane until they were almost touching.

"Dex..." Despite Sloane's concern, he didn't push Dex away. No one seemed to care about their proximity. It wasn't all that different at the office. No one batted an eye when Dex flirted with Sloane or joked about their closeness. Then again, it was hard to be suspicious of Dex. The guy was genuinely affectionate and playful by nature. Sloane supposed to their teammates, Dex was simply being himself around Sloane, and Sloane went along with it because Dex was his partner. Everyone was aware they'd become close friends. Sloane didn't feel offended their teammates chalked that up to Dex's likeable personality rather than any effort on Sloane's part. Apparently, not even Team Leader Sloane Brodie could resist Agent Daley's charms. Well, they were right.

"Hi, Dex. Hi, Sloane."

"Lou, you made it." Dex hugged Lou and gave him a squeeze, making Lou chuckle. Seeing Dex so affectionate toward his ex-boyfriend didn't bother Sloane. It had been a different story that first night Lou had shown up at Bar Dekatria and started flirting with Dex under the pretense of "talking." Dex had been the only one who seemed to have any interest in talking. But that had been before Lou walked in on Dex and Sloane making out in one of the empty hallways. Sloane had decided getting to know Lou and his intentions would be wiser than trying to scare Lou off. It had paid off, and now that Sloane was certain Lou posed no threat, the guy had become a friend. He was also a fountain of knowledge when it came to Dex, which, of course, drove Dex nuts.

"I couldn't miss one of your crazy pre-birthday-party parties. You sure it's okay I'm here? I don't know anyone except you guys and the team." Lou glanced around the room and fidgeted—his demeanor at odds with his outward appearance. Lou was attractive, like one of those Hispanic soap stars. He dressed fashionably and gave off an air of utter confidence. He was lean and toned with a body that said he worked out often. He had dark hair with dark eyes and long lashes, full lips, and was a few inches shorter than Dex. Sloane estimated roughly five seven. He was also a few years younger than Dex. Lou was the opposite of Sloane in every way. Sloane could see Dex caring for Lou, but there was something missing, and Sloane could see that too.

"Of course it is," Dex replied cheerfully. "Want something to drink? It's open bar."

"Speaking of bar... Isn't that the bartender from Bar Dekatria?" Lou motioned over to the far end of the room where Bradley was serving in his signature snug black T-shirt. His bare arms displayed impressive tattoo sleeves. At that moment, Bradley looked up and flashed them a big smile followed by a wink.

Dex waved at Bradley before turning back to Lou. "Yep. I invited Bradley, and he insisted on bartending. Said he wouldn't come otherwise. It might have had something to do with the fact that when he asked what kind of beer I'd be serving, I said 'cold.' Seriously, you should have seen his face. Like I insulted his mother."

Lou and Dex both laughed. They started chatting, and Sloane offered to get Lou his JD and Coke. On the way to the bar, Sloane caught sight of Beta Pride's team leader, Agent Levi Stone, heading his way.

"Hi, Sloane."

"Hey, man." Sloane shook Levi's hand. "Having a good time?"

Levi held up the bottle of beer in his hand with a smile. "I'm not much of a party guy, but it's nice to get out and mingle every once in a while. I appreciate Dex inviting me. Can I—would it be all right if I asked you to introduce me to your friend? The one talking with Dex."

"You want to meet Dex's ex-boyfriend?" Sloane certainly hadn't expected that.

Levi nodded. "You don't think Dex would mind, do you?"

"I think he'd be okay with it." He sure as hell hoped so. Sloane motioned over to the pair, and Levi followed him over. The two stopped chatting when Sloane and Levi approached.

"Hi, guys. I wanted to introduce Lou to Agent—"

"Blarney," Levi finished, his expression unfaltering.

Dex gaped at him. "Your name's Blarney Stone?"

There was a short pause before Levi answered with a solemn, "No," causing Lou to burst into laughter.

What the...? Sloane and Dex exchanged puzzled glances. They watched Levi hold his hand out to Lou.

"Agent Levi Stone. It's a pleasure."

Lou smiled widely and took Levi's hand. Sloane might not have known Lou for long, but he could tell the younger Human was interested.

"Louis Huerta. You can call me Lou."

"Would you like to dance, Lou?"

"I'd love to."

Levi led Lou away, and Sloane noticed Dex was frozen to the spot. Sloane stepped behind him to look at the pair over Dex's shoulder. "You okay? Do you mind him dancing with Lou?"

Dex seemed to snap out of it. "No, it's not that. Levi's a Therian. Not just a Therian, a white tiger Therian. Huge. I really thought Lou was going to bolt. Instead, he went all swoony." Something seemed to strike him, and he gasped. "Dude, the guy smiled!"

"Who? Lou? He's always smiling."

"No, Levi. Did you know his name was Levi?"

"Of course I did. I've been working with the guy for the last ten years. You've probably noticed that his team and Taylor's are usually the ones sent in to back us up. Beta Pride and Beta Ambush have been around almost as long as Destructive Delta. They haven't changed team leaders since."

Dex went thoughtful. "Considering how long you've known him, how come you don't call Taylor by his first name?"

"Because unlike Levi who's a nice guy, Taylor is a certified jackass. Always has been."

"No arguments there," Dex muttered. "This is the first time I've seen Levi smile."

Sloane shrugged. "It's been known to happen. Or so I've heard. Now I know the rumors are true." Stranger things had happened. Like Sloane going all these years without kicking Taylor's ass.

"He made a joke, and Lou laughed."

"I was there," Sloane replied with a chuckle.

"And he dances too." They both watched Lou chatting and dancing with Levi, doing his flirty, playful smack-on-the arm thing. "Look at him. A few months ago he was ranting about Therians, and now he's flirting with one."

Sloane wrapped his arms around Dex's neck from

behind and leaned on his shoulders, his head coming to rest against Dex's. "Well, he's been hanging around us a lot. Maybe he's coming around to the fact Therians aren't as bad as he thought. Has he talked to you about why he feels that way about Therians?"

"No." Dex sounded troubled by the thought. "I brought it up once, and he got really pissed about it. Said he wasn't going to get into it."

"Well, I hope whatever it is, he's leaving it behind. He seems happy now." Sloane hadn't given his affectionate gesture any thought until he heard Ash's growl behind them.

"What the fuck are you two—"

Dex cut Ash off, pointing to the opposite end of the room.

"Don't look now, Ash, but Herrera's about to take a piss on your fern."

"What?" Ash looked over his shoulder. "Motherfuck. Herrera!" Ash darted off, and Sloane pulled away from Dex. He shoved his hands into his pockets.

"Shit." What the hell was wrong with him? They were in a room filled with coworkers, and he was hanging off Dex. He hadn't even realized what he'd been doing. Dex gave him a wink and playful nudge.

"Take it easy, big guy. Crisis averted."

"I'm sorry. We need to be more careful. *I* should be more careful." No one would suspect anything if it was Dex hanging off him since his partner did the same with everyone else on the team—with the exception of Ash. Other than the occasional reassuring hug or companionable arm around the shoulder, Sloane had never behaved that way toward any teammate. Not even Gabe.

"You two look hot together. Ever think of having a little fancy feast, Daley?"

Jesus. The guy was like a bad rash. He was going to have a serious talk with Taylor as soon as he sobered up. This had to end before Sloane ended up planting one in Taylor's face. Then Sloane would have to explain himself to his sergeant. He doubted Maddock would be happy with Sloane punching out a fellow team leader, even if it concerned Dex. "Fuck off, Taylor. Go back to humping the couch."

"Only if I can have Dex with me while I do it."

Dex grinned broadly at Taylor. "Yeah, all right." Sloane eyed Dex, wondering what his partner was up to. Dex pointed to a cream-colored door past the kitchen. "But not the couch. Go wait for me in the laundry room."

Taylor looked from Dex to the door and back. "Really?"

"Yeah, why not."

"Okay." Taylor sped off.

Dex turned his attention back to Sloane. "What the fuck is a fancy feast?"

Sloane cleared his throat, feeling somewhat embarrassed. "It's a threesome. Two Felid Therians and a submissive Human in the middle."

"Man, you Felid Therians are kinky," Dex teased.

"No, Taylor's kinky. I don't like to share." Sloane wrapped an arm around Dex and brought him hard up against him.

"Weren't you just freakin' out about getting close like a second ago?" Dex asked, subtly pressing his crotch against Sloane's thigh.

Sloane craned his neck to the agent beside him practically dry-humping an equally enthusiastic female agent. "Hey, Gerry?"

The wolf Therian looked around before realizing where the voice was coming from. "Yeah?"

"What's your mom's name?" Sloane asked him.

"Uh..."

"It's okay, don't hurt yourself."

"Okay." Gerry went back to what he'd been doing.

Dex let his head fall back with a laugh, and Sloane had the fiercest urge to sink his teeth into that deliciously exposed skin. It was true, he had been freaking out and telling himself he'd made a big mistake, how he had to be careful. Then he'd thought of someone else's hands on Dex, and he didn't like it. At all.

"We need to find somewhere private." Sloane felt a shiver go through his partner at the implication, and Dex's gaze fell to Sloane's lips. His voice was low and husky when he spoke.

"Your pupils are dilated."

"Then you better do something about it," Sloane warned, his hand slipping away from Dex before it ended up somewhere it shouldn't. At least not in public.

Dex licked his lips. "Bathroom. Upstairs. Two minutes."

Sloane released Dex and went to the bar where Bradley gave him a knowing look. The guy was too perceptive for his own good.

"What?"

"I didn't say anything," Bradley said holding a hand up.

"Just give me a shot of something."

Bradley slid the shot glass over with a wicked grin. "If you're going to go upstairs, I'd do it now while Ash is busy putting the fear in the lovebirds he caught making out on his kitchen counter."

Sloane threw back his shot and gave Bradley a pointed look before he made a quick but subtle dash up the stairs.

There was a short line outside the main bathroom at the end of the hall, but Dex was smarter than that. His partner was also crazy. Sloane stood with his back to Ash's locked bedroom door—his partner had undoubtedly broken into it—and reached behind him to give a knock. Something clicked, and he was hauled inside. Dex closed the door behind him and locked it before launching himself at Sloane.

"Fuck. If Ash catches us in his room using his bathroom—"

"I locked the door. Just a quickie." Dex slipped his hand into the back of Sloane's jeans to cup his ass cheek and give it a squeeze, drawing a low groan from him. Unable to hold himself back any longer, Sloane captured Dex's soft lips with his own. He kissed Dex greedily, taking everything he could and demanding more. He could taste the beer on Dex's tongue, feel the heat coming off his partner, and Sloane's body threatened to catch fire. He continued to kiss Dex feverishly as he led him into the bathroom, closing the door behind them and locking it before pushing Dex up against it.

"Do you know why I don't dance?" Sloane said breathlessly, his hands finding the hem of Dex's shirt and pushing it up his body.

"Why? You're good at it."

"I don't dance because I like to watch you," Sloane admitted, loving the whimper that escaped Dex as he cupped Sloane through his jeans, his hand kneading and massaging Sloane's hard dick. "Also, if I dance with you, I'm going to want to touch you. And then touching leads to us having sex in Ash's bathroom."

"It's a chance I'm willing to take," Dex replied. He let out a gasp when Sloane grabbed him, turned him, and bent him over the sink. He handed Dex a towel. "Here, bite on this." Dex didn't argue.

"Stay," Sloane demanded. Fucking Dex brought out the wilder side in him, and he loved it. He rummaged in the sink's drawers and found a bottle of lube and a box of condoms. Ash wouldn't miss one. He returned the box to its place exactly the way he'd found it and put the bottle of lube on the sink beside Dex. With both hands, he reached under Dex and undid his belt. Dex loved it when he was a little rough, and Sloane was happy to give his lover exactly what he wanted. He tugged Dex's jeans and boxer briefs down to his thighs and grabbed the bottle of lube to pour some on his fingers. They had to be quick, but Sloane had no intention of hurting Dex.

He pushed Dex's T-shirt up his back and planted quick kisses on his partner's smooth skin before pushing a finger into Dex. His lover squirmed beneath him, his hips thrusting against the sink in his growing desperation for release. They didn't have all that long before Ash came looking for them, so Sloane picked up his pace, adding a second finger and soon a third as Dex groaned around a mouthful of towel, his back arching. Sloane leaned in, talking quietly in his ear.

"I'm going to fuck you fast and hard." Sloane pressed the head of his cock between Dex's ass cheeks. "You're going to feel me inside you for hours. Just how you like it."

A low whimper escaped Dex, and Sloane pushed himself in, slowly at first. His teeth gritted as the tight heat enveloped him. Dex nodded and Sloane plunged the rest of the way in, grateful for the towel that muffled Dex's surprised cry. He arched his back, his fingers gripping the edge of the sink. Grabbing Dex's hips, Sloane pulled out and drove himself back in. The sound of Dex's muffled groans, his heavy breathing, his flushed face had Sloane desperate for more. He pounded into Dex hard and fast, as he'd promised.

"Fuck. You feel so damn good." He watched his dick driving into Dex's ass for a few seconds before folding himself over Dex and wrapping his arms around him. He thrust deep, the sound of skin on skin sending him over the edge. His muscles tightened, and he thrust hard twice more before he emptied himself into the condom with a low growl. With a smile, he nuzzled Dex's hair, inhaling the sweet smell of his partner's citrus shampoo. He continued driving himself into Dex until it became too painful, and then he pulled out, removed the condom, tied it up, and quickly wrapped it in some toilet paper before chucking it in the wastebasket. He gently turned Dex around and got on his knees to pull Dex's hard cock into his mouth, a soft moan escaping him. He loved how Dex tasted, the smell of him, the feel of him.

Sloane sucked and licked, feeling Dex's hands in his hair. His tongue pressed against the base of Dex's cock, and his partner gasped. Knowing just what drove his partner wild, Sloane swirled his tongue over the head of Dex's cock before pressing his tongue into the slit, his hand giving the base a squeeze. Dex groaned and shivered. He leaned back against the sink, his eyes meeting Sloane's. With his favorite audience watching his performance, Sloane devoured Dex like a hungry man having his first meal after days without food.

Seconds later Dex was coming. Once his partner had finished, Sloane stood and helped him with his clothes before giving him a languid kiss.

"Mmm," Dex hummed against Sloane's mouth.

Sloane held Dex close, kissing his lips before nuzzling

his nose and brushing his lips across Dex's jaw. "We should go."

"To bed?" Dex asked hopefully.

"Soon," Sloane promised, chuckling at Dex's dreamy sigh. "This is your party, remember?"

"Exactly. It's my party, and I'll sigh if I want to."

"You won't be if Ash catches us." He put Dex's hand to his lips for a kiss when he noticed the blue-and-black band on his lover's wrist. "What are you wearing?"

Dex gave him a cheeky smile. "A wristband."

Sloane eyed the Pac-Man wristband and held back a smile. "You know that's not what I meant." How hadn't he noticed it before? Maybe he'd been too busy trying not to ogle his sexy partner.

"What? It's a classic. I'm the fucking king of Pac-Man." Dex gave him that wide boyish grin of his, and Sloane couldn't resist kissing those lips again. As silly as his partner could be, Sloane hoped he never changed. It wasn't that Sloane felt old, because he didn't and he wasn't, but he'd been through a lot in his life. Being around Dex made him feel lighter, stopped him from taking himself too seriously. They had fun together. He never thought his lover could also be his closest friend.

"King of Pac-Man, huh?" Sloane gave Dex a wicked grin. "We'll see about that."

Dex gasped, his eyes lighting up. "You play Pac-Man?"

"Are you kidding?" Sloane let out a snort and backed away from him before pointing to himself. "Prepare to be dethroned."

"I think I might have come in my pants." Dex thrust a finger at him. "It's on. You're going down."

"I already went down," Sloane replied with a wink before spinning on his heels and leaving the bathroom. He headed for the bedroom door unable to keep the smile off his face knowing Dex was following his every move. Tonight, he'd have a few more moves to show his lover. He might just come to enjoy these pre-birthday-party parties.

"Fuck." Dex stood staring at the door Sloane had disappeared through. Just when he thought he couldn't find the guy any hotter. What were the chances Sloane would be a total geek? Dex was so excited at the prospect that he practically bounced over to the door. Remembering where he was, he carefully checked to make sure the coast was clear before slipping out into the hall. He was about to head down the stairs when someone stepped in front of him, blocking his path.

"Hey. There you are, sexy."

Dex was seriously regretting inviting the guy. "Dude, you stink."

"How come you keep turning me down?" Taylor ran a hand down Dex's arm. "The things I would do to you."

"Wow. How can I not drop my pants with a line like that?" Dex moved to get around Taylor, only to have his path blocked again. "Seriously? Let me rephrase my rejection so there's no misunderstanding. I do not want to have sex with you." He motioned to Taylor's general personage. "I do not want anything of that, coming anywhere near any of this," he said and motioned to himself. "No. *Nyet. Nein. Nahi. Ni. Non.*"

"You're so adorable." Taylor gave a snort and stepped up to Dex, cupping him through his jeans. Dex gave Taylor a harsh shove away from him. He stared, stunned as Taylor stumbled back. Was this guy for real? Why was there always that one asshole in every office who thought himself to be irresistible when he was really a giant douchebag? Taylor was one and then some.

"What the fuck, man? What part of back the fuck off did you not understand?"

"Please. I know a cocktease when I see one."

"What?" Since when did not being interested in someone make him a cocktease?

"You think I don't see the way you flirt around the office?" Taylor scoffed. "The way you flirt with Brodie? Admit it. You want that big dick up your tight little ass, but Brodie won't give it to you. He's too busy playing hero. Plus, he's got that stick permanently shoved up his own ass, which must be hell on his sex life."

"Stay away from me. I'm serious." *Un-fucking-believable.* Dex turned to leave, only to have Taylor grab his arm. "I'm warning you, Taylor. I don't give a fuck if you're a team leader. You're out of line."

"How do you know you won't like it if you don't try it? You know what they say. Once you go Therian..." He ran a hand down Dex's back toward his ass.

The last of Dex's patience snapped, and he punched Taylor square across the jaw, the sound resonating through the hall. Everyone who'd been standing in line waiting to use the bathroom went silent, their stunned gazes on Dex and Taylor, who was now on his ass.

"You asked for that, you dick," Dex growled and backed up when Taylor pushed himself to his feet. He swayed for a moment before getting his bearings. The guy's expression went from confused to pissed off. What the fuck did he have to be pissed about? Dex had given him plenty of warning.

"Dex?" Sloane appeared beside him, his hand on Dex's shoulder. "What the hell's going on?"

"Nothing," Taylor spat out.

Sloane didn't hesitate. "Bullshit. What did you do?"

"Your partner just punched a team leader, and you're asking me what *I* did?" Taylor rubbed his jaw where Dex had clobbered him.

"I bet he had a good reason for it."

Taylor gaped at Sloane. Had he been expecting Sloane to agree with him? The guy seemed to be considering his options. He clearly reconsidered making a move against Dex because he seemed to deflate, jutting his bottom lip out pathetically. "I was only talking to him."

That only succeeded in pissing Dex off. He'd heard that shit before, and it wasn't going to fly. Not with him. "Oh, fuck you, Taylor. I don't know how many others kept their mouths shut, but I'm not letting this slide. I couldn't have said 'no' any fucking clearer. I told you how many times to keep your hands off?"

"You son of a bitch!" Sloane grabbed Taylor and shoved him up against the wall. "I warned you to keep your hands off of my team, didn't I?"

"Your team or your partner?" Taylor sneered, pushing Sloane away from him. "That's fine. I can take the hint."

Dex opened his mouth, then shut it. What was the point? He'd never met anyone who exhausted him the way Taylor did.

"Maybe I'll find me a sweet little cheetah Therian who'll be less of a pain in the ass. At least not a pain in *my* ass. His will be another story."

The suggestion Taylor meant Cael would have pissed Dex off, but when a shadow caught his eye, he cringed instead. He almost felt sorry for the guy. Almost. "Now you done fucked up twice."

Ash materialized behind Taylor like some otherworldly specter, his hand slapping down on the smaller agent's collarbone before giving it a squeeze that had Taylor hissing.

"Join me outside for a chat, will you?"

Shit. Ash was being civilized. That could only mean Taylor was lucky he didn't get tossed over the balcony. Taylor had no choice but to accompany Ash. Dex headed downstairs with Sloane at his side.

"What a dick. Whatever Ash gives him, he deserves."

"You okay?" Sloane asked, pulling Dex over to one side when they reached the kitchen.

"Yeah. Guys like Taylor annoy the fuck out of me. They think they can put their hands wherever they want when they want. Like it's somehow okay because you're a dude. They don't give a fuck what the other guy wants as long as they get laid."

"Dex?"

"Sorry. Reminds me of this asshole in high school. He was hell bent on making me his fuck toy. He thought because he was the star of the school and I was the class clown that it was okay for him to be all over me. That I should be grateful he handpicked me. And since I was gay that automatically meant I'd be okay to fuck anyone ready and willing."

"What happened?"

Dex grinned widely. "I told him to meet me in the locker room after school in one of the stalls. Naked. I snapped a picture of him in his birthday suit and told him if he didn't want the whole school to see how small his dick was, he'd leave me the fuck alone. I reminded him I was friends with the photography club's president and could easily have the picture blown up, which would be necessary in order for anyone to find his dick."

Sloane laughed. "I bet you'd have gone through with it too."

"Fuck yeah. I spent so much time in the principal's office that the man started penciling me into his schedule. We even shared lunch on occasion. He was pretty cool. He knew who the assholes were at school and didn't exactly disapprove of my methods. I avoided fist fights, so when I had to fight back, I did it in my own way." Dex leaned back against the counter. "I bet no one messed with you in school."

"I never had that problem. But then again, I hung out with Ash. We weren't really the most approachable guys on campus."

"Speaking of unapproachable. Here comes the king of."

Sloane turned to Ash who was looking even more miserable than usual. "Where's Taylor? Alive, I hope."

"I put him in a cab and sent him home," Ash grumbled. The guy looked tired. Like he hadn't been sleeping. Well, Ash *had* called in sick a couple of days ago. Dex couldn't understand why the guy had insisted on having the party at his place if he was feeling crappy.

"Thanks for dealing with Taylor," Dex said.

"I didn't do it for you."

"I didn't think so, but thanks anyway. I don't want that jackass anywhere near my brother." For all of Ash's faults, Dex couldn't deny the guy was always there to back Cael up, and he appreciated that.

"Won't be a problem." Ash leaned against the counter, his expression somber. Which wasn't unusual, but there was something else. He was looking out into the throng of agents dancing, drinking, and enjoying themselves.

"You look tired, man. You feeling okay?"

Ash seemed to snap himself out of it, and he gave Dex a nod. He ran a hand over his face and sighed. "Yeah, I'm good. Just need some sleep."

"Maybe it's time to wrap up this shindig," Dex suggested. A look of relief crossed Ash's face before his signature glower returned.

"Thank fuck for that." Ash pushed away from the counter and headed for the crowd undoubtedly to inform them they were to all fuck off.

"I hate to admit it, but I'm kind of worried about him." Dex caught his lover's concerned expression. Looked like Dex wasn't the only one. "You're worried about him too."

"Not sure yet. Maybe it's whatever bug he's getting over. He gets grumpy when he's sick."

Dex arched an eyebrow at Sloane. "I'm sorry. Are you implying that what we experience on non-sick days is him in a good mood?"

"That is correct," Sloane replied, completely serious.

"Fuck me."

"It would be my pleasure."

Dex's cock twitched in his pants. "Let's get everyone the hell out of here." He went off into the crowd and worked the room, joking and teasing as he ushered them out. When there was only Sloane, Ash, Dex, and Cael left, Dex thanked Ash for the party, receiving a grunt in response.

"I'll help you clean up," Cael said only to have Ash usher them all toward the door.

"It's fine. I can manage."

Dex was certain Cael's offer had more to do with hanging out with Ash than actually cleaning.

"Are you sure?" Cael asked. The others might not have noticed his brother's disappointment, but it was clear as day to Dex.

"Positive." With a brief good-bye, Ash closed the door on them. The three of them stood quietly in front of the closed apartment door. Dex wished he could say Ash's behavior surprised him, but it didn't. He turned to Cael.

"You got a ride?"

"Yeah, I brought my car. I'll see you guys tomorrow." Cael headed off before Dex could utter a word. Well, so much for that.

It was a breezy night, cool but not enough to warrant a jacket. Soon the leaves would be turning. It was hard to believe it had been almost a year since his life had been turned upside down and he'd joined the THIRDS. It seemed like a lifetime ago. Climbing into the passenger seat of Sloane's Impala, Dex felt as if he'd known the guy for years rather than months. He loved that he got to hang out with Sloane at work and out of it. He didn't know if that would change further down the line, but right now he'd make the most of it.

"Do you want to stay the night?" he asked Sloane. His partner preferred to stay over at his house and slept over at least three to four times a week while Dex slept over at Sloane's maybe once a week. Dex didn't dare mention that Sloane should have his own key to the house. It wasn't long ago the word *boyfriend* had scared the ever-living fuck out of Sloane. Dex had to remind himself to take things slow. Not an easy task. Dex was crazy about the guy.

"You mind staying at mine? I have to do laundry."

"Sure."

As they headed for Sloane's apartment across town, Dex held back a smile when he felt Sloane take hold of his hand as he drove. It was hard to gauge how comfortable Sloane was with their relationship, seeing as how they spent a good portion of their time hiding it from their fellow teammates.

"Did you enjoy your party?"

Dex nodded. "I did."

"You look unsure."

It was strange. He *was* unsure. "Ever since I was a kid, I'd have these huge birthday parties. I didn't even care who came as long as there were lots of people. I had a blast. I don't remember a lot of my college parties, so I'm going to assume they were pretty sweet. Thing is, tonight, I don't think I would have cared if no one showed up as long as you, my brother, and the team were there."

"Really?" Sloane sounded surprised.

"Yeah. Don't get me wrong. I had an awesome time. But I enjoyed myself most when I was with the team. With you."

"Wow."

"I know."

"Does that mean you know what you're going to do for your actual birthday party?"

"I've got an idea." Dex was going to have a chat with Bradley, see if he could arrange to have his party at Bar Dekatria. He didn't know what it was about the place, but he felt at home there. A huge part of that most likely had to do with the fact that Bradley not only put up with his eighties karaoke but encouraged him. The guy had even added new songs just for Dex.

They spent the rest of the car ride the same way they spent every other car ride together, with Dex attempting to change the station to *Retro Radio*, Sloane threatening him with grievous bodily harm, and Dex ultimately getting his way. Sloane would pretend he still had some form of control by forbidding Dex to sing along to whatever cheesy eighties song came on, Dex would pout, and within seconds he'd be singing along to "King of Wishful Thinking."

"You are most definitely the king of wishful thinking," Sloane teased.

"I'm going to take that as a compliment. Did you know in the film *Pretty Woman* the opera they go to is *La Traviata*, which is about a prostitute falling in love with a wealthy man?"

"You're like a walking, talking version of Trivial Pursuit. The 1980s edition."

Dex donned his snootiest voice. "First of all, *Pretty Woman* was 1990. Second of all, I believe it's called Trivial Pursuit Totally 80s."

Sloane's eyes widened. "Oh my God. You own it, don't you?"

"One of the player pieces is a Care Bear," Dex admitted.

"Why haven't I seen it around the house?"

"Because it's stored in the basement," Dex said, turning his gaze outside the window. He really should have kept his mouth shut. Now Sloane would probably ask—

"What else is down there?"

Yep. He'd really stuck his size tens in it this time. Talk about opening a can of worms. Not the sugary rainbow-colored sour ones or the gummy ones. Those were good. He could have sworn he'd had a pack of the sour ones in his sweet stash at work only three days ago. It was probably Cael. That gummy-worm-thieving little—

"Dex?"

"Huh?" Dex blinked at him. "Oh, sorry. What's in my

basement? Um, stockpiles of toilet paper in case the zombie apocalypse ever comes."

"What else?"

Dex could feel his face going red. "Stuff."

Sloane gave him a shrewd smile. "Am I going to find neon legwarmers and Richard Simmons workout videos?"

"Don't be ridiculous," Dex scoffed. "Like I need workout videos."

"I'm going to find something worse, aren't I?"

"No. Maybe. I don't know. There's a lot of stuff down there." *A lot* was an understatement. Dex's basement was crammed with boxes, crates, bags, storage bins, and all manner of containers stuffed to the brim with all his old belongings. When he'd started college, he'd bought himself a house with a portion of the life insurance money from his parents' deaths. In their will they'd left a note stating they didn't want him feeling guilty about using the money. They just wanted him to be happy. The house was the second big purchase he'd made. The first being his precious car.

On moving day, he'd taken all his stuff from his adoptive dad's house, including a load of boxes from Tony's basement, and moved them to his new home. Eighty percent of it was still in boxes in Dex's basement. When Lou left, some items had made it out to his living room, but there really wasn't an appropriate place for his collection of 3-D glasses.

"You're a hoarder?" Sloane gasped. "You gave me shit for being a closet geek, and you're a closet hoarder!"

"I'm not a hoarder. I just like keeping stuff."

"Same thing."

"Nope."

"How's it different?"

"My stuff's cool. Like my collection of 3-D glasses and Rubik's Cubes. I have a mint-condition Armatron. You know that was fucking mind-blowing at the time. Cael and I would spend hours—*hours*—on that thing just trying to pick up a fucking pencil."

Sloane was laughing so hard by now, Dex was afraid the guy was going to hurt something.

"Laugh it up, but when my Star Wars collection pays for a retirement villa off the coast of France, we'll see who's laughing then."

"What is it with you and the eighties?"

Dex shrugged. "I don't know. I guess... After I lost my parents, I was scared of my own shadow. For a while, I was even too scared to leave the house. When Tony left for work, I was terrified he'd get killed like my dad. I went through six babysitters. Tony was amazing though. He was patient and understanding. Then a few months later he brought home this pink little thing with big gray eyes, and he said, 'Dex, this is your new baby brother. You need to be a brave boy because he's gonna need you to take care of him. He's all alone in this world.' And I remember looking down at Cael and thinking he wasn't alone anymore because he had me and Tony, and I was gonna be the bestest big brother ever. Then Cael spit up on me." He chuckled at the memory. Then he thought about what came after.

"It was tough for a while. People were giving Tony shit because he adopted me, saying he only did it to get his hands on the insurance money. Bunch of assholes. Then they gave him shit for adopting a Therian, saying all kinds of crap, like he had an agenda or something. Cael and I were little kids. We'd lost our families, and the only one who gave a shit was Tony. They kept coming to his house, checking up on us, like they might catch him out, find us tied up in the basement or beaten." He balled his fists on his legs, feeling his anger boiling up inside. Back then he'd been too small to understand why it was such a big deal. Why everyone was always on their case. Sloane's hand on his shoulder snapped him out of it.

"Hey, it's okay."

"Sorry. It still pisses me off. It all came to a head when some dickbag news reporter showed up at my school trying to talk to me. He started asking me if Tony ever hit me or touched me where he shouldn't. I ran, and the bastard ran after me. It's probably no surprise that my penchant for ending up bruised was growing strong even then. I tripped on my laces and fell down the stairs. Luckily, I only banged myself up. Though I did lose a tooth."

"Your dad must have been pissed."

"My dad brought out the fucking army. I shit you not. He had a bunch of buddies who'd fought in Vietnam, and they brought their buddies, and let me tell you, after that day, none of those assholes dared to go near our block, much less one of us. Tony made an announcement on the news. He was fine with assholes messing with him, but if some jack-off tried to come near his kids, he was going to turn their kneecaps inside out. A year later, the Chief of Therian Defense personally recruited him to the THIRDS. You're probably thinking that has fuck all to do with your question, but it has everything to do with it. During all that shit, Tony was the best dad a kid could ask for. Don't get me wrong, if we were out of line, we'd be in trouble, but Tony never stopped doing everything in his power to give me and Cael the best family he could.

"We had pizza nights and video games, music, vacations to Disney World, camping trips, Slip 'N Slides in the backyard. He'd chase down the ice cream truck if we didn't get outside in time, read us bedtime stories, made snow angels in the winter, and in the summer, he'd let us bury him in sand at the beach. I guess, whenever I hear a song from back then or watch some cheesy movie I grew up with, it makes me feel... good. Like the world isn't such a shitty place."

"Like when you were a kid, with Tony and Cael," Sloane said, nodding his understanding.

"Yeah. When you ask me how I do it, how I stay so upbeat all the time? That's how. When the job starts getting to me, I go to my happy place. I know it's nostalgic bullshit, and I'm a grown man—"

"Fuck that."

Dex arched an eyebrow at his partner. The conviction in Sloane's voice took him by surprise.

"You had a great childhood, Dex, with a family that loved you and accepted you. There was, and still is, a whole lot of love in your family. If listening to your music makes you think of those good times, makes you feel good inside, then forget everything else. Who gives a shit what anyone else thinks?"

"Thanks." Dex felt his heart flutter, and he squeezed Sloane's hand.

"I'm still going to tease you about it," Sloane said and gave him a wink.

Dex smiled warmly at his lover. "I wouldn't want it any other way."

THREE

"That was so good."

The only way Dex's shower could have felt even better was if he'd had the company of a certain sexy someone. Except that someone was being all grown-up and responsible and doing laundry. Seriously? Who chose laundry over shower sex? Or at the very least a blowjob. Not that they needed a shower for any of that. He'd even lingered a bit hoping Sloane would join him, but no such luck. Dex wrapped a towel around his waist and walked out into Sloane's empty bedroom. Where were his clothes? He strolled out into the hall and called down the stairs. "Sloane?"

"Yeah?"

"You know where my clothes are?"

"In the dryer. I washed them. They smelled like booze and sex."

And that was a bad thing? "Okay. Mind if I borrow a T-shirt and some pants?"

"No prob. Dresser. Second drawer. The black pants with the white stripes going down the sides have drawstrings. They should fit you. There should be a faded gray THIRDS T-shirt in there somewhere. It's a bit snug on me, so it should fit okay."

"Awesome." Dex went to the dresser, found the pants, and slipped them on. He had to roll them up at the waist so he wouldn't trip on them. Then he searched for the T-shirt Sloane had mentioned. He found it, held it up in front of him, and let out a snort of disgust. "Snug? It's a fucking blanket. Bastard." He put on the T-shirt and was about to shut the drawer when he spotted something fluffy and black. Obviously, his first thought went to sex toy. He'd almost missed it, what with it being all black and camouflaged amidst a load of black clothing. Picking it up, he discovered it wasn't at all the kind of toy he'd been expecting, and his heart squeezed in his chest when he realized it was a black jaguar.

Swallowing past a lump in his throat, he walked over to the bed and sat down, the toy cradled in his arms. It was the white bandages wrapped around each paw that broke Dex's heart. How long had Sloane had this? Dex noticed the white label under the tail with the initials *S.B.* written childishly in black marker. "Oh, Sloane." Had this little fella sported his bandages the same time as Sloane?

"Everything okay?"

Dex's head shot up, and his face felt like it might go up in flames. Sloane's expression was guarded, and his gaze went from Dex to the toy in his hands and back. Crap. Dex quickly held the stuffed toy up. "I wasn't going through your stuff. I was looking for the T-shirt, and I came across this little guy."

Sloane gave him a nod, stepped up to him, and gently took the stuffed toy from him. "I found it in Shultzon's house when we first thought he was Freedman. It was in his closet. I couldn't leave it behind."

"Was it yours?"

"Yeah. I'd always wondered what happened to it. It's from my time at the facility. They heavily sedated me after... You know." He held up his wrist. "They were afraid I'd try to pull out the stitches or something. Make a second attempt. When they felt it was safe to let me go back to my room, I found this little guy on my bed. He didn't have bandages on. I added those." Sloane took a seat beside Dex, his eyes on the soft toy.

"I'd just finished putting the bandages on my little friend, when Dr. Shultzon came in with this scruffy kid." Sloane smiled warmly. "I remember thinking the kid was scary and mean looking. Dr. Shultzon told me his name was Ash Keeler. Shultzon seemed to think we were going to be great friends. Neither of us believed it at first. We sat there for hours glaring at each other." He laughed, seeming to get lost in some memory. "I remember the way I'd sat on my bed hugging my stuffed toy, glaring at the boy sitting at the end of the bed. It turned into a fierce staring contest until I lost by yawning and then hiccupping. It was hard to pull off a tough-guy routine when every time you hiccupped you sounded like a baby bird. I watched Ash trying hard not to laugh, but in the end, he gave in."

Dex climbed onto the bed and drew his knees up, studying his partner. "How *did* you two become friends? Sounds to me like Ash hasn't changed much since he was a kid." He still found it hard to believe the two were so close.

A smile tugged at Sloane's lips. "He hasn't changed at all. He's still mean-looking and angry, but he's as fearless now as he was then. Well, I'm sure he did get scared, but he never showed it, especially around me. They moved us into one of the bigger rooms so we could share, and I remember our first night. I woke up screaming and couldn't stop shaking and crying afterward. Ash didn't say anything. He climbed into bed with me and hugged me close. I knew then that I wasn't alone. What's more, I knew we'd always be there for each other."

"I can't imagine Ash as the hugging type."

Sloane cast his partner a shrewd glance. "He has his moments."

An image of Ash hugging Cael popped into Dex's mind, followed by guilt. He'd promised his brother he'd talk to Sloane about Ash, and two months later, he still hadn't. Well, now was as good a time as any. "Speaking of Ash. Has he ever... been with a guy?" That didn't sound awkward. At. All.

The question caught Sloane by surprise. "Why? You interested?"

Dex hoped his uninspired expression was answer enough, not that he believed Sloane actually thought Dex harbored some secret feelings for his archnemesis. "I'm asking because I have a friend—"

"Brother," Sloane corrected.

"Man, nothing gets past you." Damn. His partner was too clever for his own good.

Sloane stood and propped his little friend on his dresser. "Nope. It's best you remember that." He came back and stopped in front of Dex to give him a quick kiss before climbing onto the bed. Dex flopped down beside him and rolled onto his back.

"Your brother's got a thing for Ash. Has for years. You should have seen him when I introduced them. Cael went all red in the face, got tongue-tied, and then tripped over his own feet."

"Awkward runs in the family," Dex muttered as he turned onto his stomach and propped himself on his elbows. "Unless you're Tony. Then 'awkward' cowers in the corner. Must be a sibling thing. So has Ash ever been with a dude?"

Sloane shrugged. "To be honest, I don't know. I don't get involved in his love life or, in Ash's case, sex life. He's only ever slept with women, that I know of. We've been best friends since we were kids, but we've always valued our privacy. As long as he stays safe, whatever Ash does with whoever is no one's business but his."

"In other words, you have no idea."

"That's why I said I don't know. What makes you think he might be into guys?"

"The way he is with my brother makes me wonder."

"He is pretty hands-on with Cael. I admit I was surprised the first time I saw Ash behaving so affectionately toward your brother. From day one, he's never cursed him out, threatened him, or even told him off. He's like a different person. I got used to it after a while. Figured it was something the kid brought out in him. But he's never mentioned any guys. Plus, he's told me several times he's not gay."

"After you asked?" Dex wiggled over to Sloane and let his head rest against Sloane's stomach. It's like he couldn't be near the guy without obliterating any space between them. Whenever he touched Sloane, his belly filled with butterflies, and his pulse sped up. Either Sloane didn't notice Dex's slight flush, or he chose not to bring it up, which was fine with Dex. He didn't want to make Sloane uncomfortable.

"I've never asked," Sloane said, absently stroking Dex's hair. "He's sort of volunteered the information. Now that I think about it, there was that night at Dekatria. Ash had had a little too much to drink, and he was going on about how the fact he liked hanging out with Cael didn't make him gay. It was weird. Then again, it might have been the alcohol talking."

Dex wriggled his brows, making Sloane laugh. "Methinks the scary agent doth protest too much." He rolled onto his back, and Sloane followed, landing on top of Dex. He gave Dex's lips a kiss before trailing kisses down his jaw to his neck and making Dex's toes curl. A hum escaped him, which seemed to encourage Sloane.

"You planning on asking him?" Sloane teased before taking Dex's earlobe between his teeth.

"Fuck no. Like he would tell me the truth anyway." Dex went quiet, and Sloane pulled back to look down at him.

"You're worried about Cael."

"Yeah. He has a habit of falling for the wrong guys."

Sloane's smile returned, the desire burning in his amber eyes mixed with warmth and affection. "Something else that runs in the family?" He squeezed Dex under his arms, and Dex let out a laugh before trying to push his hand away.

"Maybe it did," Dex said, trying to hold back his laughter while pushing at Sloane. "Stop tickling me, you dick." Sloane stopped, and Dex rewarded him with a lengthy kiss. "I think I broke my unlucky streak."

"Always the charmer, aren't you?" Sloane lay on top of him. The feeling of his weight on Dex felt so damn good. He could stay like this all night. His hands slid around Sloane's torso, down the curve of his spine and the dip before his gorgeous ass.

"I try," Dex murmured, arching up against Sloane.

Sloane smiled knowingly before kissing Dex. "And succeed. Unfortunately." His lips returned to Dex's, hot and soft, his scent driving Dex crazy. God, he wanted

Sloane so badly. He pulled off Sloane's T-shirt so he could enjoy the feel of Sloane's firm muscles and the softness of his skin. It struck him how perfect this moment was. How happy he was right here, right now. Something in his chest tightened, and he suddenly found it difficult to breathe. He pulled away and gave Sloane the most charismatic smile he could muster.

"Does that mean you're charmed enough to make me some chocolate chip cookies to go with my glass of milk?"

Sloane stared at him. "It's nearly midnight."

"They're premade. Just cut 'em up and pop 'em in the oven."

"You stocked my fridge up with your unhealthy snacks again, didn't you?"

Dex smiled widely so his dimples would appear. "I did. So... cookies?"

"And if I say no?" Sloane arched an eyebrow, and Dex let out a heavy sigh.

"I guess I could go to sleep without the taste of warm, gooey chocolate chip cookies fresh from the oven made by the gentle hands of my tender lover—"

Sloane burst into laughter. "Okay. Jesus. Fine. I'll make you cookies." He kissed Dex one more time before rolling off the bed. Dex gave him a sappy grin before getting up on his feet, walking to the edge of the bed, and motioning for Sloane to turn around.

"Seriously?" Sloane planted his hands on his hips. Despite his stance, the light in his eyes told Dex he was amused.

"The floor is made of hot coals."

Sloane backed up to the bed, and Dex jumped on him, his arms coming to wrap around Sloane's neck and his legs around Sloane's torso. "I see. So, you get to save your feet while I burn for you?"

"That's the idea."

"You skipped puberty, didn't you?"

Dex let out a wistful sigh. "It wasn't for me."

Sloane laughed as he carried Dex out of the room. "You're hopeless."

"I'm also nonrefundable."

"Surely there's a return policy."

"Forget it. You're way past the thirty-day refund period. You're stuck with me now. And before you ask, I'm also nontransferable and nonexchangeable. If you donate me to charity there's no tax write-off because technically that would be considered Human trafficking."

"Wow. You've got your bases covered."

"You bet. Should have paid more attention to the Dexter J. Daley boyfriend agreement."

Sloane dropped him onto the counter and stepped between his legs to pull him close. "I don't recall this boyfriend agreement."

"You might have been sleeping at the time, but sleeping during the reading of the DJDBA is covered in the fine print. As long as you have a pulse, you're considered present and accounted for."

"Duly noted." Sloane slipped his hands under the too-big T-shirt when something seemed to occur to him. "What's the *J* stand for in your middle name? It's not stated in your file."

Dang it. He should have known it would come up sooner or later. Dex pretended to be giving the question considerable thought, and Sloane decided to get to work on those cookies. He went to his fridge and groaned when he opened it. From his perch on the counter Dex could see all the tasty, unhealthy snacks he had snuck into Sloane's fridge. There were rolls of cookie dough, a bottle of chocolate syrup, candy bars, pizza, white bread, and a score of other foodstuffs that were full calorie, full fat, high in sugar, and screaming with carbs.

"I feel faint," Sloane muttered, grabbing one of the tubes of chocolate chip cookie dough. "I think the only way I can feel remotely better about this is if you tell me your middle name."

"You'll laugh."

"Why?" Sloane removed a baking sheet from one of the cabinets and prepped it before opening the tube of cookie dough.

Dex shrugged, his eyes on his dangling feet. "Because it's corny."

"Come on. I won't laugh."

"Fine. It's my great-great-great-grandfather's name. He was a Pinkerton back in the late 1800s. The men in my family have always been lawmen dating to way back when."

"And his name was...?" Sloane put the tube on the counter and turned to him with a smile. "Come on. It can't be that bad."

"This is me we're talking about."

"True. Still. You know I won't laugh."

Might as well get it over with. "Justice Daley."

Sloane blinked. "Your middle name is Justice?"

"Yep."

"That is—" Dex narrowed his eyes at him and waited. With a laugh, Sloane gathered him up in his arms. "The cutest thing I've ever heard."

"Yeah, well, the kids in school didn't think it was so cute. That's why I started using 'J' instead. It kind of stuck." Dex wrapped his arms around Sloane's neck and leaned in for a sweet kiss. His lips pulled into a dimple-forming smile. "If you tell Ash, I will kick your ass."

"Now why would I do that when I could coerce you into more pleasant things to ensure my silence?" Sloane wriggled his eyebrows, and Dex couldn't keep himself from laughing.

"Blackmail, huh?"

Sloane let out a hum as he kissed Dex, his hands finding their way under Dex's shirt again. Dex pulled back and grinned at him. He didn't even have to say anything.

"If I put the cookies in the oven, can we make out until they're done?"

"Absolutely," Dex promised. He sat enjoying the view of the sexy Therian prowling about the kitchen in only his tight black boxer briefs. It was astonishing how, even in his Human form, Sloane moved like a powerful Felid. As Sloane bent over to pop the cookies in the oven, Dex jumped off the counter unable to resist doing some pouncing of his own.

WHAT WERE they going to do to him now?

Sloane was strapped to the chair. His ankles, wrists, waist, and head restrained. It always hurt. He'd wanted to hide when they came to his room, but he didn't want to look like a wimp in front of Ash. Ash never looked scared when the nurses came for him. Now Sloane wished he had hidden. Not that they wouldn't have found him. There were only the two beds in their room. It wasn't that he wasn't grateful. Dr. Shultzon was nice, and he brought them toys and ice cream and let them paint their room however they wanted. Sometimes when Sloane was playing with Ash, he would forget where they were, what they were. Until it was time for the tests.

This time he'd been stripped down to his underwear. The sticky little white pads were fixed to his skin all over his body, wires coming out of their centers. The pads were cold and sometimes sent little shocks through him. The wires led to different machines and monitors. One machine monitored his heartbeat, one his brain, and the others—he didn't know what they did. They looked like the machines in those Sci-Fi movies Dr. Shultzon rented for them from the video store. If only Ash were here, Sloane might not feel so scared, then.

"All right, Sloane. Like I instructed. Ready?"

No. "Yes."

"Okay. You may begin."

Sloane closed his eyes and called upon the wild animal inside him. The Felid woke from its slumber and answered Sloane's call. The transformation started, and Sloane gritted his teeth against the pain. The moment the first bone slipped out of place, Sloane pushed it back. His Felid side cried out, confused about why he was being shoved back when Sloane had called for him. The machines around them beeped wildly, and Sloane cried out, his body telling him he shouldn't try to stop the transformation so suddenly once it started. Doctor Shultzon pressed a button, and the pads stuck to Sloane's body sent pulses through him.

"It hurts! Please, stop. Please," Sloane begged. The pulses hurt. They curdled his blood and angered his Felid half. Sloane hissed, his fangs starting to elongate. He fought desperately, pushing the Felid back.

"It's okay, Sloane. You're a very brave boy. You can do this."

"I can't," Sloane cried, tears streaming down his cheeks. "It hurts so bad." Whatever they were doing to him, it made

his other half very angry. It wanted to come out and hurt them. Sloane arched up violently, his whole body convulsing as the Felid tore through him. His vision sharpened, and his claws started to pierce the tips of his fingers. Sloane couldn't stop crying.

"I know it hurts. Just a little longer."

"I can't hold him back!"

"You can. Your Human side is the dominant species, Sloane. You tell him what to do, not the other way around."

They didn't understand. Sloane shook his head, his body slammed down against the chair as if by some unknown force. "It's not like that," Sloane blubbered, his nose running and sweat dripping down his face. Sloane didn't know what he was, but he did know he wasn't Human. Dr. Shultzon had told him he was a Therian when he'd first brought Sloane here from the hospital where they'd locked him up for being a freak.

Shultzon put his hand to Sloane's head, tenderly stroking his hair. "It's all right. Tell him you're okay. It's over."

Sloane did. He tried to soothe the beast inside him. Told him it was okay. The worst was over, even if only for today. The Felid protested but slinked back into the shadows. Sloane clenched his jaw, his eyes shut tight against the sting and pain of his claws and fangs retracting. A few heartbeats later, the Felid slumbered once again. Shultzon wiped Sloane's nose with a tissue, then ran a damp cloth tenderly over Sloane's face before he undid the straps restraining him. Sloane's bottom lip trembled, and big, fat tears rolled down his flushed cheeks.

"I know what you're thinking." Shultzon put a hand under his chin and tilted his face up so he could look into Sloane's eyes. "You're not a monster. Just a regular thirteen-

year-old boy like any other. Maybe a little different, but that's not a bad thing."

Sloane nodded even if he didn't agree. Maybe he wasn't a monster, but he was a freak and a killer. He'd killed his mom. His dad hurt him and then killed himself. They'd thrown him away. Locked him up and told him he was... an abomination. Sometimes he felt so alone, he wished...

"Sloane, that's enough!"

The harsh tone startled Sloane, and a sudden sharp pain drew his gaze down to his wrist where he'd dug his nails. Eyes wide, he shook his head frantically. "I didn't mean to!" He didn't want to go back into observation. What if they tied him to the bed again? "I swear!"

"Hush. It's okay." Shultzon sat next to him and drew him into his arms, rocking him gently like his mother used to do when there was a bad thunderstorm and the lightning scared him. "I know you didn't mean to. But you have to be more careful, or I won't have a choice."

Sloane nodded. "I promise." He didn't want to hurt anymore. Everything always hurt. His head, his body, his heart. A shuddered breath escaped him, and his voice sounded so small when he spoke. "I want to go back to my room."

"Okay."

Shultzon led him down the bright white halls and into the elevator where they soon stepped out into another white hall. Every floor looked the same, always white and far too bright. The door to his room opened, and Ash stepped out. As if he'd known Sloane was near. Without waiting for the doctor's okay, Sloane took off down the hall and threw himself into Ash's arms. Despite being the same age, Ash was bigger, and when his strong arms squeezed Sloane, the tears started once again. He hated crying so much, but he couldn't seem to stop.

"It's okay," Ash said gruffly, leading Sloane inside and shutting the door behind him. He walked Sloane over to his bed and sat down with him, holding him while he cried. When Sloane's eyes and head hurt from crying so much, his nose stuffed and his throat sore, he pulled back and wiped his face with his sleeve.

"I'm sorry. I'm such a wuss."

"You're not a wuss."

"I am. They do the same to you, but you never cry."

"It's good you cry," Ash said somberly. He turned to look at Sloane, and for the first time in two years, he looked... sad. "It means you're not broken."

Sloane frowned at him. "You're not broken."

"Yes, I am. I only ever feel angry."

"That's not true!" Sloane took Ash's hand in his. "You smile and laugh. If you were broken, you wouldn't do that."

Ash seemed to think about that, then shrugged as if giving in. Sloane pushed on.

"You're my best friend in the whole world, Ash."

"I'm your only friend."

Sloane laughed. "Okay, but if you weren't my only friend, you'd still be my best friend. We're going to always be best friends, right?"

Ash smiled broadly. "You bet."

The door to their room opened, and two doctors stood by. "Ash. It's time."

"Okay." Ash breathed in deep, puffing up his chest. It was as if he weren't afraid of anything.

Ash walked to the door, and Sloane looked on worriedly. He crawled onto his bed, grabbed his favorite stuffed toy, and drew his knees up. Ash stopped to look over his shoulder at

Sloane, a grin on his face. "If you touch my stuff, I'll kick your butt."

"Got it." Sloane couldn't help his smile. Then the door closed, and he was alone again.

Ash would be back soon. He had to be. It was the only thing Sloane had to hang on to. Shutting his eyes tight, Sloane dreamed of the day they'd be free. He even dared to hope he'd have a normal life with someone who cared about him, who wasn't afraid of him. Who maybe even... loved him.

"Sloane..."

Sloane rolled over and opened his eyes. It was dark, but that wasn't a problem for him. Pale-blue eyes filled with concern and affection gazed back at him.

"I'm sorry," Sloane said, his voice rough with sleep. "Did I wake you?"

Dex reached out and swiped a thumb across Sloane's cheek. Only then did Sloane realize it was wet. "Were you crying in your dream?" Dex asked softly.

"I cried a lot when I was back there. The first couple of years, anyway. I was such a mess."

"You've been dreaming a lot about that place recently. More than usual. Is it because of what happened at the facility with Isaac or everything else?"

Sloane pulled Dex up against him, needing to feel his warmth, grateful for the way Dex offered his quiet strength without hesitation. Dex laid his head on Sloane's shoulder, his hand coming to rest over Sloane's heart. With a smile, Sloane covered Dex's hand with his and gave it a squeeze.

"Every time I go to sleep, I'm a kid again, back there strapped to that chair. I never expected to step foot in the facility again, much less see Dr. Shultzon. I think that's what's triggered the dreams. Plus knowing the place was in use doesn't help." He shivered, and Dex planted a kiss on his skin to soothe him. It would be in his best interest to forget. Who knew what the hell else they'd been working on? If the scopolamine concoction was anything to go by, it couldn't be anything good. Sloane put that thought away for now, not wanting to worry Dex. His partner only had the faintest idea what had gone on during the First Gen Recruitment Program.

As if reading his thoughts, Dex spoke up somewhat hesitantly. "You never talk to me about what happened to you there."

"I don't intend to change that. And it's not because I don't want to confide in you or don't think you can handle it, but what would be the point of telling you all the terrible details? What are you going to do with that information other than feel angry and hurt for what I went through? You can't change what happened. No one can." He kissed the top of Dex's head, closing his eyes at the now familiar scent of citrus. He nuzzled Dex's hair and murmured sincerely, "I appreciate your concern, but some things are better left unsaid."

Dex was quiet for a moment before nodding. He delivered another kiss to Sloane's neck and murmured, "Okay."

With a smile, Sloane turned onto his side so he could face Dex. He leaned forward and put his lips to Dex's for a kiss, enjoying the way his partner opened up for him. Sloane had never cared much for kissing, but he could lose himself in kissing Dex. With a low moan, Sloane rolled Dex over to face him and deepened their kiss. His hand slipped under Dex's boxer briefs to palm Dex's hard cock, and Dex returned the favor. They continued to kiss as they thrust into each other's hands. It was slow and excruciating, but Sloane forced himself to keep a steady pace. He wrapped a leg around Dex's to pull him closer and keep him against

Sloane as their pace picked up. Dex shivered, and he gasped before spilling himself into Sloane's hand. A few seconds later, Sloane's climax hit, and he shuddered from head to toe.

As Sloane dozed off, he heard Dex say something about being glad he was here. Sloane gave his partner a squeeze and kissed his brow before murmuring, "Me too."

FOUR

SLOANE EYED the newest addition to his partner's desk with mixed feelings. It was a coffee mug. Of course, this was Dex, so it wasn't any old coffee mug. It had a silhouette of a guy jumping against the backdrop of a sunny day. Sloane read the black text underneath the leaping man out loud without the excitement the exclamation mark suggested.

"I pooped today."

Dex grinned as he typed away at his desk's interface. "What a coincidence. So did I."

"I was reading your mug, wise guy." He immediately regretted opening his mouth. This was going to go to weird places. He just knew it.

"So you didn't poop today?"

"I'm not going to discuss my bowel movements with you." Yep. Weird places.

The smile never left Dex's face despite his attention not moving from his report. "You don't think we've reached that stage in our relationship?"

"I don't know what stage that's supposed to be, but I have no intention of ever reaching it." There were just some body fluids he wasn't comfortable with. Which was why he was so useless around babies. Babies scared the hell out of him. They were so tiny and fragile. It's like they knew he was freaked out by them because they always screamed and wailed when they saw him or he was forced to hold one. He frowned at the thought.

Dex gave him a curt nod. "No discussing poop. Got it."

Were they still having this conversation? "Stop saying that word."

"What word?"

"Poop." This had to be the strangest conversation he'd ever had at the office. He was hardly surprised he was having it with Dex. His partner cackled and sat back in his chair, his eyes sparkling with mischief.

"Jackass." Sloane stood and snatched up his *normal* THIRDS issued coffee mug. "I haven't had nearly enough caffeine to deal with you this morning."

Dex held out his empty mug. "How about being a good partner and grabbing me a cappuccino?"

Sloane stared at him. "You want me to walk into the canteen with *that*?" He stepped up beside Dex and started rummaging through his partner's desk drawers, ignoring the stash of sweets.

"What are you looking for?"

"Your marbles. I think what was left of them slipped out of your head." Sloane shut the drawer and headed for the door. "Make sure no one trips on them when they walk in here."

"Wait, I'll come with you." Dex jumped to his feet, mug in hand. "I have to talk to you about something serious."

"*Me*-serious or *Dex*-serious?" They headed into the bullpen, past the many offices occupied by Unit Alpha's Defense teams, and out to the reception area. It was pretty quiet at this time of day, which wasn't unusual. With everything going on lately, their department was busier than ever. Even with the Coalition case hitting Threat Level Red and all other cases getting shuffled around, it didn't mean new cases weren't being opened. Crime didn't reschedule because THIRDS agents were being run off their feet. In fact, it's when criminals decided to put in some overtime. Sloane greeted the team of receptionists before heading down the corridor toward the elevator.

"How are the two different?" Dex asked.

Unsurprisingly, there was a big difference. After all his years in the field, Sloane was still running across surprises and situations he'd never been faced with. Granted, those instances were usually provided courtesy of his partner. Every day on the job was like opening a mystery box. He never knew what he was going to get. One particular incident from the previous week jumped out at him.

"Dex serious is 'Uh-oh, I dropped a gummy bear inside the grenade launcher.'" He glanced over at his partner and wondered how the guy always managed to look innocent no matter how devious a scheme he'd just pulled off.

"I hadn't realized it was stuck to my visor until it fell in. Then it was too late."

"You almost took that perp's eye out," Sloane reminded him.

"Luckily the evidence was edible."

"That's gross. You're damn lucky it didn't fuck up the grenade launcher. Letty would have kicked your ass." As much as Letty loved Dex, she loved her toys just as much and got mighty pissed off when someone broke something through carelessness. Especially since she'd then have to explain to Maddock why the team had gone over their equipment budget and the reason for the equipment malfunction.

They walked into the elevator that was thankfully empty, and Sloane provided his handprint along with his badge number to get them descending to the thirteenth floor. It occurred to him his caffeine intake had nearly doubled in the last few months. His eyes landed on the likely cause.

Dex held his hand up in promise. "No more gummy bears while my visor's down. Got it. What I was going to talk to you about is *you*-serious."

"I like how you glossed over the whole eating gummy bears out in the field infraction with your offer of not eating them with your visor down." His partner was the king of evasive tactics. Well-suited for government work.

"Do you want to hear what I have to say?"

"If I must."

"Cute. I think you should take Dr. Shultzon up on his offer."

That brought Sloane up short, and he turned to find Dex was serious. "You do?" He thought about his first day back at work after the few days he'd taken off to take care of Dex following the incident at the facility. He'd been surprised to find a voice mail from Shultzon asking if Sloane wanted to meet up for coffee and a chat. He'd left his phone number, which Sloane had programmed into his phone but hadn't so much as looked at.

"When was the last time you spoke to him?"

"Aside from the few words at the facility, when I was sixteen and started with the THIRDS. We weren't allowed contact after that." The elevator doors opened, and Sloane stepped out with Dex on his heels. "I wouldn't have known how to get a hold of Shultzon even if I wanted to."

"Maybe it'll help."

Sloane didn't bother giving it any thought. "Okay. I'll call him when we get back to the office."

"You want me to make myself busy?"

"Actually, you mind staying?" He felt a little embarrassed asking, but Dex's broad grin set his mind at ease. Having Dex nearby would help him feel less nervous. After the incident at the facility, Sloane had tried his best to put it all behind him. Then again, he'd thought he'd put it behind him once before, and it all came crashing down around him thanks to Isaac Pearce. Still. Maybe Dex had a point. If seeing Shultzon had triggered his dreams, maybe the doctor could help stop them. It was worth a try.

"'Course not." Dex beamed up at him.

"Thanks." They walked into the expansive canteen, which was laid out more like a giant mall food court than an employee canteen. Sloane spotted their team at their usual table over by the window. It was nice to see Hudson and Nina had joined them. Monday mornings were especially busy with caffeine in high demand whether in the form of coffee, tea, or energy drinks. From the moment their day started until lunch, agents needing their fix packed the place. Calvin and Hobbs seemed to be the only ones missing, which really was no surprise. Hobbs tended to avoid large, crowded places, and wherever Hobbs went, Calvin followed.

Sloane greeted some of his fellow Defense agents while they joined the drink line. It moved quickly, and Dex got his ridiculous frothy cappuccino sprinkled with chocolate powder. Impressive, seeing as how the canteen didn't offer chocolate powder. While Dex was distracted chatting with Levi who was adding a packet of sweetener to his very plain, very black coffee, Sloane quietly ordered a sugar-free vanilla latte. He didn't need Dex knowing his coffee tastes were rubbing off on him.

After saying good-bye to Levi, Dex and Sloane joined their team at the long gray table. It was like any other day. Rosa and Letty were chatting away in Spanish, Cael was on his tablet, and Hudson was in the middle of a rather animated debate with Ash who appeared to be back to his old self, stirring up trouble and sending tempers flaring. The only difference today was the space between Ash and Cael. The two were usually attached at the hip, even when they were in the canteen. Today Ash was sitting on one end of the bench, flanked by Rosa and Nina, while Cael sat on the other side of the table toward the opposite end. He also looked miserable. Sloane took a seat beside Hudson with Dex sliding in next to him.

"Absolutely ludicrous." Hudson let out a frustrated huff before taking a sip of his milky tea. "There is no room for vigilante behavior in a civilized society."

Ash sat forward, jamming his finger down against the table to emphasize his point. "If you haven't noticed, Doc, we don't live in a civilized society. We live in a fucked-up world swarming with stupid people doing stupid shit. How many bodies have you wheeled into your shiny lab this week alone?"

Hudson arched an eyebrow. "What you're suggesting would merely add to that body count. These are armed Therians going around shooting and assaulting Humans. Simply because they do so in the name of justice, does not make it acceptable. Violence is never the answer."

"How about you come out in the field with us when the shit's hitting the fan, and then tell me violence isn't the answer. Maybe it isn't in your tea-drinking, I-do-beg-your-pardon country where some asswipe isn't handed a gun for opening a bank account, but not here. Do you know how old I was when I fired my first gun? Six. Now you tell me, Doc. What the fuck is a six-year-old doing being taught to shoot a gun?" Ash let out a snort of disgust. "Say what you will, but the Coalition is doing us a favor rounding up these assholes. We've become a society of walking contradictions. We bitch and moan about how bad things are, but the second someone makes a suggestion, we're shouting bloody murder about our civil rights."

Wow. Ash was on a roll today. Sloane didn't know what had ticked his best friend off to warrant the epic rant, but it must have been serious.

"Are you fucking kidding me?" Dex gaped at Ash, and Sloane stifled a groan.

Here we go.

"Yeah, I'm serious. Those guys have rounded up more members of the Order in the last three weeks than we have in months."

"There's a reason for that," Dex ground out. "I don't know if you recall, but we operate under this nifty little thing called the 'law,' which the Coalition wipes their asses with. If we went around shooting down and beating up whoever the hell we felt like, dragging them in without evidence or regard for the law, I'm sure we'd round up plenty of assholes in no time. How can you defend those guys?"

"I'm not defending them. I'm simply saying whether we like it or not, they're getting the job done."

"And leaving us to pick up the pieces and sort out their mess," Dex argued.

"Whatever." Ash removed his phone from his pocket and stood. He turned when Cael got up.

"Ash, can I talk to you a sec?"

"Not now, Cael. I've got to take this call." Ash walked off, and Cael sat back down. He stared at his tablet for a moment, the entire table having gone quiet. Apparently, Sloane wasn't the only one to have noticed the brush-off. What the hell was that about? Ash had never brushed Cael off like that.

"Excuse me." Cael grabbed his tablet and hurried off in the opposite direction Ash had gone. Sloane felt Dex squeeze his leg before he took off after his brother.

"What the hell was that?" Letty asked.

"I don't know. Ash has been... off lately." Rosa turned to Sloane. "You should talk to him. He's been in his own world for weeks, and he won't talk about it. Not that he's ever been big on sharing, but I'm worried. He hasn't said anything remotely inappropriate to me in ages."

"I'm rather disturbed we gauge Ash's wellbeing through his lack of inappropriate comments," Hudson muttered, taking another sip of his tea.

"Everyone has their little telltale signs," Rosa said. "For instance, the more cups of tea you have in a day, the more stressed you are."

Hudson's teacup came to a halt in midair. He frowned and glared accusingly at the brew before setting it down. "Betrayed by my beverage."

"This is his fourth cup this morning," Nina chipped in with a broad smile.

"Thank you, love." Hudson sighed and carried on drinking his tea.

Sloane didn't like the sound of that. Hudson was nothing but steady and calm. Granted, attempting conversation with Ash was a surefire way to spike your blood pressure, but judging by Nina's comment, Hudson seemed to have been feeling agitated far before his debate with Ash. "Everything okay, Hudson?"

Hudson's cheeks flushed slightly, and Sloane wondered what he'd said to bring about such a response.

"Everything's perfectly fine. Thank you, Sloane. It's just one of those days."

Nina leaned forward, talking quietly. "One of those days when Sebastian Hobbs walks into the lab to pick up lab results looking all fine and muscly."

Hudson's teacup clattered against the table. "Oh, for heaven's sake, Nina."

"What?" Nina blinked innocently.

Ah. That explained it. Sloane gave Hudson a sympathetic smile. If there was ever a cautionary tale regarding the dangers of falling in love with your teammate, *that* was it. The irony wasn't lost on Sloane. However, Sloane wasn't Sebastian Hobbs. Seb had been madly in love with Hudson, so much so it led to him being careless, disregarding protocol, and the results had been catastrophic for everyone involved.

An agent had to fuck up pretty badly to get transferred off a team, and Seb had not only fucked up, but done so with flying colors. The incident had destroyed Hudson and Seb's relationship, though it was clear the two still harbored deep feelings for each other. It was a shame. They had been sweet together.

Sloane had tried to help his friend and teammate at the time, but love had turned Seb inside out, and in the end, Sloane watched an exceptional agent break down and lose it. Sloane would never allow himself to follow such a path to ruin. He cared about Dex very much, and there was little he wouldn't do for him. But to be blinded by love to the point where he'd risk everything? The career he'd worked so damn hard for? The safety of his team, of those around him? He'd like to think he had better sense than that. Besides, he and Dex were doing just fine as they were without bringing love into it. They'd only started officially dating a few months ago, and it had been rough getting there.

The rest of the table broke off into conversation again with Rosa changing the subject much to Hudson's obvious relief. Sloane excused himself, reluctantly took Dex's mug, and headed back to the office, his thoughts going to his own relationship. At times, he wondered if things were moving too fast between them. There had been a strong, sexual attraction from the start, and that attraction had turned into affection. If Dex hadn't asked for more, would Sloane still be lingering on the edge of commitment? Would he have taken the next step in their relationship? His earpiece beeped, cutting through his thoughts. He tapped it and answered.

"Brodie here."

Lieutenant Sparks's voice came over the line. "Sloane, would you stop by my office for a moment?"

"Yes, of course. I'm on my way."

"Thank you."

Sloane stepped into the elevator, wondering what the lieutenant wanted to speak to him about. Maybe they finally had a break in their case. A few minutes later, he walked into Lieutenant Sparks's office. She motioned for him to close the door. Doing so, he took a seat in one of the chairs in front of her desk and waited for her to finish typing something into her desk's interface. Once finished, she leaned back in her chair and smiled at him. Her eyes went to the mugs in his hand.

"Interesting choice of drinkware."

He followed her gaze to the two mugs, completely

forgetting about Dex's "poop" mug. His face probably looked as red as it felt.

"I'm going to go out on a limb and say that's Agent Daley's mug."

Sloane cleared his throat and nodded. "You would be correct."

She chuckled. "I knew he would be a good fit for your team."

Funny how everyone had known that before Sloane. It had taken him longer than most to see it, but now he couldn't imagine being partnered with anyone else. The lieutenant's smile fell away, and she was all business.

"I called you in because we haven't had a chance to talk since the incident at the facility. I wanted to know how you were doing."

"I'm fine. Thank you for asking." Although he did appreciate his lieutenant's concern, why was it coming now and not months ago when the incident had occurred? Regardless, he was happy she'd taken the time to talk to him personally. "I appreciate you not suspending me," he added.

"I think we both know you were never in danger of getting suspended. However unorthodox your methods are at times, you get results. You always do. The Chief of Therian Defense knows it too. He's very impressed with you."

Sloane couldn't help his surprise, considering he'd all but implied the guy was a jackass over the phone with him. "Is that so?"

"You did an exceptional job, Sloane. Not only did you retrieve Dr. Shultzon, but you also rescued your partner and eliminated the threat without the loss of any civilians or officers." She tilted her head to one side, her penetrating gaze never leaving his. What wasn't she saying?

"I had no choice." His gut tensed. He knew her well enough by now. She was searching for something. Then it occurred to him. "Wait. What exactly is at question here? My order to neutralize the threat or the motive behind it?" And why the hell was it coming so late? He'd followed all the required protocol at the time. Given his statement, filled out the report, passed his eval, and even saw his THIRDS appointed psychologist, which was customary after a shooting that resulted in loss of life.

Sparks shrugged. "I think you stopped a very dangerous Human who hurt a lot of innocent citizens as well as two of your partners."

It was best he ignore her statement on Isaac hurting his partners. She knew damn well Isaac had done more than hurt them. Actually, now that he thought about it... "My partner and Dr. Shultzon wouldn't have been put in danger if the THIRDS had been honest about the status of the facility. You said it was no longer in use."

"That was the information I had at the time. We discussed this during your briefing, Sloane."

"Yes, and I wasn't given any answers then either." Much like he wasn't getting any answers now.

"I'm afraid I can't give you any more information. All you need to know is that the facility has been permanently decommissioned. Everything has been either shipped out or destroyed. The building is under lease."

"And the drug?"

Lieutenant Sparks met his gaze head on. "None of your concern. You're a Defense agent. Your responsibility is to your team and the citizens of New York City. Anything you need to know, you will be told."

Sloane kept his mouth shut. He should have known he wouldn't get any answers. "You'll have to forgive me, Lieutenant, but I'm not sure why you've called me in here." It clearly wasn't to see how he was doing.

"This organization was built on agents like you and Agent Keeler. You don't shy away from making the tough decisions. You do what needs to be done."

Sloane was confused. Why was she telling him this? He opened his mouth to ask as much when she stood, straightened out the jacket to her pantsuit, and motioned to the door.

"Thank you, Sloane. That will be all."

What the hell? Sloane stood and gave her a nod. He headed for the door when she stopped him.

"Sloane?"

He turned to face her and was taken aback by what he saw. The pupils of her deep-blue eyes were dilated, making them almost appear black. Her piercing gaze and icy demeanor sent a chill through him despite the smile on her face. It was the look of a Felid who'd been to hell and back. He might not know all that much about Lieutenant Sparks's past, but something told him the two of them weren't all that different. Sparks had her demons, and for reasons unknown to him, the death of Isaac Pearce seemed to be holding them at bay. At least for a little while. Sloane knew too well how it felt.

"Between you and me, Sloane? We both know you could have taken Isaac Pearce alive."

Sloane's jaw muscles clenched. "Thank you for inquiring after my well-being, Lieutenant." With that, he left the office.

Lieutenant Sparks had been trying to tell him something, and he'd figure out what it was. One thing he did know was that she wasn't wrong. Like she'd said. He'd done what needed to be done, and that was the end of it.

Sloane walked into his office in a dark mood. At least until he saw Dex. He smiled at the serious frown on his partner's face. It was strange how just the sight of him could lighten Sloane's mood, even when Dex was driving him out of his head. Sloane playfully flicked Dex's ear, chuckling when his partner gave a start.

"For the love of Lucy, you're going to give me a heart attack one of these days."

"Nope. Your fried Mars bar wrapped in bacon is going to do that." He took a seat at his desk. That didn't even earn him an acknowledgment. Whatever his partner had been lost in thought about was really bugging the man. Sloane had an idea what it was. "How's Cael?"

"All over the fucking place because of that dickbag. I don't know what the hell's going on with him. Cael won't talk to me about it."

"Rosa's been worried about them too."

Dex sat back, his fingers resting on his stomach and drawing Sloane's gaze to his partner's lean figure. "Do you really think Ash believes all the bullshit he spouted about the Coalition?"

"You know Ash. He likes to stir things up."

"I agree. But to think those guys are doing a better job than we are?"

"Dex, Ash likes to push buttons. And he succeeds spectacularly when it comes to you. I keep telling you not to let him get to you." It was easier said than done, but sometimes Sloane wondered if Dex even tried to ignore Ash's taunts. It was a good thing his partner was usually cheerful and lighthearted because sometimes Sloane could swear he saw a little darkness under Dex's shiny surface. He knew his partner had a bit of a temper, but it rarely showed itself unless he was exceptionally pissed off about something.

"I can't help it. It's like he has some superpowers of annoyance."

Sloane removed his smartphone from his pocket and swiped the entry pattern before tapping his contacts and searching for Dr. Shultzon's number. There was no point in putting this off any longer.

"Are you calling Shultzon?"

"Yeah." His finger hovered over the call button. He glanced up, and Dex gave him a cheesy grin before thrusting his thumbs up. Sloane couldn't help but chuckle. Feeling slightly better, he took a deep breath and tapped the screen. Two rings later, and the doctor answered.

"Yes?"

"Hello, Dr. Shultzon?"

"Sloane, how lovely to hear from you."

Sloane played with the strap of his thigh rig while he talked in the hopes of relieving some of his anxiety. "I hope you don't mind me taking you up on your offer to call."

"Not at all."

"I thought maybe we could meet. Have a chat over coffee."

"Of course!" Shultzon sounded excited at the prospect. "Whenever you're free."

"How about this afternoon?"

"That would be wonderful. Would you mind stopping by the house? I'm waiting for a courier."

Almost done. "Not at all. I'll give you a call when I'm on my way."

"Wonderful. See you soon."

Sloane hung up. He'd done it. He'd actually called and set up a meeting with Shultzon. God, if he was this nervous from just speaking with the man over the phone, how would he feel when he was faced with him? He was about to tell Dex about his meeting with Shultzon when he heard it.

Snip

It couldn't be. Sloane stared at Dex who was gaping, mouth hanging open, his gaze just over Sloane's shoulder. Heart pounding, Sloane slowly turned his chair, his worst fear confirmed. Sloane let out an inhuman sound before letting out a wail.

"Oh my God, Sarge!"

Maddock stood with a wide grin on his face, a pair of scissors in one hand, and a chunk of Sloane's hair in the other. Sloane frantically felt the back of his head, coming up short on the left side. He opened his mouth, but only a strangled cry escaped.

"I told you two weeks ago to get it cut. Now you have no choice."

"You butchered my hair!"

"Shoulda gone to your barber, or stylist, or whatever the hell you young people call 'em these days. Get your hair cut, or I'm coming back for the other side." Maddock placed Sloane's hair on his desk and walked off humming and singing a song about getting a haircut.

With a whimper, Sloane picked up his fallen locks.

"I swear I didn't see him until it was too late," Dex said, coming around to inspect Sloane's head. "Damn."

"I can't believe he did that." Sloane was dumbstruck. "After all these years of threatening to do it, he actually did it." It was true. He had no one to blame but himself. Maddock had warned him repeatedly. Sloane wore his hair far longer than THIRDS policy allowed and always waited until the last possible moment to get it cut.

Dex sat on the edge of Sloane's desk. "I'm sorry, man. That was harsh. What can I do?"

"Can you put the room in privacy mode?"

"Sure." Dex walked over to the panel and typed in his badge number and security clearance. The walls went white, and the room was secure. Then Sloane let it rip, cursing up a storm. He let loose with everything he had, using swear words he hadn't even been aware he knew. When he was done, his face was hot, and he felt out of breath.

"Your dad's evil," Sloane murmured pathetically. Dex sat on the edge of Sloane's desk and slid over. He stopped in front of him and held his arms out. With a pout, Sloane wheeled his chair forward so he could rest his head on Dex's lap.

"There, there." Dex petted Sloane's head, soothing him. "That was quite the outburst. Didn't know you had it in you. I'm not even sure I know what the last two were."

"German, I think. I heard Sasha over in Recon go off once when his hard drive got wiped by some rogue virus. I don't know what it means, but it sounded... appropriate for this moment." He lifted his head and propped his chin on Dex's leg. "I have to get it cut, don't I?"

Dex winced as he ran his fingers through the butchered hair on the side of Sloane's head. "Yeah. There's really no way to pull this off as trendy."

"Thanks." Sloane stood and gave Dex a kiss. "Tell the evil overlord I left early. I'm going to go see Marcus to get this fixed and then head over to Shultzon's. I'll call you later. If anything comes up, ring me."

"Okay. Good luck on both accounts."

Sloane gave Dex a wink before walking out of the office. On the way to the elevator, he tried to think only about his haircut and not the appointment that would follow. There was no reason to feel nervous. Shultzon had been a huge part of his life once upon a time, but that had changed a long time ago. He could do this. He had to. It was the only way to restore some kind of normalcy after the disorder his life had been thrown into since revisiting the research facility. At least now he could take comfort the nightmares were only in his head.

FIVE

SLOANE WAS FORCED to see his stylist thanks to the horror inflicted upon his flowing locks by his sergeant. When the man had seen Sloane's butchered hair, he'd all but shouted bloody murder before praying to some saint in Spanish. At least Marcus had been sympathetic and mourned the loss along with him. A few snips and a quick blow-dry later, and Sloane felt better. He could still run his fingers through his hair, though only on top. The sides of his head were cut short, making the little silver hairs reflect the light like tiny solar panels. At least that's what it felt like. Marcus had offered to shave his growing beard, but Sloane decided he'd leave it to bug Maddock. At least this time, if his sergeant came at him with a razor, Sloane would see it coming. The man was sneaky, even for a Human. He'd most likely honed his stalking skills over his years raising two mischievous boys.

The locks clicked on the other side of the door, and Sloane braced himself. For fuck's sake, he wasn't a kid anymore. Despite being out of uniform, the badge clipped to his belt and the sidearm tucked into the shoulder holster under his jacket reminded him of who and what he was now. When the door opened and he was faced with the man who was both his savior and personal bogeyman, remaining unfazed became more difficult than he'd expected.

"Sloane." Dr. Shultzon greeted him with a broad, warm smile and a hug. "It's so good to see you."

Sloane gave him a curt nod. "Sir."

"Please, come in." Shultzon stepped aside so Sloane could enter. It felt odd being back here on a personal visit. As Shultzon locked up behind him, Sloane took a quick look around the elegant surroundings, remembering how different it had looked a few months ago when Isaac and his men had ransacked the place before they'd kidnapped the doctor. Now it was immaculate, looking almost comfortable and peaceful. Shultzon motioned for Sloane to enter the living room, and as he did, Sloane took stock of the room, how the bookshelves along the walls were once again filled with books, the lamps were upright, the cream-colored couches and armchairs sat pristinely with their cushions in place, and the wood floors gleamed.

"Nice haircut. Sergeant Maddock's doing?" Shultzon asked, his smile causing creases at the corners of his eyes. He took a seat in one of the armchairs and motioned for Sloane to sit on the couch across from him.

"How'd you know?" Sloane sat slightly forward, his arms on his legs, fingers laced, and his eyes everywhere but on the man before him. Maybe coming here was a mistake. He hadn't talked to Shultzon in years, and now here he was opening the floodgates to God only knew what.

"Sloane, we're only going to talk. You don't need to look so uncomfortable. Sit back, relax. And the answer to your question is that I make it my business to know."

Sloane sat back and studied Shultzon. "About agents' haircuts?" The man hadn't changed at all since Sloane had hugged him good-bye his last day at the facility, right before he'd been blindfolded and deposited on the THIRDS's doorstep like a baby left on the steps of a church. Shultzon's hair had a lot more white than it once had, but other than that, he hadn't changed overly much. He was still tall, kind looking with sharp gray eyes that missed nothing, and a soothing voice that could turn commanding and fierce at the drop of a hat. There was one difference Sloane found comforting. Shultzon no longer had power over him.

"I make it my business to know what goes on at the THIRDS. I may be retired, but I'm still valued there and often consulted. Thank you for coming to see me. I hoped you would."

"Did you?"

Shultzon nodded. "I've followed your progress. I was so proud of you when you made team leader. Despite what you may believe, I care about you. You were like the son I never had."

"Son?" Sloane sat up with a hiss. He'd told himself he wouldn't get angry, but he should have known better. Shultzon may have saved his life, but that didn't mean Sloane could forget the price he'd paid. "I still have nightmares. I haven't been able to stop dreaming about that goddamn place since returning there."

The smile slipped off Shultzon's face, his expression turning remorseful. "I'm sorry. I understand your resentment."

"Do you? I trusted you. And you..." Sloane pressed his lips together, willing himself to calm down. "You tortured me. You tortured Ash. All of us. I endured physical and psychological agony nearly every day." He wanted to blame his lost childhood on Shultzon, but that wouldn't be fair. The man hadn't stolen Sloane's childhood. Being a Therian, what happened to him, losing his mother... He never stood a chance at a normal life after that. He felt his anger wavering.

Shultzon leaned forward, his hands clasped in front of him. "Sloane, I know you think of it as torture, but it was necessary to run those tests in order to understand you. To understand your limits. I protected you and Ash."

Shultzon's sincerity and regretful tone irritated Sloane. "We could have died."

"I would never have let that happen to either of you."

"What about the others? Are you telling me no one died strapped to one of those goddamn chairs?" Sloane jumped to his feet and paced. It was the only way he'd maintain a grip on his temper. The memories flooded back and slammed into him from every direction. The needles, the drugs, the shocks going through his body. When the world looked at him, they saw nothing but an animal. That's what they'd called him at the asylum. Then the Therian First Gen Research Facility had made him feel like one. He looked down at his hands. "I was just a boy."

"Sloane, it's because of you that we have Post-shift Trauma Care. Therians were dying hours after they shifted back to their Human forms, and no one understood why. Most were perfectly healthy. Because of you, we learned how vastly different the Therian metabolic rate was to that of a Human's. And all you did was say two little words. Do you remember what you said to me?"

Sloane nodded. How could he forget? He'd shifted back to his Human form, and he felt as though he were dying, wasting away to nothingness. It had all been so terrifying. His body had felt brittle, and he feared it would shatter if he so much as breathed. Then he'd looked up at Shultzon and he'd quietly said, "I'm hungry."

"That's right. Those two words saved countless lives, Sloane. I asked you what you wanted, and you asked for meat. Four double quarter pounders later, and you were good as new. As soon as we made that discovery, the rest fell into place. Think about it."

Sloane didn't know if that was true. He didn't know how much to believe. Shultzon had been good to him when he wasn't running tests, but he'd been the head doctor at the facility. How much of what he'd been told had been the truth, and how much had been to get Sloane to cooperate? The only thing that kept the Therian children from escaping had been fear. In their Therian forms, they were physically stronger. Fear of the outside world—of being alone—kept Sloane from trying to escape. Every child in that facility had been discarded. Treated like rabid animals.

Behind him Shultzon was going on about everything Sloane had supposedly done to help his fellow Therians, but it was hard to hear past the screaming in his head. He flexed his fingers, forming fists as he tried to shut out the memories of his own screams. The cries of agony became louder, and he felt the Felid inside him stir. His heartbeat sped up, his pulse soared, and he balanced precariously before the abyss. If he didn't regain control...

"Dex."

Sloane's eyes snapped open, his vision sharp. When he turned, Shultzon was smiling warmly at him. "What did you say?"

Shultzon hadn't moved from his position, looking calm and collected as always. "I was asking how your partner Dex is."

For a moment, Sloane stood staring dumbly at the man.

His brows drew together, and he frowned. Why was Shultzon asking about Dex? "Dex is fine."

"He seems to be doing very well. I thought he might have trouble making the leap from homicide detective to Defense agent."

Sloane walked to the couch and sat down. "He's done great, considering he was thrown into the HumaniTherian murder case his first week on the job." Why were they talking about Dex all of a sudden?

"How's he handling being unable to carry out his own investigations?"

"It frustrates him," Sloane admitted, chuckling when an image of Dex looking stumped came into his mind. Not being able to chase down every lead they received frustrated the hell out of his ex-detective partner. So while Recon did the investigating, Sloane had started distracting Dex with training sessions and puzzle games during their down time. His partner would get absorbed in them, and then when they were called out, Dex was raring to go. "We've found a way around it."

"Would you like some coffee?"

"Sure." Sloane sat back, thinking about Dex and all his crazy little quirks while Shultzon disappeared into the kitchen to make coffee. Although Dex was technically still a rookie, he'd come a hell of a long way. He was a quick learner. During training sessions, he'd watch Sloane sparring with Ash and Hobbs and quickly pick up the moves. What Dex lacked in strength compared to his Therian teammates, he made up for in cunning. He was also good at catching his opponents off guard. Shultzon returned with a tray and handed Sloane a cup of coffee. Sloane added a little milk and sugar to it, which was all Dex's doing. He used to be content to drink his coffee black. As he sipped his coffee, he could feel himself relaxing.

"I've been meaning to ask. How long have you and Dex been together?"

Sloane nearly choked on his coffee. So much for feeling relaxed. He wiped at his mouth and met Shultzon's gaze. "Excuse me?"

"Dex. You two are together, aren't you?"

Sloane observed Shultzon as he tranquilly stirred his coffee. "He's my work partner."

"Ah, I see." Shultzon nodded and took a sip, as if those three little words explained everything. It was obvious he didn't believe Sloane.

"What?"

"You were always very good at hiding the truth, even if it was from yourself. But you could never hide from me." Shultzon nodded to where Sloane had stood minutes ago. "You were seconds away from going feral, but you didn't."

"I don't lose control that easily." Maybe that had been true once upon a time when he was younger and had trouble controlling his emotions, but not now. Sloane didn't go feral unless he wanted to.

"I was losing you. I could tell. Nothing I said was getting through. Until I said his name."

Sloane vaguely remembered Shultzon talking, but for the life of him couldn't recall what about. He did recall Dex's name. Was it possible he had been going feral and not known it? Shit, that wasn't good.

"That and the fact Isaac chose Dex to use against you tells me the young man means a great deal to you. I'm sorry I put him in such a difficult position. I hope he forgives me."

"He's pretty pissed he can't remember, but he's not angry with you."

"Then you haven't told him everything, or he would be."

That much was true. "He knows enough. There's no point in worrying him with the gory details." Sloane had spent enough time around Dex to know how personally he took the pain of those he cared about. Knowing the details of what Sloane had suffered would only bring his partner heartache. Was it selfish of Sloane to want to always see Dex happy? His partner didn't seem right without a smile.

"You're protecting him." Shultzon nodded his understanding. He placed his coffee on the table and sat back to study Sloane. "After everything we've been through, do you really believe I'm going to tell Lieutenant Sparks about your boyfriend?"

Sloane scowled but didn't answer. Let Shultzon think what he wanted. Sloane wasn't about to give up his relationship.

"Either way, I'm glad you're happy again. You deserve to be happy."

Happy. That was something Sloane hadn't thought he'd ever feel again after Gabe. It was true Dex did make him happy, even if at times Sloane felt their relationship was moving a little too fast. Of course, he wasn't about to discuss it with Shultzon. "Lieutenant Sparks said the facility's been closed for good. Is that true?"

"What's your gut telling you?"

Sloane cursed under his breath. He'd come to trust his instincts and listen to his gut. The THIRDS was hiding something regarding the facility. They might not be using the same building, but that didn't mean they'd stopped doing whatever the hell they'd been doing.

"We both know how these things work, Sloane."

"And the drug? You saw what it did to Dex. He would

have killed you and then—" Sloane cut himself off, unable to even say the words. He closed his eyes in an attempt to get the image out of his mind, but that only made it worse. It hit him like a Mack truck just then. He'd told Dex he would do everything he could to preserve civilian life, even if it meant losing Dex. Now he wasn't so sure about that, and it scared the hell out of him. He'd never felt this nervous about his relationship with Gabe. Being with Dex was certainly an adventure. Except sometimes he felt as if it were an adventure he was ill-equipped for.

"Sloane, look at me."

Sloane wanted to refuse on principle, but some part of him still felt like that scared little kid when Shultzon spoke to him. He did as asked.

"Right now, there is no need for concern. Should that change, you'll be the first to know."

"Why would you tell me?" Shultzon had no reason to care about Sloane or what happened in his life now. Had he really come to care about Sloane, or was it something else? Could he really trust the man? As if reading his thoughts, Shultzon nodded.

"I trust you. The moment I laid eyes on you, I saw all the potential you possessed. You started out a frightened child and turned into an extraordinary young man. You're an exceptional team leader, and I have no doubt that you'll continue to achieve great things. You're stronger than you think, Sloane. You always have been."

Sloane stood, feeling awkward at Shultzon's kind words. He remembered how much the man's praise had meant to him once. How he'd put himself through so much just to have Shultzon smile at him and tell him how good he was.

"I should go."

Shultzon extended a hand, the look in his eyes genuine.

His tone was sincere when he spoke. "Please say you'll visit again. Maybe you can even bring Dex along. I'd love to meet him."

"I'll tell him." Sloane took Shultzon's hand and thanked him for the coffee and the chat. He left the house and stood for a moment out on the sidewalk. It was so peaceful. He barely even heard the traffic. The evening was breezy. Sloane walked to his car, glad he'd listened to Dex about coming here. He'd been incredibly uncertain at first, almost sure he'd be making a mistake, but he'd trusted Dex. The thought of his partner made him smile. He climbed in behind the wheel thinking about how understanding Dex had been since the very beginning and how every time Sloane felt unsure about anything, his partner was there to help him figure things out. For all of Dex's joking around, the guy was incredibly astute.

As he drove toward Dex's house, he decided he'd take a little detour. He wanted to get something for Dex. He drove around for a while trying to figure out what exactly. Whatever little token he got, he knew his partner would love it. Dex was definitely one of those it's-the-thought-that-counts kind of guys. He was also easy to please. But Sloane didn't want to get him just anything. He wanted to get something that would make Dex smile that brilliant smile of his. The one that reached his sparkling blue eyes. He thought about what Dex went crazy over, even if it was silly or something that drove Sloane crazy. A thought popped into his head, and he smiled at himself. His partner was in for a treat.

DEX TAPPED his foot along to the electric guitar and beating drums while Asia sang about the heat of the moment and teenage ambitions. Only moments ago, Dex had been on a video chat with his little brother, and now he was attempting to make sense of the Coalition case file in front of him. Although he didn't have the clearance to access Themis offsite, he could access his desk's interface and its files. Sloane had sent him a text while at Shultzon's to let Dex know he wouldn't be getting home in time for dinner so to go ahead and order the pizza he knew Dex wanted. He also reminded Dex he'd be working it off during their next training. Silly Sloane. Like that would deter Dex from gorging out on New York's finest slices loaded with extra cheesy goodness and a crunchy crust. He patted his full belly and let out a contented sigh. Next training session would suck, but it had been so worth it.

He propped his sock-covered feet on the coffee table in front of him and scrolled through his tablet. According to Cael, Themis had raised no flags on any unauthorized access. Although algorithms had been set up in the hopes of catching any agents attempting to access information they had no business accessing, it was proving almost impossible. Thousands of agents accessed Themis from HQ alone. Recon agents had more access to classified information than Defense. They could also make amendments and deletions that Defense agents couldn't do. Hence why Dex and the rest of his team's Defense agents were always bugging Cael or Rosa when files needed altering. Intel agents had access to high-level clearance information that even Recon didn't have access to. What Dex couldn't understand was why Sparks seemed so chill.

The THIRDS had a mole in their organization. One that was feeding intel to a vigilante group, and other than Unit Alpha looking into it, there had been no briefings regarding it, no visits from the higher ups, no assemblies or discussions. As if every day was like any other. That sent Dex's curiosity into high alert. What was going on behind the scenes? What were they not being told? It was the THIRDS damned "need to know" policy that frustrated the hell out of him.

Information trickled down, and Dex wasn't the type to sit around waiting to accept what morsels he was given. As much as he loved his brother, whenever he heard the words "Recon's working on it," Dex wanted to smack someone over the head. Recon could work on it all they wanted. That wasn't going to stop Dex from trying to work things out on his end. Which was why he was sitting on his couch with his tablet and a digital map of New York City. There were scores of color-coded dots and pins scattered about, each one pertaining to an unconfirmed or confirmed Coalition sighting as well as Coalition activities.

From what he could see, there was definitely more activity in Brooklyn and Queens than there was in Manhattan. That wasn't surprising, considering Isaac had been operating out of a base somewhere in Brooklyn. Austen was working on getting them the location since THIRDS priority had shifted from the Order to the Coalition. They'd also received intel stating most of Isaac's followers who'd been stationed with him had jumped ship after his death.

Dex stared at the dots on the map until his eyes hurt. There was absolutely no pattern in the locations. So far, the Coalition had sent over a half dozen members of the Order to the hospital with injuries ranging from bruises to broken bones. How long before they had another corpse on their hands? When the Ikelos Coalition hit the headlines, the Order decided they needed to be armed and ready. Now whenever the two sides clashed, there was gunfire with no consideration for innocent bystanders. Dex turned off his tablet and put it on the coffee table. He sure hoped Austen was as good as everyone said he was, because they needed some kind of lead soon.

There was a knock on the door, and Dex let out a yawn before shuffling over. It was almost nine. He'd had dinner, showered, changed, and was ready to veg on the couch.

Dex couldn't help his dopey grin at seeing Sloane. "Hey —" He was cut off when Sloane stepped inside, kicked the door closed behind him, and then grabbed Dex in a fierce hug. Dex didn't question it. He slipped his arms around his partner and held him, smiling when Sloane nuzzled his face against Dex's neck. Sloane pulled back, and he was smiling.

"Thank you."

"For what?" His partner certainly seemed to be in a good mood, considering he'd had his hair chopped off, though the sexy new cut he was sporting sent tingles through Dex just the same. He'd also gone to meet with a man who wasn't exactly on his Christmas card list.

"Just because." Sloane kissed Dex, and when he pulled back, Dex's heart did a flip at Sloane's shy smile. He handed Dex a small white paper bag. "I bought you something. I know I'm going to be paying for it later, but I just wanted to get you something to say thank you."

Dex took the bag. He could barely contain his smile. "You bought me something?" If only Sloane knew how much his tiny gestures meant to him. Man, he was turning into such a sap.

"I know I could have gotten you flowers or I don't know." Sloane shrugged looking embarrassed. "Truth is, I'm not exactly sure what makes an appropriate boyfriend gift. So instead I thought about what would make an appropriate Dex gift, and this is what I came up with."

Dex opened the bag and gasped. "Sweet baby Jesus."

"Is that okay?"

"Okay?" Dex wiped an imaginary tear from his eye before reaching into the bag and pulling out the rainbow-colored, sugar-coma-inducing pastry. He whispered reverently. "You got me a Fruity Pebbles donut. Do you know how much sugar is in this?"

"Enough to make me diabetic just by looking at it."

"I know," Dex replied in awe. "You're so good to me." He gave Sloane a kiss and headed for the kitchen to fetch a glass of milk. Sloane followed. "I take it your visit with the doc went well?"

"Yeah. I don't know if it'll change anything or stop the dreams, but I do know that by the end, I felt... better. Maybe talking to him does help. Either way, I promised I'd drop by for another chat sometime soon. He'd like for you to come, if you don't mind."

Dex gingerly put his donut on a piece of paper towel and smiled at Sloane. "Of course I don't mind." He sat at the counter with his donut and glass of milk, eating while Sloane told him about the visit and what they'd talked about. Once they'd finished, Dex was stuffed. In a little while he'd be on a sugar high so fierce, he would probably be able to hear colors. That worked out for both of them because Sloane decided to put Dex's energy to use. They had sex in the living room, kitchen, on the stairs, and in the shower. It had been fast and hot as fuck. They showered and Dex came crashing down from his sugar high as they lounged on the couch.

Sloane was stretched out beside him, his head on Dex's lap, while Dex absently stroked his partner's hair.

"I can't believe your dad actually went through with it," Sloane grumbled. He'd been lamenting over the loss of his hair for hours.

"He did warn you he was going to take a pair of scissors to it if you didn't cut it," Dex replied. It wasn't as if Dex hadn't tried to warn Sloane. Anthony Maddock did not make idle threats. He simply bided his time, waiting for the right moment to make good on them.

"Yeah, but I didn't think he'd actually butcher it!"

"You should've known better," Dex said with a laugh. "At least it's still long enough to run my fingers through. Either way, you still fiiine. I like it. Marcus did a great job. It's kind of rockabilly."

"I don't know what it is. I just tell Marcus to deal with it and he does. I'm glad you like it though." Sloane leaned his head back and smiled, prompting an upside-down kiss from Dex. He didn't say so, but Dex enjoyed these moments where he got to do nothing but be with Sloane. Being in a secret relationship was more difficult than he'd thought. At work Dex had to be constantly on alert, making sure he didn't accidently let something slip that would give them away. Friday nights were date nights, and although Dex looked forward to those days every week, it usually involved a lengthy car drive outside the city. They couldn't afford to be caught by a fellow agent, or worse, the media. At times he wished they could have a normal relationship out in the open, but for now, he'd take what he could get. Which reminded him...

"So I've been thinking."

"Uh-oh."

"Dick," Dex chuckled. "We've been exclusive awhile."

"We've been exclusive always. Unless we count your unhealthy affair with coffee."

Dex gave a sniff. He wasn't about to disagree with it. "The goddess of java shall not be denied."

"I worry about you sometimes."

"You sound like my family."

"No. They worry about you *all* the time. I know. Cael should have it embroidered on his uniform to save him from grumbling it every few hours."

Dex worried his bottom lip, telling himself he should just spit it out, or he'd obsess over it until he did something stupid and blurted it out at the most inappropriate moment. "Anyway, I was thinking that maybe we should... ditch the condoms." Dex braced himself. There was a long pause before he heard Sloane let out a shaky breath. Damn it. He should have known it was too soon. Just because they had awesome sex and Sloane seemed happy to go along with most of Dex's crazy ideas didn't mean he was ready to—

"Okay."

"Wait. What?" Dex looked down into Sloane's amber eyes. "Really?"

"We've both got a clean bill of health, get tested every quarter, don't mess around with anyone else, so why not?" Sloane gave him a smile, though Dex wasn't fooled. He could see Sloane was nervous about it. But he could also see how much Sloane wanted to do this for them, and Dex didn't take the gesture lightly.

"Wow."

Sloane tilted his head to one side, studying Dex. "You thought I was going to get cold feet?"

Dex felt his face grow hot. "To be honest? Yeah."

"You're so cute."

"I don't know what to do when you say things like that."

"Should I make a serious face when I say it?" Sloane's brows drew together, and he schooled his expression, his voice gruff. "You're so cute."

Dex let out a laugh. "And you're such a dork."

"Says the guy who owns Star Wars lightsaber chopsticks."

"Sushi tastes better when you use the Force."

"You're only strengthening my case," Sloane said with a wink.

"Does that mean you don't want the ones I ordered for you?"

Sloane peered at him. "You ordered me lightsaber chopsticks?"

"Yep. But if they're too dorky for you..." Dex tried hard not to laugh at Sloane's wary expression.

"Which ones?"

"I have Luke's, so I ordered you Yoda's." Dex held back a smile, watching as Sloane thought about it before giving him a curt nod.

"I approve."

Dex rubbed his fingers over the stubble on Sloane's jaw when he heard it. *Wait, was that...* No, it couldn't be. Could it? He discreetly lowered his gaze to Sloane's, meeting his lover's wide eyes and confirming Dex wasn't hearing things.

"Holy shit, you're purring!"

Sloane bolted upright, turning to stare at Dex. "I was, wasn't I?"

"I take it that's sort of a new thing for you."

"I... I've never done that before. Not while Human anyway. I didn't even know I could do that. I shouldn't be able to do that! It's..." Sloane looked like he was at a loss for words.

"A little creepy?" Dex offered sympathetically.

Sloane nodded.

Dex reached out, and Sloane pulled back, eyeing him. "What are you doing?"

"I want to see if you do it again."

"I can't make it happen, Dex, it simply… does. You can't force a Felid to purr."

"Okay, then, lie down."

"Dex," Sloane huffed.

"Come on. Aren't you curious?"

With a heavy sigh, Sloane lay down, his head on Dex's lap.

"Relax," Dex said, running his fingers through Sloane's hair. "Close your eyes, take a deep breath, and relax." He continued to run his fingers through his lover's hair, caressing his jaw and stroking his cheek until Sloane's breathing evened out. Then Dex heard it again. A faint rumbling coming up from Sloane's chest, vibrating against Dex's leg. Sloane opened his eyes, his bottom lip jutted out.

"I'm fucking purring."

"But you know what?" Dex lowered his head toward Sloane's and cupped his face.

"What?"

"It's kind of adorable."

Sloane's frown deepened. "You would think that wouldn't you. You're weird."

"And you're a Therian who can purr while he's Human."

"Shut up." He pinned Dex with a glare. "If you tell Ash, so help me I will reassign you and make you his partner."

Dex put a hand up in promise, though he felt a hint of pride in the fact he was the only one to have brought that out in his partner. Sloane was able to lose himself to the point where even his Therian form—no matter how deeply buried, was able to express its content. He leaned forward and kissed Sloane. Inside he was doing a jig. Sloane turned and sat up so he could pull Dex against him. Their kissing grew more urgent when Sloane's phone went off. With a growl, Sloane snatched it up off the coffee table.

"Brodie here. Yep. We're on it. Pick us up and bring our gear." He hung up and sighed. "I've never worked for an organization so set against me getting laid."

Dex laughed and got to his feet, pulling Sloane up with him. "Come on. Hobbs will be here any minute. I swear that dude was like a NASCAR champ in another life. Where are we heading anyway?"

"Someone called in a Coalition sighting."

"If someone called it in, they'll probably be long gone by the time we get there."

"Either way, you be careful." Sloane pulled him close, and they kissed until they heard a deep honking. Hobbs arrived in record time, stopping just long enough for Sloane and Dex to lock up, rush out into the street, and hop into the back of the truck. Once inside, they both got into their uniforms and gear.

According to Tony, the 911 dispatcher stated armed Therians in masks were spotted on Pitt Street just a block away from the HPF's Seventh Precinct. These guys had balls. Even if the HPF didn't have jurisdiction, it wasn't as if they were going to sit back and twiddle their thumbs while a bunch of armed thugs gunned people down.

Hobbs parked the BearCat off Delancey and Clinton Street where the Williamsburg Bridge started, making sure to stay away from the parking spots right beside the stone structures, a.k.a. the pigeon crapper. Hobbs detested pigeons, mostly because they had a habit of shitting on the BearCat within moments of it getting washed and waxed. Everyone readied themselves while Sloane addressed the team.

"Cael, I want you and Hobbs in your Therian forms.

Remember what Austen said. The Coalition always travels with two members in their Therian forms. I want to be prepared."

Cael and Hobbs gave Sloane a curt nod before Cael hit the release button on the privacy screen and Rosa stood by to assist. They moved fast with the rest of the team scrambling out of the truck while Cael and Hobbs finished shifting. Tony stayed behind to provide surveillance. Cael jumped down from the truck and circled Rosa, rubbing against her leg with a purr. She chuckled and scratched him behind the ear, giving it a playful tug when Hobbs joined them. Just as Calvin joined his partner, a series of pops resounded. Everyone quickly fell into formation behind Sloane who tapped his earpiece.

"Shots fired. Destructive Delta, we're moving in." They used the cars parked down the street to give them cover before crossing to the other side and rushing toward the gunfire. "Sarge, what can you see?"

Maddock's voice came in over their earpieces. "Five Therian suspects are heading your way. They should be coming up Delancey Street any minute. Looks like they're chasing a couple of Humans. Be careful. Two of the Therians are in their Therian forms. We've got a tiger Therian and cougar Therian." As soon as Maddock finished talking, they saw two men sprint onto the street two blocks ahead of them. The two Felids and three Coalition members quickly followed them.

"Move out!" Sloane ordered, and they all broke into a run after their suspects with Cael speeding off ahead and Hobbs close behind. If Cael managed to get close enough to one of the Therians in their feral form to trip him up, Hobbs could move in. Since the rest of the team didn't stand a chance of catching up to the tiger and cougar, they concentrated on the other members. A series of gunshots echoed through the air, and any pedestrians who were around cleared out. There was a loud roar, and the Coalition members split up. "Shit. Everyone fan out!"

Dex took off after one of the masked Coalition members running down Delancey Street. He was forced to duck behind a parked minivan when the large Therian aimed at him and shot off a round. Not hearing a second round of gunfire, Dex peeked out from behind his cover and saw the guy make a left onto Willett Street under the Williamsburg Bridge. Shit. He couldn't lose this guy. Dex resumed the chase, spotting the Therian climbing the fence into the enclosed area under the bridge where there were plenty of places to hide. Dex followed, letting his tranq rifle hang from its strap so he could jump on the fence and climb up. He deftly scrambled over it, landing on his feet. His boots kicked up dust and dirt when he landed. For a moment he thought he'd lost the guy, but he caught movement ahead of him and took off, his rifle once again in his hands.

"THIRDS! Stop or I'll shoot!" Dex called out, speeding past rusted metal containers, parked trucks, and street maintenance equipment. His warning went unheeded. In fact, Dex was forced to make a sudden detour to avoid getting struck by a bright orange cone. Fucker threw a traffic cone at him! Back on course, Dex came skidding to a halt, aimed his tranq gun, and fired. The roar of the Therian told Dex he'd hit his target. Unfortunately, he realized too late that one tranq wasn't enough to bring the nearly seven-foot Therian down, only enough to give him a limp as the drug went through his system. Hoping to catch up, Dex made a run for his perp. He was close. A little more and—

A hard body slammed into him, knocking the wind out of him when Dex hit one of the metal containers. His adrenaline and training kicked in. Dex thrust an elbow up, catching the new masked Therian in the chin. Not allowing his larger opponent to recover, Dex delivered a right hook. He was going for a left when a fist came at him. Dex used his left arm to block the punch and came back with a right uppercut, satisfied by the painful growl released by the large Therian. The bulletproof vest the guy wore made it difficult for Dex to get a good shot in. In the distance, Dex saw his quarry. The guy had stopped to see what was going on, and that's when Dex saw Ash coming his way. Dex struggled with the Therian in front of him but motioned frantically to the one he'd shot. "Suspect is tranqed!"

"Affirmative."

Dex watched Ash take off after the guy and ducked just as the Therian in front of him threw a punch at Dex's head. The guy's fist collided with the container instead, and he let out a fierce howl. Jackass. Austen had been right. These guys were trained but not officially. Had the guy really been expecting Dex to stand there and get punched in the head? He grabbed the guy's wrist, sidestepped, and twisted his opponent's arm behind his back before kicking the back of his knee and shoving him up against the container. He moved to grab the perp's left arm to twist it behind his back when it came at him with a gleaming blade. Dex pushed out of the way, the edge of the blade slicing at Dex's sleeve and leaving a sting behind. In the next instant, Dex was kicked in the thigh with enough force for his leg to go dead. He hit the ground hard, but he refused to stay down. As he pushed himself to his feet, his assailant made a run for it and disappeared into the shadows.

"Motherfucker!" Dex punched the gravel beneath him and forced himself to sit up. Moments later, Ash showed up looking out of breath and sans Therian suspect. "What the hell happened?" Dex pushed himself onto his right leg, hopping back so he could use the container to steady himself.

"I lost him."

Dex stared at his teammate. "What do you mean you lost him?"

"Do I need to draw you some pretty pictures in crayon?" Ash snarled. "I fucking lost him."

"How could you lose him? He was right in front of you!"

Ash got up in Dex's face, pissing Dex off further. "Next time, you go after the perp, and I'll stay back to get my ass kicked. Oh wait, that won't happen because I'm not a fucking Hobbit!"

"Fuck you, Simba!" Dex shoved Ash back away from him or at least attempted to.

Ash pulled back a fist when Sloane materialized between them. "All right, you two. That's enough."

Dex couldn't believe it. They'd almost had one. How the hell could Ash let the guy get away? What a fucking disaster.

"What happened?" Sloane asked looking from Dex to Ash and back, the rest of the team catching up, including Cael and Hobbs who were both panting and huffing. Guess his brother and teammate hadn't had much luck either.

"Ash pulled a Wes Welker and dropped the ball," Dex spat out.

"Fuck you, Daley. Welker wouldn't have dropped the ball if Brady hadn't fucked up the throw."

Unbelievable. "Oh, so now I'm the one who fucked up? And since when are you a Patriots fan?"

"I'm not. Doesn't mean I'm not gonna call out a shitty

play, and Brady pulled a shitty play. So did you. Why the fuck are you bringing up a two-year-old game anyway?"

Dex had no idea. What he did know was that he was mighty pissed off at Ash and wanted so bad to plant one in his face. "I shot the guy!"

"Once! The guy was as big as Hobbs. One tranq dart is gonna sting and piss him the fuck off, but it ain't gonna take him down, genius. You should have gotten off at least three shots!"

"For fuck's sake, give it a rest, both of you." Sloane paused long enough to answer his earpiece. "Brodie here. Copy that, Sarge."

"What?"

"Everyone into the truck. We've got a dead body."

"Someone's going to have to carry the damsel. He's got an ouchie," Ash sneered walking off before Dex could tell him to go to hell. Sloane slipped an arm around Dex's waist and helped him hop toward the gated exit.

"How's your leg?"

"It's fine. Just needs a massage," Dex grumbled. He was aware of Sloane taking most of his weight so Dex didn't have to walk. Beside him, Cael bumped his head against Dex's hand before giving it a lick. "I'm fine. What happened to the Therians you were chasing?" Dex received a series of chirps, as if he was supposed to understand. Then again, he *had* asked. "Sorry. Did you lose them? One chirp for yes, two for no." One chirp. *Fucking great*. "Did you get close?" Again he received one chirp. Well, at least that was something. "Did they have a backup plan?" One chirp. Bastards.

Sloane helped Dex into the BearCat with Cael and Hobbs hopping in after them. Cael settled in beside Dex, purring and snuggling his head against his dead leg as they drove roughly two blocks over to Broome Street, stopping outside a deli. Sloane told Dex to sit this one out, but Dex refused. He wasn't about to give Ash the satisfaction. He told Sloane he was fine, gritted his teeth and limped over to where Hudson and Nina were inspecting the body. Cael didn't leave his side.

"What have we got?" Sloane asked, crouching down for a closer look. Dex decided he'd stand and keep watch. If he got down, he might not be able to get back up with any kind of dignity, and Ash was two feet away giving him a knowing sneer. At least until his gaze landed on Cael. With a frown, Ash turned away and Dex noticed Cael's tail give a restless twitch. He let out a soft mewl and Dex rubbed his ear like he used to do when they were kids whenever Cael needed comforting.

"Human male, Caucasian, midforties. Victim's name is Alberto Cristo," Hudson replied. "According to witnesses, our vic was exiting the deli when two Human males cut through that building there." Hudson pointed to the twenty-four-story apartment building across the street. "They were being followed by the Coalition. The Humans pulled out their weapons and fired on the masked Therians. Everyone ran and ducked for cover, and this Human ended up with one in the head. So far no one witnessed our victim getting struck."

"Anyone else injured?" Sloane asked.

"No."

"We believe he may have been hit by a ricochet," Nina offered and pointed to two bullet holes in the deli's doorframe.

"Okay. Thanks, Nina. Let me know if you find anything else." Sloane tapped his earpiece. "Sarge, can we get background info on our victim?"

"Copy that."

They left Recon and the medical examiners to do their thing and climbed back into the BearCat. The ride back was silent with the majority of the team doing its best to avoid eye contact. They'd fucked up, and now they had their first casualty.

Dex was still fuming when they reached HQ. His leg was sore as hell, and his arm stung where that asshole had cut him. Luckily his uniform had taken the worst of it. There had been very little blood and the cut didn't need more than a small bandage. Too bad his shower hadn't managed to wash away his pissy mood. He slammed his locker shut and dropped down onto the bench, his bare feet protesting the cold tiles. "We were so fucking close." Sloane took a seat on the bench beside him, and Dex leaned slightly toward him so he could feel Sloane's warmth. The locker room was mostly empty at this time of night with a couple of agents a few rows back talking quietly before they headed off.

"What's going on, Dex? I haven't seen you this pissed off in a while."

"Come on, Sloane. You know I'm right."

"Okay, and then what? What are you saying?"

What *was* he saying? He wasn't saying anything except the same damn thing, and that wasn't going to change the outcome. "I don't know. I'm sorry. This whole Coalition thing's got me frustrated. We've been after these assholes for two months and haven't caught one break. Now some poor bastard is dead." He lowered his voice for the next part, not willing to chance anyone overhearing him. "Someone out there—one of our own—is a traitor. We finally got close and fucked it all up. If I'd only gotten off more shots—"

"Okay, stop. No what-ifs. You did your best. I don't

know what happened on Ash's end, and you know what he's like when he fucks something up. He'll never admit it. He's probably feeling as shitty as you are."

Sloane was right. No one liked to admit they'd screwed things up, especially Ash. Dex wasn't so great at it either. Maybe he needed to give his teammate a break. He wouldn't be surprised if his real anger toward Ash was stemming from how the guy was treating his brother. It wasn't as if the two of them got along on the best of days. "I guess so."

"Listen. Recon's going to the hospital to check on the victims and question any witnesses. I know you hate waiting, so..." Sloane took a discreet look around and leaned into Dex, his voice hushed. "How about I take your mind off the wait? We'll head over to my place and get into bed." He gave Dex a wicked grin, and his hand slid over Dex's thigh to his crotch. "I'll help you relax."

Dex stole a quick kiss and got to his feet. "Let's get out of this one-horse town."

SIX

"YOU'RE SUCH A DORK," Sloane teased, watching his partner squirm and laugh.

"I'm sorry. You know how ticklish I am. Is it my fault you go for those exact spots?"

"But I like those spots." Sloane hummed as he trailed his tongue up his partner's inner thigh, loving the taste of Dex's soft skin. The higher he went, the more Dex squirmed. Deciding he would give his partner a break from the torture, he rose and moved up to kiss Dex. His tongue explored his partner's mouth while his hand palmed both their erections. Slowly he stroked their cocks, occasionally giving them a squeeze and enjoying the sounds Dex made as he writhed with need. His partner arched his back, his legs spreading for Sloane.

"Sloane," Dex moaned against his lips.

"Yes?" He knew what Dex wanted, but he loved hearing him say it. His partner's fingers dug into Sloane's shoulders, and Sloane groaned his pleasure.

"Please, fuck me."

Sloane smiled against Dex's lips as he deepened the

kiss. He took the bottle of lube lying beside him on the mattress and sat back on his heels. With a wicked grin, he handed it to Dex.

"Make me wet, baby."

Dex swallowed hard and sat up. He took the bottle from Sloane, the flush on his face travelling from his cheeks to the tips of his ears and down to his shoulders. Sloane resisted the urge to pounce on his partner. Instead he watched Dex intently as he squeezed a generous amount onto his hand. He closed the bottle and tossed it to one side before getting on his knees. When Sloane got on his back, Dex gave him a puzzled look.

"I want you to ride me."

"Fuck." Dex shivered from head to toe.

"That's the idea." Sloane put his hands behind his head, and Dex crawled over him. He sat on Sloane's thighs and wrapped his lubed hand around Sloane's hard cock, sliding it up to the head and drawing a sharp breath from Sloane. He loved watching his partner. The heated look in Dex's eyes, the way those plump lips were slightly parted as he slowly eased his hand down to the root, twisting as he went. Sloane closed his eyes with a moan. When Dex had slathered him up good and driven Sloane to the point where he thought he'd come, he grabbed Dex's wrist and pulled him over. He needed to taste those lips, to claim them as his, and he started by forcing his tongue inside Dex's mouth, his kisses hungry and needy. Gripping Dex's ass, Sloane moved Dex onto him, pulling away from Dex's lips long enough to demand hoarsely, "Fuck yourself on my dick."

"Oh God." Dex shifted back and reached behind him. He took hold of Sloane's cock, and Sloane felt it being pushed between Dex's ass cheeks. With gritted teeth he watched Dex gradually push himself farther back onto Sloane.

"Fuck. Dex," Sloane groaned, his hands gripping fistfuls of the sheets as he felt the tightness of Dex's ass swallowing Sloane little by little. Sloane's brow was beaded with sweat, and he gritted his teeth until Dex was sitting on him with Sloane shoved all the way in. Dex leaned slightly forward, and Sloane ran a hand up his lover's chest. "You're so fucking beautiful."

Dex gave him a wicked smile. He sat back and palmed his erection, jerking himself off unhurriedly. Just when Sloane thought the sight would drive him crazy, Dex started to move. Sloane's hands found Dex's hips, and he couldn't hold back his growl when Dex's gentle rocking turned into Dex fucking himself on Sloane just like he'd asked.

"Oh fuck." Sloane couldn't have been more grateful to Dex for bringing up ditching the condoms. In truth, Sloane had been prepared for the question even if he hadn't thought it would come up so soon. But there was nothing stopping them from taking this step, except for Sloane's own apprehensions. Now that he was inside Dex like this, every touch, every caress of skin on skin made him desperate for more. More of Dex. More of them. More of what could be. The idea terrified him, and when that happened, he focused all his energy and attention on the beautiful man in front of him. It was going to be difficult to keep this up, but he forced himself to hold back for a little while longer, to appreciate what he was being given. Dex rose and fell back onto Sloane, his moans and whimpers driving Sloane close to the edge.

Dex's moves quickened as did his hand on his own cock. "Sloane..."

Sloane was beyond speech. He simply nodded, mesmerized by Dex's face as he came, shooting his load across Sloane's chest. The way he threw his head back, exposing his neck, his lips parting as he moaned. Sloane watched Dex's whole body tremble before him, his lover's skin flushed and glistening with sweat. As Dex climaxed, Sloane was squeezed tightly, and he lost it. Dex fell forward onto Sloane's chest in exhaustion, and Sloane grabbed hold of Dex's hips, forcing his lover down as he thrust up. The sound of skin slapping skin urged Sloane on, and he lost his rhythm as he pounded into Dex. Sloane buried his face against Dex's neck and breathed in deeply, the scent intoxicating. His hips snapped against Dex's ass bringing a gasp from his lover. Dex slipped his fingers into Sloane's hair and held on tight.

Sloane's climax slammed into him, and he thrust deep into Dex. He continued to push, feeling his muscles tense and his body burn. When he'd emptied himself completely into Dex, he let his arms fall to his sides. He was dripping with sweat and out of breath, with the strength to do nothing but lie there with Dex sprawled on him, both of them trying to catch their breaths.

"That. Was. Fucking. Amazing," Dex managed, his voice muffled against Sloane's neck. All Sloane could do was nod. He told himself he should get up to clean them off, but who was he kidding. He wrapped an arm around Dex, and before he knew it, he'd dozed off. When he woke up the next morning, Dex was getting back into bed. He smiled widely at Sloane. What the hell was Dex doing up before him?

"Had to pee."

"Thank you for sharing," Sloane said with a chuckle. His chest was clean, so he assumed Dex had done more than pee. His partner was also strangely awake. "You had coffee didn't you?"

Dex hung his head in shame. "I did."

That explained it. They didn't even need to be up for another hour. No doubt his partner would be having another cup with breakfast as well. "Come here." Sloane patted his side, and Dex crawled toward him when he heard a familiar gruff voice call his name. They both froze.

Dex's eyes widened. "Was that..."

"Hey, Sloane. You up there?"

"What the hell?" Dex hissed. "Ash has a key to your apartment? Why didn't you tell me?"

Sloane scrambled off the bed and grabbed his boxer briefs off the floor. "He doesn't usually let himself in. You gotta hide." He rushed from the room and nearly collided with Ash.

"Fuck, Ash." Sloane reeled back, his hand going to his chest. "You scared the shit out of me. What are you doing here?"

"I've been calling you for the past hour. I was driving by, so I figured I'd see if you were in, except you weren't answering your door. I thought maybe something happened. You're usually up by now." Ash eyed him before cursing under his breath and storming into Sloane's bedroom. He looked around the room before facing Sloane with an accusing glare. "I fucking knew it!"

Sloane peered at him. "Knew what?"

"That you two were screwing."

"What the hell are you talking about?"

"Oh, we're going to do this are we?" Ash nodded, his hands going to his hips. This wasn't looking good. "Okay. First of all, unless you were practicing for the day jacking off becomes an Olympic sport, there's no reason you'd be that out of breath and reeking of sex. Plus, you're still in bed at this time of morning."

"I had a headache, so I thought I'd lie in," Sloane replied with a shrug.

Ash arched an eyebrow at him. "There's an open bag of gummy bears on your nightstand."

"Now I can't like gummy bears?" Yeah, that one was stretching it even for him, and they both knew it.

"Uh-huh." Ash went over to the closet, and Sloane maintained his stoic expression. There was no way Dex would be hiding in the closet. It was too obvious. Ash opened the door, looking unimpressed. "There's a fuckwit naked in your closet."

Dex looked up at Ash with wide eyes. "This isn't what it looks like. I dropped some change, it rolled under the closet door, and when I went to pick it up, my clothes fell off. True story."

"You're an idiot," Ash growled, then turned back to Sloane. "And *you're* a dick. How could you keep this from me?" He shook his head. "I knew it. My gut was telling me, but I ignored it because I figured my best friend would have the balls to confide in me." Dex slowly stood, his hands clasped in front of him, and Ash turned his face up to the ceiling. "Put some pants on for fuck's sake."

"Good idea." Dex darted to the armchair where his clothes were when Sloane caught his arm.

"Really? Your clothes fell off? That's the best you could come up with?"

Dex gave a helpless shrug. "I panicked." His partner looked like he was about to freak out. Sloane couldn't blame him. He was pretty freaked out about this whole mess too. Ash interrupted his thoughts.

"I swear if he doesn't put some clothes on that scrawny ass of his, I'm going to—"

"We had sex in your bathroom during my party!"

Sloane gaped at Dex who clamped his hands over his mouth, as if doing so might miraculously take back what he'd just blurted out. Ash's words echoed Sloane's thoughts.

"What. The. *Fuck*! You had sex in my bathroom?" Ash went from flabbergasted to disgusted in point five seconds. "Oh my God. Please tell me you didn't jizz on my towels."

Dex held a hand up in promise. "I swear we didn't jizz on your towels."

"Why should I believe you?"

"Would it ease your mind if I told you I jizzed in Sloane's mouth?"

Sloane and Ash groaned at the same time. Just when he thought this day couldn't get any more ridiculous. He should have known, really.

"No. No, it doesn't ease my mind. I'm going to have fucking nightmares for the rest of my life! I have to buy all new towels. Bleach the whole fucking place." Ash shook his head, seeming unable to accept it. "My bathroom, man. You fucked in my bathroom." He made a gagging sound, and Dex opened his mouth, but Sloane put his hand to it before his partner could say anything to make things worse because with Ash and Dex in the same room, things could always get worse.

"Dex, can you wait downstairs. Please."

Dex nodded and, covering himself with his clothes, rushed out of the room. Sloane decided it was best to wait. He had no idea what was going to come out of his best friend's mouth next. He felt a deep pang of guilt when Ash's expression fell.

"Why didn't you tell me?"

"Yeah, because it would have clearly gone so well." Lucky for him, Ash didn't deny it.

"How long?"

"Officially?"

"There's an unofficially?" Ash made to sit down on the bed, took in the rumpled state then seemed to think better of it. "Is there anywhere in this room where you two haven't done it?"

Sloane pointed to the armchair. "There. It's usually where we throw our clothes."

Ash walked over and dropped himself onto it. The room went quiet. Just when Sloane thought the silence was going to drive him crazy, Ash spoke up. "Well?"

"It started off as sex. Lots of sex."

"I don't want to be reminded of what you two were doing before I got here." Ash reached behind him, grabbed Sloane's T-shirt, then tossed it at him. "So now it's not just sex."

"Hasn't been for a while." Sloane slipped his T-shirt over his head and walked over to the bed to sit down.

"When did it stop being about sex?"

"Months ago." Sloane shrugged. "I wasn't ready to admit it."

"Then it's serious. You're serious about him."

Sloane nodded.

"He's a fucking jackass."

"Don't," Sloane pleaded. "You're my best friend, Ash, and next to him, the only other family I have. Please."

"Shit. You really care about him."

"Yeah, I do. I know he annoys you—"

"Understatement."

"But I'm happy with him. I didn't think I'd get another chance after Gabe."

Ash averted his gaze and seemed to get lost in his own thoughts for a few heartbeats. Sloane held his breath. It was difficult enough at work with Ash and Dex always at each other's throats. What would it be like now that Ash knew? He couldn't believe their cover was already blown. Their secret was quickly becoming not so secret.

"He really makes you happy?"

Sloane didn't hesitate. "Yes."

Ash went pensive once again. "I'm not going to be nice to him 'cause he's your boyfriend."

Sloane held back a smile. "Nothing has to change."

"It already has."

"Are you okay with that?"

"You and Daley?" Ash gave a snort.

"Stupid question?"

"Doesn't matter what I think. What matters is that you're happy. Just be careful. I don't think I need to tell you what'll happen if this shit gets out. I don't want them transferring you."

"Cael knows." He might as well get it out there now. "And Shultzon, though I never confirmed it. You know what he's like. I'm pretty sure Bradley knows, though he's been trying to get us together from the start. Oh, and Lou." He cringed at Ash's murderous glare.

"The fucking bartender and Dex's ex-boyfriend knew before I did? What the fuck, man?"

"I didn't tell them. I swear, I'm not making excuses, but I really didn't tell anyone. Lou walked in on us at Dekatria that night he showed up. I got into an argument with Dex, we were making up in one of the unused back-of-house halls, and Lou walked in on us. If I was going to tell anyone, you have to know you would be the first person I'd tell, even if it meant you threatening to kick my ass."

"Yeah, all right. I know." Ash rubbed a hand over his head. "Okay, well. Cael won't say anything, and I don't think the others will either."

"Dex doesn't know Cael knows."

"Those two are going to be the death of me." Ash ran a hand over his face and sat back with a heavy sigh.

"Dex I'm not surprised. But Cael? What's going on with you two?" Something was going on with his friend. Ash hadn't accompanied them to Dekatria in weeks. He barely dropped by the office. Unless they were training or out in the field, Sloane barely saw Ash.

"Nothing. It's fine."

"You haven't been hanging out with him recently."

"I've been busy."

"Too busy for Cael?" Sloane couldn't hold back his disbelief, especially when Ash snapped at him.

"What am I, his fucking babysitter?"

Sloane stood and faced his friend. "What the hell, man? First you brush him off in the canteen and now this?"

"Sorry. I'm just tired."

"Ash, if something's going on, you know you can talk to me." His friend was reserved, but Ash's behavior was starting to worry Sloane.

"Thanks, but I'm fine." Ash got up and shoved his hands in his pockets. "I came by to tell you I won't be in most of today. I've got an eval scheduled."

"Shit. Are those coming up already?" He wouldn't be surprised if that was the reason behind Ash's strange mood lately. Psych evals were never fun, especially the kind they were subjected to. The THIRDS wanted to make sure their First Gen agents weren't going to go off the deep end, so they pushed until an agent either caved under the pressure or dealt with it. Sloane always felt out of sorts the days surrounding his psych evals.

"Yeah. You know I don't like texting that shit, which is why I tried to call you."

"Thanks. I'm glad you came by."

"And here I was pissed off I got caught in a jam over on Ninth Avenue. Any sooner, and I might have caught you two—" Ash cut himself off and shuddered at the thought. He turned and headed downstairs with Sloane following close behind. Dex stood from the couch, his anxious gaze going from Ash to Sloane. When Sloane gave him a wink, Dex visibly relaxed. At least until Ash marched over to him and stuck a finger in Dex's face.

"You better hope this doesn't get out, Daley. If he gets transferred, I'm going to kick your ass."

"Got it."

"This is serious."

"Yeah, I figured. The getting my ass kicked part sort of gave it away," Dex said with a frown. "Look, I know what's at stake. I'd never do anything to screw things up for Sloane."

Ash went quiet for a moment before giving Dex a nod and storming off without saying another word. Sloane let out the breath he hadn't realized he'd been holding and then dropped down onto the couch with a heavy sigh. Dex quickly followed.

"That went better than I expected."

Sloane gave Dex a sideways glance. "We really need to work on those freak-outs."

"Yeah, I'm not very good under stressful conditions."

"What are you talking about? You work under stressful conditions nearly every day."

Dex seemed to think about that. "You're right. Let me

rephrase that. I'm not very good under stressful conditions that involve Ash."

Sloane let his head fall back against the couch with a groan. "You're lucky you're cute."

"And damn good in the sack," Dex added.

"And damn good in the sack," Sloane agreed.

"So... how about you show me how good *you* are." Dex got to his feet and removed his shirt followed by his boxer briefs. Sloane got to his feet and towered over his lover, his smile stretched wide.

"Challenge accepted."

So FAR, so good.

Sloane observed Dex as he edged up to the open doorway, pausing before entering with his rifle aimed and ready. Rosa entered swiftly behind. The two searched the room quickly and efficiently, watching each other's backs as they did. Dex silently motioned to the closed door on the other end of the living room, and Rosa gave him a nod. Dex pressed himself up against the wall beside the door, reached out, and after getting Rosa's signal, Dex pushed the door open. Rosa rushed in and assessed the room with Dex bringing up the rear. Moments later, Dex declared into his earpiece. "Clear."

"Good. Fall back. Calvin, Hobbs, what's your twenty?" Sloane's attention turned to the pair on the large monitor. Calvin inched up to the large steel door with Hobbs in his Therian form close behind, sniffing the air.

"We're about to breach the perimeter," Calvin replied. "Cael, do you have a visual?"

Sloane moved his gaze to Cael who appeared to be

staring at the monitor but not seeing what was right in front of him.

"Cael?" Calvin asked, snapping the young agent out of his trance.

"You're clear."

Sloane preserved his silence, watching with growing concern as Calvin entered a room he expected to be clear and instead met the barrel of a gun. Two shots in his leg, and Calvin went down cursing up a storm. Sloane remained quiet. Cael blinked, stared at the screen, then jumped to his feet.

"Shit."

Shit was right.

Sloane stepped to one side as the doors to the observation deck slammed open, and a very pissed off Calvin stormed in, bright red paint splotches on his tac pants where Letty had shot him.

"What the fuck, Cael!"

Cael gave a start and faced Calvin. "What happened?"

"That's what I'd like to know." Calvin marched up to Cael, his face flushed with anger. Although it wasn't like Calvin to blow up at one of his teammates, the guy had every right to be angry. "You said the room was clear."

Cael's eyes went from Calvin to the monitor and back. "I'm sorry. I must have looked at the wrong screen."

"The wrong screen?" Calvin stared at his teammate in disbelief.

Cael crossed his arms over his chest, his tone and posture defensive. "I said I was sorry."

"Sorry? Sorry's not good enough, Cael."

"What else do you want me to say?"

"How about what you'll tell my mom when you're on her doorstep to let her know her son's dead because you looked at the wrong screen! Get your head out of your ass. What the hell's going on with you?"

"What's going on with me? What the hell's going on with you? You've been acting pissy for months!"

Calvin looked as if he'd been slapped in the face. "What?"

"Please, like no one's noticed," Cael scoffed. "You've been moping and grumpy."

"That's my problem. At least it's not interfering with my job, which is more than I can say for you."

Hobbs showed up, a deep low mewl coming from him as he padded up to Calvin. He bumped his head against Calvin's leg, and Sloane watched as Calvin pushed his head away. The two young agents continued to bicker while Hobbs chuffed and mewled in an attempt to get his partner's attention.

"All right, that's enough," Sloane snapped. The three agents gave a start and turned to face him. Cael and Calvin quickly stood to attention, their hands clasped behind their backs while Hobbs sat beside his partner, his ears flattened against his head in worry. They'd been so absorbed in their argument they'd clearly forgotten Sloane was even there. "I have to say, I am truly disappointed. This has been the worst training exercise I've seen in a long time." Sloane came to stand in front of them. His agents couldn't even look him in the eye. They were supposed to be an elite team with years of experience. They were trained better than this. "Cael, you weren't even paying attention. You allowed your teammate to walk into a goddamn trap. Calvin, you shouldn't have been relying on Cael to do all the work for you. You made yourself a sitting duck, and then to make things worse, you got so pissed off at Cael, you didn't even bother to neutralize the threat after you went down."

"I got shot because of him," Calvin argued. He seemed to catch himself and tacked a quick, "sir" at the end.

"In the leg," Sloane replied curtly. "You're a fucking sniper, but you didn't bother shooting a target who was two feet in front of you." Sloane moved onto Hobbs. "And where the hell were you when your partner needed you? You should have been right behind Calvin. The moment you saw your partner unable to take the shot, you should have stepped in to neutralize the threat."

Hobbs lowered his head, a soft moan coming from him. He nudged closer to his partner, but Calvin ignored him. Usually Calvin would oblige with a scratch behind the ear to reassure him.

"I don't know what's going on with all of you, but it ends now. I'm not about to risk the safety of this team and the people we're supposed to protect because you can't get your shit together. You have personal problems to deal with, I get it. We all have shit to deal with, and guess what? The Coalition doesn't give a flying fuck about our personal problems. We still have a job to do. We have never let each other down before. Are we going to start now?" All three shook their heads somberly. "Good. This better be the last time I see such a piss-poor display." He gave a nod, and the three started to head off. "Oh, and just to be sure it doesn't happen again, the three of you are on equipment pickup duty for the next month. Have fun with that."

The agents cursed under their breaths but didn't utter a word. Equipment duty was a pain in the ass and a perfect disciplinary measure. For a month they'd personally have to inspect every piece of equipment in Destructive Delta's armory and their BearCat. Clean every nozzle, check every chamber, reload every magazine, dust, clean, disinfect, and deliver uniforms to Laundry Services along with a host of other fun tasks.

Sloane's earpiece beeped several times, and he tapped it to answer. "Agent Brodie, here."

Austen's voice came over his line. "Con Ed plant. Twenty minutes."

The line went dead, and Sloane tapped his earpiece again. "Destructive Delta, we're moving out. *Now*. Hobbs, stay in your Therian form. Calvin, you drive." Sloane ran out of the observation deck, catching up to the rest of his team as they rushed down the wide stone corridor toward the armory, connecting with Maddock along the way. "Sarge, I've just received intel on the Coalition. We're heading out."

"Copy that. Keep me posted, and take some backup with you."

Sloane grabbed his tranq rifle and tucked extra magazines into his tac vest's pockets as he addressed his team. "All right, everyone. If you get close enough to take one of these bastards down, you do it. If we can get our hands on just one of them, we might finally be able to get some information. Watch your backs and stay alert. Call for backup if you need it." His earpiece beeped, and he answered it. "Agent Brodie."

"Taylor here. Beta Ambush will be on standby. We're heading out to the location now."

That was quick. Maddock must have asked Taylor to provide backup, though he wished Maddock would have asked Levi instead of Taylor. There wasn't much Sloane could do about it now. "Copy that." As Sloane's team made for the BearCat, Dex pulled back to walk beside Sloane.

"Judging by the royally pissed-off faces, I'm going to

take a guess and say the training session didn't go as planned."

"It was a fucking disaster," Sloane admitted. He'd never faced this problem with his team before. They weren't invincible, and even Sloane had been dealt some shitty blows on the personal front, but it felt as if his team was falling apart, and he couldn't let that happen. "I need you to talk to your brother. He really dropped the ball back there."

"What about Ash?"

"Ash wasn't there. And just so you know, I'm not taking sides. If it had been Ash who'd fucked up, I would have called him out on it, but he wasn't there at the training session. Your brother was. I'm sorry, Dex, but Cael has to pull himself together before someone gets hurt. I'll deal with Calvin and Hobbs."

Dex let out a resigned sigh. "You're right. I'll talk to him."

As they climbed into the truck, Cael came to sit beside Sloane. "Where's Ash?"

"I don't know. He had evals this morning but should have been out by now." Sloane didn't tell Cael which evals Ash was having. That was up to his best friend if he wanted to tell someone. Aside from their quarterly physical and psychological evaluations, the THIRDS often pulled agents in for random screenings. It kept everyone on their toes and from doing anything stupid.

"Sloane, I'm really worried. I've been thinking about the way he's been recently, and it made me wonder if being back at the research facility got to him."

Shit. Sloane had been so wrapped up in his own little world, he hadn't thought about how Ash might be dealing with the whole thing. It made sense. After all, Sloane had been having nightmares since the incident, but at least he had Dex to help him through it. Ash wasn't the kind of guy to ask for help, and he certainly wasn't into sharing his feelings. Looked like his teammates weren't the only ones needing a good kick in the ass. Some fucking friend he was. "You're absolutely right, Cael. I promise you, as soon as I get the chance, I'll talk to him."

"Ash is always acting like such a tough guy that it's easy to assume nothing gets to him. Having all that come crashing back has to have affected him in some way. I just wish he'd say something rather than bottling it all up. I've tried talking to him, but it's like he's avoiding me."

Sloane gave Cael a reassuring pat on the leg. "I'll talk to him."

"Thanks. And I'm sorry about the training session today. I won't let it happen again."

"I'm counting on it." He gave Cael a reassuring smile, watching the young Therian look a little more at ease. Cael was right about Ash. Getting his best friend to open up was going to be no easy task. More like pulling teeth. Sloane couldn't fault him, he was no better at opening up himself, but he was working on it. Dex made it easier. Ash had been there for him all those years ago. Sloane hoped Ash would let him be there for him now. Something told him that was easier said than done.

SEVEN

It was all go from the moment the truck stopped just off the intersection of Avenue C and East Thirteenth Street. There were a half dozen masked Coalition members dispersing. They'd clearly been warned, but Destructive Delta managed to make it in time. The team had split up, with everyone taking off after a Coalition member while backup made its way there.

Dex raced down East Thirteenth Street after one particularly huge Therian, and he wondered why the hell he always ended up against the biggest guys. For a moment, Dex thought he was about to lose the guy, certain the Therian would head straight for FDR Drive. Except the masked Therian didn't get anywhere near FDR. Before Dex's eyes, the guy jumped onto the hood of a car parked beside the plant, hopped on the car's roof and then leapt onto the large garbage container before disappearing over the fence of the Con Edison Plant.

"Fuck me," Dex growled. He took a deep breath and followed, regardless of his equipment. He wasn't going to lose the guy. Not this time. He jumped onto the Honda's hood, the metal denting and protesting under his boots, before jumping onto the roof. The car had been parked nearly touching the container, and to Dex's relief, there was some kind of rectangular metal box sticking out of the container's side right in front of him. It was wide enough for him to prop the front of his boot. He reached out and grabbed the edge of the container, braced a boot on the metal box, and hoisted himself up on the ledge, praying he didn't fall headfirst into trash bags of God only knew what.

This was where being a Felid Therian would have come in real handy. If Hobbs had been here with him, he would have leapt over this thing with no problem. Dex stood and held his arms out to keep his balance as he quickly but carefully walked around the ledge of the container to the fence. It wasn't at all graceful or as easy as it looked in the movies, but at least Dex landed on the other side on his feet and not his ass.

He caught sight of the masked Coalition bastard running toward what looked like a steel bridge connected to several of the buildings. Dex gave chase, hearing nothing but the loud whirring and buzzing from the plant around them. Fuck. He sure hoped he didn't get electrocuted. *Don't touch anything*. It didn't help that wherever he looked he spotted *Danger High Voltage* signs. Dex had to catch the guy before he disappeared into the shadows, or Dex was screwed. If he stopped to remove his night-vision goggles from his backpack he'd lose the guy for sure, but if the Therian made it to the shadows before Dex caught up, he wouldn't have any choice but to stop. Walking into the darkness where a Therian lay in wait was suicide.

Pushing himself, he picked up his speed, catching up just enough to reach out and grab a strap on the guy's vest. He gave it a fierce jerk, and although it wasn't nearly enough to bring the guy down, it was enough to unbalance him momentarily.

Dex took advantage of the flailing perp. He tripped the guy and threw all his weight into the large Therian. They both hit the ground rolling. They thrashed and struggled with Dex getting slammed hard against the solid ground, forcing the air out of his lungs. He tried to get to his earpiece, but his hand was forced against the ground. With his free hand, he grabbed a fistful of the Therian's mask and pulled. Auburn hair sent his stomach plummeting, and then his worst fear was confirmed.

"Ash?" Dex rolled onto his side, unable to believe what he was seeing.

"Fuck," Ash snarled. His eyes suddenly went wide, his gaze somewhere behind Dex. "No! Wait—"

Dex's world went black.

DAMN. Again?

Dex really needed to stop turning this into a thing. Sloane was going to kill him. He stayed exceptionally still and made certain his breathing remained steady. They'd tied his hands behind his back with heavy rope, along with his ankles. He was blindfolded and gagged, but at least he could hear. From what he could make out, there were at least two others in here with him. Wherever *here* was. He listened to the voices, one of them he'd recognize anywhere. Ash was arguing with someone. Afraid they might realize he was awake, Dex didn't take any chances in testing the ropes securing him. Not yet anyway. Then he heard Cael's name.

"Look, I'm not interested in your boyfriend—"

"He's not my boyfriend," Ash replied snidely. "He's just a kid who wishes he were. The guy's got a hard-on for me. Hangs on my every fucking word. He'll do what I tell him."

That fucking prick. It took everything Dex had to remain still, his head pressed against a solid concrete floor. His left arm was starting to ache from lying on it. Dex continued to listen, trying to commit the second, unfamiliar voice to memory. It was hard to get a read on someone based on voice alone, but little things were starting to come through, like the guy's arrogance.

"And you think he'll listen to you over his own brother?"

There was some moving around before Ash spoke up. "I think if you want something bad enough, you'll do what it takes. He's young and infatuated, which means he'll do stupid things, including ignoring his big brother's warnings. I've had the kid on the ropes for days."

"You really expect us to let him walk out of here now that he's made you? He's a THIRDS agent."

"I say we get rid of him."

Shit. There was a third guy. Thank goodness Dex hadn't made a move. Who knew how many there were.

"You fucking lay a hand on him, and I'll get rid of your balls. The deal was I would get in on the action, provide you with intel, and in return, the Coalition would stay away from my team."

Dex stifled a scoff. How very considerate of Ash. This whole time not only had they been hunting a member of the THIRDS but their own teammate. It was like a bad dream. His thoughts went to Sloane and Cael. This was going to crush them. Dex quickly reined in his growing ire. First, he had to get himself out of this.

"Yeah, well, if we'd known what a pain in the ass your team was going to be, we would have reconsidered."

"*You* asked *me* to join, remember?"

"I'm fucking regretting it already."

The third guy chimed in again, his voice odd, like it was purposefully muffled. "Funny how shit always fucks up when you're around. You're bad luck."

"That's me," Ash said roughly. "I'm like a bad penny. I always turn up."

Was Ash quoting Indiana Jones? *Not the time, Daley.* He waited to see what their next move would be when Mr. Arrogant-Prick-Not-Ash spoke up.

"Fine. But the boss is going to hear about this. If that little shit causes us problems, it's on your head."

Okay. There was a boss, but he wasn't around, and judging by Mr. Asshat, he was most likely the second-in-command Austen had mentioned. Silence followed until Dex was abruptly hauled off the ground and slung over someone's shoulder. He was carried away, and soon Ash's rough whisper broke the silence.

"I know you're awake. I can tell by your breathing."

Fucking Therians.

"If you know what's good for you, you'll keep playing dead."

Dex did as he was told. He listened to all the sounds around him, but it was nearly impossible to tell where he was. It was cool and had an outdoorsy smell, but they were definitely indoors. There were the sounds of several footsteps from at least three others and the opening and closing of heavy doors. A door shrieked somewhere and slammed. Metal. Dex could tell the place was dimly lit. Although the bandana around his eyes was black, there was a little light coming in from underneath. A door close by opened and then closed, and Dex felt a breeze against his face and heard the distant sound of busy traffic and blaring car horns. They were outside. Then Dex was dropped on a seat. Ash's truck. The ropes binding his ankles and wrists were sliced off and the gag removed.

"Keep the blindfold on until I say so."

The door slammed to his right, and Dex sat unmoving, his temper simmering under the surface. He heard the engine of Ash's monster pickup truck roar to life, and a seat-belt was roughly pulled across Dex's chest. It clicked into place, and then the truck was moving. A few minutes later, the blindfold was yanked off, taking some of Dex's hair along with it.

"Fucking shit." Dex was seething, especially since Ash was sitting there looking so goddamn calm. "How long have you been a traitor?"

"Don't be such a fucking drama queen."

"Are you kidding me?" He didn't even know where to start with how pissed off he was. If he didn't think punching Ash across the jaw might get them killed, he'd have done it by now. "You son of a bitch! How could you do this? To Sloane? To Cael?"

"I don't need Sloane's permission. And Cael—Cael's just a kid. He's a teammate. That's all."

"Bullshit. I don't believe that. You care about him. Everything you said about him back there was bullshit." That much Dex believed. "And I know it. You want to know why?"

"Not particularly."

"Well you're going to hear it anyway. Because there was no way you were pretending back in the hospital when Cael was there. I saw you. From the moment I joined the team, I've seen how you are with him."

"Ever heard the expression, mind your own damn business?"

"How is this not my business? My teammate, my boyfriend's best friend, the guy my brother's totally crazy about is a traitor. How—"

"Cael's crazy about me?"

Dex opened his mouth, then closed it. "Seriously? Some asshole knocked me out and kidnapped me, wanted to off me, and you're working with the Coalition, but you want to talk about your love life?"

"Did Cael say he was crazy about me?"

It was like talking to a fucking brick wall. But Ash's grave expression told Dex he was serious about this. Fine. As long as he had Ash's attention, he'd go with it. "I don't know how you did it or why the hell you deserve it, but yeah, he's got it bad for you. I thought you knew. You told that asshole as much."

"I figured as much, but it's different hearing it confirmed by you." Ash's stern expression never wavered.

Dex shook his head, feeling a lump form in his throat. "Doesn't matter though. Whatever you do, you're going to end up breaking his heart." The verdict on Ash's sexuality was still out, though the whole *straight* image was swiftly crumbling. Even if Ash did feel something for Cael, he had bigger problems right now than relationship issues.

"What the fuck do you know about me?"

"Clearly not as much as I thought," Dex snapped. "I might not have liked you, but at least I had some goddamn respect for you." The truck came to a skidding halt, and Ash lunged across the seat. He grabbed Dex by the collar with both hands and jerked him close. His amber eyes were glowing and dilated, his fangs elongating.

"Now you listen to me. This isn't one of your stupid karaoke nights. These guys don't fuck around. Right now, I'm the only thing keeping them from putting a bullet in you. You want to keep our team safe? You shut the fuck up. And keep Cael away from me."

Before Dex could utter a word, Ash unfastened Dex's seatbelt, opened the door behind Dex, and shoved him out. Dex flailed and turned, landing painfully on the sidewalk with a groan. He heard a door slam and the sound of screeching tires. Ash was gone.

Dex sat up and rubbed his arm where he'd landed. He stared down the street, watching Ash's taillights get farther and farther away. For the longest time, he sat there in a daze. It took him a while to realize he was on his street. Ash had dropped him off at his house.

Not caring who saw him, Dex drew his knees up and let his elbows rest on them. He dropped his head into his hands and tried to figure out his next move. For the first time in his life, he was at a loss. When his ex-partner had killed that young Therian, Dex had known what the right thing to do was, despite knowing what it would do to his career. Now here he was again, facing the betrayal of someone close to him. Someone who he'd trusted with his life. He might not have gotten along with Ash, but he was big enough to admit he admired certain aspects of the fierce agent. The right thing to do would be to step forward and tell the truth.

But what if Ash was telling the truth about their team being in danger? Had it been an idle threat to get Dex off his back? To scare him? He'd never seen that side of Ash. He'd all but gone feral inside the truck. Dex had almost been... intimidated. Dex pulled out his phone, scrolled through his contacts until he reached his dad's number. His finger hovered over the Call button. What made Ash any different from Walsh? What if Ash had hunted alongside his fellow Coalition members and joined in on beating the shit out of the Order's followers?

"Fuck me," Dex groaned. Why was this shit always happening to him? Why couldn't someone else have discovered Ash's little secret? "Fuck this. Fuck that. Fuck everything. *Fuck*!" He fell onto his back, glowering at the tree branches above him. It was a nice night. A little orange-and-brown bird chirped and hopped down a branch, coming to stop over Dex's head. "If you shit on me, I will shoot you." The little bird chirped and Dex sighed. "I won't shoot you, but I will definitely get pissed." Well, wasn't this just awesome. He heard an indignant scoff and tilted his head back.

"Good evening, Mrs. Bauman."

The tiny old lady and her equally tiny dog huffed as they went on their way. The poor woman must think he was on something, though she didn't so much as blink at the rifle lying across his chest. It seemed every time she saw him he was either standing half-naked on his front steps or lying on the sidewalk, contemplating his life and the utter clusterfuck it was. He sat up and tapped his phone.

"Hey, it's me."

"Dex? Where the hell are you? Are you okay? We lost your signal."

"Yeah, I'm uh... I'm home." He felt like an idiot, but just the sound of Sloane's voice helped soothe him.

There was a long pause. "What do you mean you're home?"

"I'm home. My house."

Another pause. "I'll be there in fifteen minutes. Do I need to call for backup? Medics?"

"No."

"Okay, then. Hang tight."

Hanging up, Dex headed inside to wait for Sloane. He locked the door, and when he went to sit on his couch, he realized he was still in his uniform and had all his equipment. He removed his rifle from its clip and laid it on the coffee table followed by his thigh rig. Piece by piece he removed his equipment, the process calming his nerves.

There was a pounding on the door, and Dex gave a start. "Who's there?" What was he expecting? Like the Coalition was going to knock on his door and answer.

"It's Sloane. Open up."

Dex had been expecting to be chewed out when Sloane came barging through the front door. Instead, his partner closed the door and threw his arms around Dex, squeezing him tight before changing gears. He pulled back and inspected Dex, caressing the bruise on Dex's cheek. "Jesus, Dex. What the hell happened to you? You scared the shit out of me."

As much as Dex wanted to give in to Sloane's embrace, he had to get it out. "I got knocked out, ended up... somewhere. I was blindfolded, bound, and gagged."

"You really need to stop getting yourself kidnapped." The words were softly spoken, even if Sloane meant it as a tease.

Dex gave a sniff. "You started it."

"It happened once. You're going on three now."

"Okay, we can debate my amazing luck later. I need to talk to you." He took Sloane's hand and led him over to the couch where they sat.

"What is it?"

"First, did you manage to catch up to any of the Coalition members?"

"No. We went after them when they split up but lost them after they ran into the Con Ed Plant. They must have had a getaway plan. I'm surprised they were still there when we showed up. What happened to you?"

Dex held fast onto Sloane's hand, grateful his partner didn't pull away or question it. "I saw an opportunity to go after one of the Coalition members, and I chased him into the plant. At first, I wondered why the hell he was running when he could have been shooting at me. Then I tackled him, managed to unmask him, and saw why."

Sloane stared at him. "You saw his face?"

"Yeah. He's one of ours all right."

"Shit. You found the mole? We have to tell Lieutenant Sparks." Sloane grabbed for his phone, and Dex stopped him, his gaze never leaving his partner's. "What aren't you telling me?"

It took Dex a moment to find his spine. He so didn't want to do this, but Sloane deserved to know. Whatever happened after that was anyone's guess. "It's Ash."

Sloane frowned, looking puzzled. "What about Ash?"

"The mole is Ash."

"That's impossible. Ash would never—" Sloane shook his head, his expression unfaltering. "No."

"Sloane, I saw him. Before I could say anything, I got knocked out. When I woke up, I heard him arguing with some guy. I think it was the main guy's second-in-command. A true asshole." Dex relayed everything he'd heard, and when he finished, he watched his partner closely. After a good few minutes where Sloane didn't say a word, didn't so much as blink, he finally spoke. His tone was hushed, and he sounded less certain.

"It has to be a mistake."

"I saw and heard him," Dex replied gently.

"Look, I understand how you feel about him, but this is serious—"

"You think I'd make something like this up?" Dex couldn't believe what he was hearing.

"No, I'm not saying that."

"But you are. Or that I'm delusional, or mistaken, or whatever equals you not believing me." How could Sloane dismiss him so quickly? Dex had just been kidnapped, threatened, and had the biggest fucking shock of his career, and Sloane didn't believe him?

"It's not that I don't believe you." Sloane sat back with a heavy sigh, and Dex felt the anger melt away. He hated seeing his partner looking so... heartbroken.

"Then what is it?"

"Ash is the only family I've had since I was a kid. We've stuck by each other through everything. Through the First Gen Recruitment Program, college, the THIRDS. After Dr. Shultzon patched me up, I was so scared. Thinking back, I know Ash was too. He just never showed it. He did it to take care of me. He's the only reason I hung in there. He's my best friend. I can't..." Sloane closed his eyes, his brow creased with worry. Dex felt like a complete asshole.

How could he have been so callous? Ash had been Sloane's whole world at one point. His only reason to get through the pain and fear of another day at the facility. A place where two young boys had been tested, studied, poked, and prodded. All for the "greater good" of their species. Dex remembered how terrified he'd been after he'd lost his parents. He might have been younger than Sloane, but he'd been much luckier. He'd ended up in a loving family with a great dad and awesome little brother. Dex leaned over and put his hand to Sloane's cheek, hating the pain he saw on his lover's face. Sloane had already had enough pain in his life.

"I know what I saw. *But* we should give him the benefit of the doubt. Let's not jump the gun. We should find out what the hell's going on before taking this to the lieutenant."

Sloane opened his eyes and sat forward. "No. It's my job to report it in. I've been on your ass from the start about not letting your emotions cloud your judgment, and it's exactly what I'm doing now. I won't be one of those do-as-I-say-not-as-I-do team leaders."

"This is different. If it had been Cael, I would have asked you for the same chance." His partner looked uncertain, so Dex leaned in to give him a kiss. "We're not holding back information, just looking for more evidence. Like we'd do with any other case. Except instead of handing the reins over to Recon, we sort it out ourselves. Okay?"

Sloane appeared to think about it for a moment. "Okay." He let his head rest against Dex's with a soft sigh. "Thank you, Dex. If we get any shit for this, I'm taking responsibility."

"What? No—" Sloane's lips cut off Dex's protest, and at that point, Dex didn't care. He opened himself willingly, allowing Sloane to pull him close and deepen the kiss. Whatever Sloane needed, Dex was happy to give. Sloane unclipped his rifle and dropped it onto the carpet beside the couch before removing his tac vest. He leaned into Dex and crushed him down against the couch cushions. His lover's kisses grew ardent and desperate. If this was what Sloane needed right now, Dex would do everything he could. He gripped Sloane's biceps and pulled him down against him, craving the feel of Sloane's weight on him. They were both hard, their erections rubbing against each other.

Dex groaned and reached down to unzip Sloane. He pulled his partner's dick out of his pants and pushed Sloane onto his back so Dex could get between his knees. He swallowed Sloane's cock, his hand squeezing the base as he came back up. He sucked Sloane off, licking and nipping, pressing his tongue to the slit. Sloane moaned and writhed, his hand clutching the couch in a fierce grip. Dex doubled his efforts, determined to make Sloane lose himself even if it was just for a little while. Not long after, he heard Sloane gasp, felt his body stiffen before releasing himself inside Dex's mouth. Dex swallowed around Sloane's cock, drawing out his lover's orgasm. Once Sloane had gone tender, Dex pulled off him. He lay half-on, half-off Sloane, his arm around Sloane's chest. Sloane reached down to cup Dex, but Dex moved Sloane's hand up to wrap around his waist.

"It's okay," Dex said softly. "Just lie here with me."

Sloane nuzzled Dex's temple, a small huff ruffling Dex's hair and making him smile. He closed his eyes and shortly after felt the steady rise and fall of Sloane's chest. Dex told himself it was too soon. Too soon to be feeling like this. He pushed those thoughts aside, feeling his pulse beat wildly. Eyes closed, he concentrated on Sloane's breathing, telling himself everything would turn out fine. They'd find out what was going on with Ash, and everything would go back to normal.

EIGHT

DEX WAS on his third cup of coffee, and it wasn't even ten a.m. He had training in a few hours and somehow had to find the energy for it. He'd barely slept last night. How could he knowing what he knew? He couldn't stop worrying about Sloane, Cael, and this whole business with Ash. Had he made the right decision? Regardless, he couldn't turn Ash in. He had to find out more. Ash might be a jerk, but could he really be working with the Coalition after serving the THIRDS as long as Sloane? Did he think he could get away with it? Was it worth risking his career and friends over? Even if Ash truly believed that what he was doing was for the greater good, how could he allow innocent people to get hurt in the process? Of course, not everyone who they believed to be innocent was.

That morning the intel on Alberto Cristo had come in. Cristo hadn't been in the wrong place at the wrong time as they'd originally believed, and the theory a ricochet had killed him was looking very unlikely. Cristo had been a member of the Order. The algorithms Themis had run on him pulled up surveillance video of Cristo among fellow members of the Order at rallies and protests held by the Order, one in particular resulting in aggravated assault against a Therian citizen. There was a warrant out on Cristo, but the guy had disappeared. It looked like the Coalition had found him. There was no doubt in Dex's mind that Cristo had been in exactly the right place at the right time, and how convenient that no witnesses had come forward to explain how Cristo had ended up with a bullet in his head.

Sloane's voice snapped Dex out of his thoughts, and he watched his partner tapping away at his desk's interface. He scrolled through panels, bringing up glowing blue windows and high-level access screens. He swiped his hand across his desk, and everything slid over to Dex's. Man, he loved THIRDS technology.

"It's all set up. Anything Ash accesses on Themis will send me an encrypted alert. Once I access the file, I can delete my log-in activity, so if he goes back, he won't know I'm on to him."

"Great. So can we do a scan to see if he's accessed anything so far?" Dex looked through the open windows of Ash's activity on Themis. There was a log file of all his reports, web searches, incoming and outgoing phone calls, texts, connections on his earpiece, offsite connections to Themis, even what snacks he purchased from the vending machines, which were also connected to Themis. Dex wasn't sure how he felt about the government monitoring his snack preferences. "That sneaky bastard!"

"What is it?" Sloane stood and ran over to Dex's side. "Did I miss something?"

"He gives me shit for eating gummy bears, and he buys a pack nearly every day."

Sloane stared at him. "Seriously? Do you ever not think about food?"

"Of course I do," Dex replied with a smirk. "When I'm thinking about sex. Though sometimes I like to think of both at the same time." He wriggled his eyebrows, but his partner remained unimpressed.

"Am I going to have to give you a time-out?"

Dex pouted. "No."

"Besides, you're wrong about the gummy bears."

"But they're right here on the list."

"Who else do you know who loves gummy bears as much as you do?"

Dex thought about it. "No one loves gummy bears as much as I do. I'm not ashamed to say I used to steal them from Cael when we—Oh." Now Dex felt even worse. "He buys them for Cael." Why did the guy have to be so damned nice to Cael? It would have made this so much easier if Ash treated his brother the way he treated everyone else. Instead he bought Cael his favorite snack.

Sloane nodded and resumed his seat. He studied the screen, his expression turning somber. "Looks like the last time he bought gummy bears was six weeks ago."

"When he started acting like even more of a douche. What am I going to tell Cael? I feel shitty for having lied to him about last night." After Sloane and Dex had cleaned themselves up, they'd headed back to HQ where Dex had lied to his dad during his debriefing. He'd explained how he'd gotten lost in the Con Ed Plant chasing after a Coalition member and ended up knocked out. When he'd woken up, he was dazed, couldn't find his team, and somehow made it home. His communicator's signal was likely scrambled while he was in the plant surrounded by dozens of buzzing high-voltage units.

"Hopefully we'll get to the bottom of this, and you can tell him the truth. Speaking of, I need Cael to forward me his reports on Cristo and set up some additional algorithms. Now that we know he was with the Order, I want to know why he ended up executed and why the Coalition would want him dead."

"I'm going to swing by his office, see how he is," Dex said, getting up from his chair. "I'll ask him to send the info over." Just as he said the words, Cael ran past their open door calling for Ash. Dex went to the door to peek out into the half-empty bullpen. Ash stopped and turned to Cael. The hairs on Dex's neck stood on end, and he walked out of the office with Sloane on his heels.

"There you are. I've been looking everywhere for you," Cael said cheerfully.

"What do you want?" Ash snarled, causing Cael to flinch. His smile fell off his face, and he took a small step back.

"Sorry. I thought you might want to get a drink after work."

"I'm busy."

"Oh. What about tomorrow?"

"I'm busy tomorrow and the next night and the night after that. Find some kids your own age to play with." Ash started to walk off when Cael grabbed his arm. Dex didn't like where this was headed.

"What the hell? What's going on? Why are you being such a jerk?"

"Because if you haven't heard, I'm an asshole. You should have listened to your brother. I don't want to fucking hang out with you, Cael. I've got adult shit to deal with that doesn't include video games, pizza, and learning to shave."

"Something's wrong. You know you can talk to me," Cael pleaded. "I've been worried about you."

Ash jerked his arm out of Cael's hold. "I don't need you worrying about me. I'm a big boy. Worry about yourself. You've been slacking lately. Your head's up in the clouds."

"Because I've been worried about you, you jackass!"

"I can handle myself fine. I'm doing my fucking job just like you should be doing yours. You're going to get someone killed." Ash poked Cael in the shoulder, and Dex took a step closer. What the fuck was Ash's problem? And why was he taking it out on Cael?

"I know what I'm doing," Cael snapped.

"No, you don't. It's our asses on the line while you stay in the truck playing with your computers." Ash let out a frustrated sigh and threw a hand up. "Fucking useless."

"What?" Cael's eyes grew glassy.

Dex had seen enough. He pushed himself in front of Cael and faced Ash. "What the fuck is your problem, man?"

"You and your pain-in-the-ass kid brother. I'm tired of dealing with your shit. This is a tactical team, not a fraternity. All the shit that's going on out there has reminded me of why I'm here. And it's not to babysit the Wonder Twins. The simple fact is I got bored of both your shit." Ash made the mistake of getting up in Dex's face.

Dex landed a hit square across Ash's jaw. The large Therian reeled back, caught off guard by Dex's punch. With a fierce growl, Ash threw a hook that Dex ducked under. He pulled back a fist only to have Cael latch onto his arm and yank him back.

"Dex, stop!" Cael ran in front of Dex, but it was Ash Cael was protecting.

Dex gaped at his brother, both hurt and fuming. "Are

you fucking kidding me? After all the shit he just said, you're defending him?"

"Please." Cael put his hands together, and Dex was stunned. Ash stormed off, and Dex spun around to head back to his office. He was seething and cursing under his breath. All that shit Ash had said to his brother and not only had Cael taken it, he'd defended the asshole? He thought his brother was better than that.

"Un-fucking-believable." He stormed into his office with Cael and Sloane quickly following. The walls around them going white, telling Dex they were in privacy mode—obviously Sloane's doing. His partner was probably expecting Dex to blow at any moment, and Dex could feel it bubbling up. He couldn't keep himself from pacing the room. He was so goddamn fucked off. Ash's words regarding Cael listening to him over Dex rang in his ear and there was nothing he wanted more than to find the guy and land another punch. How could his brother be so blind?

"Dex, please don't be mad at me." Cael took hold of Dex's arm to stop him from pacing, but all he could see was Cael getting hurt. Having his heart broken, or worse, having the Coalition come after him. All because of that asshole.

"How is it the people I love the most are the ones listening to me the least? First Sloane. Now you. Next thing you know, Dad's going to be—"

"*Stop.*"

Dex stilled. His eyes on Sloane. Now what?

"What did you just say?"

Had Sloane not heard him? Dex opened his mouth ready to repeat himself when he realized what he'd said, and by the look on Sloane's face, what he'd done. *Fuck. Oh fuck.* What had he done? He'd fucked up. That's what he'd done. Big time. Maybe he could play it off. "I was just—"

"Did you say... you love me?" Sloane took a step back, and Dex held his hands up, praying his partner didn't do what he looked like he was about to do. Then he remembered his brother was in the room. Double shit.

Sloane seemed to sense his thoughts. "Cael knows about us."

"What? When the fuck did that happen?" What in the ever-living fuck of fucks is going on around here?

Cael glared at him. "Thanks, bro."

Dex didn't have time to answer his brother because something in his gut told him he had to do something fast. Sloane was about to bolt. Dex could see it in his eyes.

"You didn't answer my question," Sloane demanded softly. "And don't try to play it off. I know you too well by now."

What was he supposed to do? Lie? He could lie. No, he was a shitty liar. But he could... Fuck it. "Yes. I love you."

"When?" Sloane asked, his voice growing more distant.

When? "I don't know? It's not like I marked it on my calendar."

"Don't." It was a subtle but grave warning. Dex wasn't trying to be a smartass. It's just what his brain went to when he was on the verge of freaking out about something. And if there was ever a time to freak out about something, this was it.

"I know it's too soon, which is why I wasn't going to say anything, but with everything going on, it just slipped out."

"So you were going to keep it from me?"

Dex felt himself deflate and he shrugged. "What's the right answer here, Sloane?" There was none. They both knew it. He took a step toward Sloane, his heart breaking when Sloane pulled back.

"I need some air," Sloane said, backing up until he hit

the security panel. He turned and entered his security code. Dex could feel it all crumbling around him, and he felt sick to his stomach. Even then, he stayed where he was, refusing to force Sloane.

"Can we please talk about this?"

"Not right now. I need some space." The door had barely finished opening before Sloane squeezed through it and was off, taking Dex's heart with him. He didn't know how long he stood there staring at the open door. Outside the office agents went about their business. The sound of chatting, doors closing, and speakers relaying information blurred and faded. Numbly, Dex dropped down into his chair, doing his best to calm the encroaching fear. Instead, he turned his attention to his brother. "How long have you known?"

"Since I was in the hospital after the Therian Youth Center bombing."

"How could you not tell me? How could either of you not tell me?" Had they even planned on telling him? All this time he'd been pretending in front of his brother, feeling absolutely shitty about hiding his relationship from him, and the little turd had known the whole time?

Cael crossed his arms over his chest. "Really? You're going to be pissed at me for knowing?"

"It's not that I didn't want to tell you. I did. I felt shitty not being able to."

"It's fine. I understand. I wish you could do the same for me." Cael approached Dex and knelt beside his chair, his silvery eyes pleading. "You know how I feel about him. He's not himself right now, and I'm asking you to cut him some slack."

"Cut him some slack?" Dex shook his head. "Cael, I'm sorry. I know how you feel about him, and believe me, I understand, but the guy's been treating you like shit, and you're following him around like some lovesick puppy. How could you take that from him? You're better than that. You're better than *him*."

"Screw you, Dex." Cael jumped to his feet, his fists balled up at his sides. "Your commitment-phobe boyfriend just bailed on you because you let slip that you love him, which by the way, has to be the shittiest declaration of love I've ever heard. And you're going to lecture me on relationships?"

"Ouch, man." Wow. That stung.

"Stay out of it, Dex." Cael stormed out of the office leaving Dex wondering when the last Jenga piece of the precariously skewed tower that was his life had been plucked. A glowing red reminder popped up on his desk. It was time to head down to Sparta for training. At least something had gone right. It was just what he needed. He felt as if he was going to explode if he didn't let loose on something. He marched out of the office and headed for the elevator.

Dex had never been so eager to start his daily training session. Down in Sparta, he changed in the male locker room, swapping his uniform for his black Led Zeppelin T-shirt, loose jogging pants, and sneakers. He grabbed his boxing gloves from his locker and slammed it shut.

The bays were pretty busy at this time of day, but there was plenty of free boxing equipment in the boxing bays. He chose one of the emptier ones, and as he got ready, all he could think about was Sloane. The moment Dex had seen his face, he'd known. Sloane was going to run. *I'm so stupid.* He finished wrapping his hands and made straight for the punching bag.

After some quick stretches and warm-ups, he started

pummeling the red leather bag, hoping to release some of his frustration, but the more he punched the bag, the angrier he became. He'd told himself not to get so close. His head had known far longer than his heart what would happen, had tried to warn him. But Dex hadn't listened. He'd been a lovesick idiot, trailing after Sloane, getting on his knees, content to let Sloane bleed him. Maybe a part of Dex enjoyed it. Enjoyed being stripped, his vulnerability exposed. Why else would he continue to put himself through this? Why did he keep waiting? Because he'd promised Sloane he would. And what had Sloane promised in return? Dex remembered the words as if they'd been said yesterday. *I can't make any promises.* Sloane had made it clear. Dex had no one to blame for his heartache but himself.

"Well isn't that cute."

Dex froze. He closed his eyes and breathed deeply. Someone up there was conspiring against him. Was this a test to see how much he could take before he lost his shit? Any other day, Dex would have walked away. But not today. He turned and faced Ash who was dressed similarly in a T-shirt and loose jogging pants. Letty was beside him looking worried.

"Come on. You and me," Dex said through his teeth.

Ash let out a laugh. "Are you fucking kidding?"

"Does it look like I'm kidding?"

"Sloane wouldn't be happy about that."

"Well Sloane's not fucking here, is he?" Dex snapped. He expected a smart-ass remark, but instead Ash seemed to be thinking it over, so he pushed on. "You've wanted this since I joined. Now's your chance. No one here's going to stop you. You want to beat the shit out of me, now's your fucking chance."

"Okay."

Dex nodded and swiped his boxing gloves off the side of the mat. He held them out to Letty. "Help me out here."

Letty took one glove from him and helped secure the strap before taking the next one. "Dex, are you sure you want to do this? You know he won't hold back."

"I'm counting on it."

Letty cursed under her breath, saying something in Spanish Dex didn't understand. He tapped his hip where his pocket was, and Letty reached in. She pulled out the small box containing his mouth guard and opened it, looking as if she was going to try again to convince him not to do this, but instead, she held the mouth guard up to him. He leaned over and closed his mouth around the rubbery piece. He could tell she wasn't happy, but he needed this.

He hopped on his toes, rolled his shoulders, and waited while Letty helped Ash with his gloves and mouth guard. As soon as Ash was ready, they both stepped onto one of the larger empty blue mats. Looking at Ash, all the anger came flooding back, and no matter how hard he tried, he couldn't stop thinking about Sloane.

You really thought he wouldn't run? He'll always run. From you.

"Come on," Dex said around his mouthpiece.

Ash shook his head, but there was no way Dex was letting him back out now.

"Come on!"

Ash gave him exactly what he asked for. The first punch landed across Dex's jaw and sent him reeling. He fell hard against the mat, his face in a world of pain and stars in his eyes. How the hell Dex hadn't been knocked out by that one hit was beyond him. *Fuck. That hurt. Okay, maybe this wasn't your brightest idea.*

"That all you got, Daley? One hit? That's pretty fucking pathetic."

Bastard. Dex pushed himself to his feet and shook himself off. Would Sloane come back this time? He had to. They worked together. What if that's all he came back for? *You fucked up. The first guy you could see yourself spending your life with and you fuck it up within months.* A new record. Ash grinned at him, and Dex lost it.

He came at Ash with everything he had, mindful of Ash's fierce hooks. He maneuvered around him, ducking under hooks and jumping out of the way when Ash swiped at him. Ash threw both arms out to grab him, and Dex dropped down to the mat and rolled. He popped back up and took a swing, catching Ash on his shoulder. Then Dex remembered what Ash's proficiency was. Close-quarter combat. The guy had been toying with him. Letting him land blows, waiting for Dex to realize the mistake he'd made.

Ash got in his space, all sharp elbows, swift punches, and knees. Somewhere between taking the pain and protecting his body, Dex managed to land a blow against the larger Therian's left ribs, but his retreat was denied. Ash's gloves came down hard against Dex's back, and he was on the mat again. This time Dex wasn't allowed to get up. Ash straddled him and pinned him down with his full weight.

The first blow hit his shoulder, and Dex let out a sharp cry at the pain. He put his gloves together doing his damnedest to protect his face from Ash's assault. A blow landed against his abs, and the wind rushed out of Dex. He took a chance at leaving himself open to thrust his glove up, catching Ash in the chin and succeeding in pissing the guy off even more. An uppercut clipped Dex's jaw, and his head snapped back. He could taste the blood in his mouth and started wheezing. The weight lifted, and Dex rolled onto his side, spitting out his mouth guard and drawing in large gulps of air. His lungs burned, and his body was on fire. But none of it hurt more than his heart. He stayed on his side, his forehead pressed against the mat as he tried to catch his breath.

"It's okay, Letty. I got this." Ash's tone was almost gentle, and Dex looked up in time to see Letty snap herself out of it. With a nod, she headed off. Dex realized the room was empty except for him and Ash. A hand appeared before Dex's face and he glared at Ash.

"Don't do that."

"Do what?" Ash asked, insisting Dex take his hand.

"Act like a decent person. Like you give a fuck." Reluctantly Dex accepted Ash's help and sat up, his arms resting on his knees and what was most certainly the most pathetic expression ever on his face.

"I do give a fuck. He'll come back."

Dex shook his head, his lips pressed together to keep himself from sounding like the drama queen Ash was always accusing him of being. Why was he even sitting here talking to a guy who might possibly have betrayed them all? As much as he was fine with ticking yet another box on his list of reasons to dislike Ash, something in Dex's gut fought the idea of Ash as a traitor, simply based on the guy's relationship with Sloane. Man, he was such a goddamn mess. "How fucked up is this? I'm pissed, and you're comforting me. If that isn't a sign the apocalypse is coming, I don't know what is."

"He *will* come back." Ash sat beside him, mirroring his pose. Dex wasn't sure what he found more disturbing, Ash being... not a dick or him taking comfort in Ash's words. In the end he gave in and went with it. He was too tired not to.

"I know. That's not the problem."

"It's the running. I hate to tell you, but... he always runs."

"Unless it's a fight. He'll run headfirst into that. But if it's me?" Dex threw a hand toward the open bay doors. Something occurred to him, and he swallowed his pride. If he had to look to Ash for answers, so be it. "Did he run from Gabe?"

Ash shook his head. "No."

"So it *is* me. What do you know, I can feel shittier."

"Think about it for a moment, Dex."

"He loved Gabe, but he never ran." Dex racked his brain for a reason. Why hadn't Sloane run from Gabe? He'd loved him. Why did the thought of Dex loving Sloane have the guy taking off? Ash answered for him.

"It didn't scare him."

Dex thought about his relationship with Sloane. He'd been the one to push things forward, but it wasn't as though he'd forced Sloane into a commitment he didn't want or wasn't ready for. Dex had wanted more and took the plunge in telling Sloane as much. If Sloane hadn't been ready, he wouldn't have taken that step, and Dex would have found a way to work around it. "What does that mean?"

Ash shrugged. "Gabe was the first one Sloane let in, and yeah, he loved Gabe, but he could do it while still holding some of himself back. The facility, his past, his nightmares? Gabe never knew about that shit. Sloane told you what happened to his mom."

Dex flinched, his heart squeezing at the memory. "He told you?"

"That he'd spilled everything to you? Yeah. The only ones who knew were me and Shultzon. He's not scared of opening up to you, Dex. He's scared of what you might find if he does. We didn't exactly grow up around functioning relationships. Hell, our friendship was a result of fear and loneliness."

"But we've talked about his past. Whatever happened doesn't change the way I feel about him."

"Doesn't change the way he feels about himself either." Ash let out a heavy sigh, and Dex had a feeling the guy wasn't referring to just Sloane. "I'm sure the fact you love him despite all his baggage means a hell of a lot to him, but that shit doesn't get left behind. Some of it—his mom's death..." Ash pursed his lips and shook his head. "He might be able to think back on it one day and not feel guilty, but he'll never forget. What happened to us back in that facility might get more bearable with time, but it fucked us up. It made us what we are. The way we are. Damaged."

Dex turned to Ash and met his gaze. "You're not damaged. You've had it rough and were dealt a really shitty hand, but you pushed through it. You took all that anger and pain and you used it for something good. To make a difference." There was no response from Ash who simply averted his gaze, his eyes on his fingers. "So now what? I keep bracing myself, waiting for the next time he walks out on me?"

"Don't give up on him, Dex."

"Funny. He said something similar about you."

Ash studied him for a moment, before his eyes clouded over. "You told him. I figured you would."

"I wasn't trying to be a dick." And that was the truth. Even if at first he'd acted like a jerk about it. He hadn't been intent on turning Ash in simply because it was Ash. Sure, they weren't exactly friends, but it was because of Cael, Sloane, and the rest of the team that Dex had been so angry. "I couldn't keep something like that from Sloane. I'm not about to start keeping secrets." *Except the part about you loving him. You kept that one, and look how well that went.*

"So why haven't you told Sparks?"

"Because it would crush Sloane. I told him I would give you the benefit of the doubt. For him."

"Aren't you sweet." Dex opened his mouth, but Ash stopped him. "There isn't jack shit to talk about, so don't bother."

"Okay. How about you tell me why you were such a dick to my brother? And don't bullshit me, man. You can say you don't care, but I know you do."

Ash got to his feet and started for the exit when Dex called out after him. "You really hurt him." That brought Ash to a stop. Dex waited, holding his breath. *Come on, Ash. Give me something.*

"Good," Ash ground out through his teeth. "I told you. He needs to stay away from me."

Not the something he was hoping for.

Dex got to his feet, feeling sore as hell. "Whatever's going on, I hope it's worth it."

Ash grumbled something under his breath, and Dex could have sworn he'd heard Ash say "me too." But it was too late to ask because Ash was gone. Dex sucked in a sharp breath and headed for the showers. Wherever Sloane was, Dex hoped he found the answer he was looking for. Hopefully, that answer would lead him back to Dex.

NINE

*H*OW LONG CAN *you keep this up?*

How long could he keep running? It felt as though he'd been running his whole life. Sloane looked down at his wrists and the evidence left behind of his first attempt to escape. He'd grown stronger since then, but he was still running.

The dangers of his job never bothered him. It was different. He told himself he wanted to make the most of the time he had, and he should, considering the dangers they faced every time they went out in the field. Then Dex would take another step closer, Sloane's chest would tighten, and he would balk. His guilt was eating at him, but he'd told Dex from the beginning that he couldn't make promises. And this was why. He'd never expected Dex to become such a big part of his life so quickly, and he sure as hell hadn't expected Dex to fall in love with him.

Gabe had loved him, but it had been different with Gabe. Like they were both holding something back. It was the way they'd been built. But Dex... He smiled at the thought of that dopey grin, those sparkling blue eyes, and that infectious laugh. Something in the air changed, and Sloane couldn't help his smile.

"How'd you find me?"

Ash took a seat on the bench beside him. "It's what we do. Besides, I know you better than you know yourself."

"In that case, maybe you can tell me why I keep doing this?" He looked up at the starless sky, feeling the breeze against his skin, hearing it rustle the leaves of the trees around him. There was nothing but their voices and the sounds of traffic on the other side of the fence a few yards behind him.

"You're scared."

"That it?"

"No. You're scared because for the first time in your life, you found someone who sees you, all of you. He can see the cracks, the missing pieces, the one's too broken to be salvaged, and despite all that, he still wants to be with you. What did he say to make you bolt? Must have been big." Ash leaned his arms on his legs so he could look at Sloane.

"He let it slip that he loves me."

"Daley's in love with you?" Ash stared at him, and Sloane braced himself for a barrage of insults regarding Dex, how Sloane should bail or some unhelpful remark, but they never came. Instead, Ash looked him right in the eye and in his most sincere voice said, "Stop running. You've got something good. Don't fuck it up."

Sloane opened his mouth, but nothing came out.

"He knows all your hang-ups, your demons, all the fucked-up shit you come with, and not only does he stick by you, he fucking bleeds for you, man. I've seen it. For fuck's sake, he got in the ring with me because of you."

"What?" Sloane went to get up, but Ash grabbed his arm.

"Relax. He's still in one piece. I only beat him up a little." Sloane arched an eyebrow at him, and Ash winced. "Okay, a lot. But he's okay. I went easy on him when I realized it was because of you. Figured you'd left. It was the only thing that could set him off like that. We talked after."

"About me?" Sloane didn't know what to think about Dex challenging Ash to a fight. He must have been so angry and hurt.

"What else?"

Sloane clasped his hands between his knees until he couldn't take it anymore. "What did you tell him?"

"Not to give up on you."

"Thanks."

"S'okay."

They sat there in companionable silence when an old memory crept up on Sloane, and he started chuckling. "Remember when we were kids, we used to play Indiana Jones, and you'd throw pillows at me, and we'd pretend they were boulders falling from the mountains?"

Ash laughed, and for the first time in a long time, his best friend's smile reached his amber eyes. "How could I forget? You were so obsessed with those movies, wanting to be Indiana Jones. It's all you talked about. Remember when Shultzon got you the hat for Christmas? You were so excited, I thought you were going to hurt something."

Sloane couldn't help his laugh. "That's right! I forgot about the hat. Who didn't want to be Indy back then?"

"Me," Ash replied with a grin.

"That's right. Because you wanted to be..." Sloane trailed off, and he smiled at Ash's cringe. His friend's face turned red reminding Sloane of how, once upon a time, his world had revolved around Ash, and Ash's world had revolved around his. They'd huddled together under the blankets while the storm that was their lives threatened to break them, promising each other they'd never let go.

"Just say it," Ash muttered, averting his gaze.

"The Man in Black, a.k.a. Westley."

"So what?" Ash's lips turned up into a wide smile. "He was cool. Running around swashbuckling, fighting rodents of unusual size. I got to wear a mask and carry around a sword. You had a whip. Did you know you were gay then?"

"Fuck off," Sloane laughed, giving him a playful shove. "Dick." His expression softened when he thought back to those days. "I remember when you got sick from one of the tests and they kept you in the infirmary for observation. When you got back, I said I thought I'd never see you again, and what did you do? You grabbed my Indy hat, popped it on your head, and said..."

"I'm like a bad penny, I always turn up." Ash smiled warmly. "I remember."

"It became a thing after that. When I'd get scared, you'd say it to reassure me. Our secret."

They both reminisced about their youth, talking of only the good times. When they'd jumped on their beds wearing capes, pretending they could fly. They'd painted their ward-room to look like a forest with a night sky on the ceiling complete with stars and constellations. Then they'd lie on either his or Ash's bed and stare up at the star-covered ceiling, their nightlight serving as a campfire as they talked about how one day they would sleep under real stars.

"I can't believe we were ever that young," Ash said, his voice soft.

"I know." Sloane tried to swallow past the lump in his throat. "Ash?"

Ash's eyes darkened, his expression turning cold. "Don't ask questions you don't want to know the answers to."

"You're a lot of things, but a traitor isn't one of them. I don't know what you've gotten yourself into, but promise me you'll be careful." Whatever was happening, Ash wasn't a traitor. Sloane would bet his life on it.

"Shouldn't you be arresting me?"

Sloane shrugged. "I have no proof."

Ash arched an eyebrow at him in surprise. "But you have a witness. And not just any witness, a fellow agent."

"No, I don't." Sloane looked out ahead of him, aware of Ash studying him. "What happened with Cael?"

"Fuck, man. What is it with you and Daley? First you're connected at the hip, now you're thinking the same? I swear if you start eating gummy bears, I'm going to punch your lights out."

"Ash."

"None of your business, all right?"

Sloane turned to meet his friend's gaze. He might be willing to give Ash the benefit of the doubt, but things couldn't continue the way they were going on his team. Destructive Delta had the highest rate of success of any other team in Unit Alpha, and it reflected in their budget, the leeway they were given, and the trust put in them to get the job done. Sloane couldn't allow his team's performance to suffer, and right now, Destructive Delta was teetering dangerously close to being exposed. "Since it's happening on my time and involves my team, it is my business. You know I can't let Sparks find out what's going on. If she gets wind, we'll be under the microscope. I won't allow Destructive Delta's reputation to fall to ruin. How could you say all that shit to Cael? You're crazy about him."

"What the fuck are you implying?"

Ash's defensive tone wasn't lost on Sloane. "Come on,

man." Sloane had been happy to ignore it as long as Ash did, but that didn't stop it from being true.

"I'm not gay," Ash insisted.

"Well you sure as shit aren't straight, so don't you fucking dare. That might fly with someone else, but not with me. We've been through too much shit together for you to stand there and lie to my face. You can deny it to yourself and everyone else. You can stay in the closet if you feel you need to. Refuse all the labels, date whoever the hell you want, I'm not going to judge you. I never have. But don't, *don't* sit there and tell me you're fucking straight. You've got a thing for Cael. Either step up or someone else will."

"Like I said, I'm not gay."

"Bullshit. What the hell is going on with you?"

Ash bolted to his feet. "You and your boyfriend need to get off my fucking back. I know what I'm doing. Just keep those two away from me, okay?" Ash gritted his teeth, his fists clenching before his expression softened. "Please. Keep them away. I know I have no right to ask you for anything, but do me that one favor."

Sloane nodded slowly, though he had no idea what he was agreeing to, only that Ash was asking him to do something for him on faith. How was Sloane supposed to keep Dex and Cael away from Ash if they were all on the same team? And why was Ash so adamant about it?

"Thanks. This was nice. For the most part," Ash said quietly. Something buzzed, and he flinched. "I gotta go."

"Okay." Sloane watched his friend walk away. The buzz had come from Ash's pocket. His cellphone. Was it the Coalition calling? Is that where Ash was running off to? He tried not to think about what his best friend would be up to tonight. He picked up the bouquet of flowers tucked beside him on the bench and started walking along the edge of

Sylvan Water. He stepped onto Sylvan Avenue, walking past the Egyptian pyramid, its entrance flanked by a statue of Joseph, Mary, and baby Jesus.

Sloane had numbly walked down this path more times than he cared to remember. Finally, he was on Lake Avenue where, after a couple of feet, he veered off to the right. He could close his eyes and still find it. Gently he laid the bouquet of flowers on the freshly cut grass and looked past his reflection to the white letters chiseled into the gleaming black marble. The familiar lump in his throat was accompanied by an equally familiar ache in his chest, and although it still hurt, the pain had dulled. His lungs no longer burned when he inhaled, and his eyes didn't sting. A part of him felt guilty for it, but his heart told him it was time. He stood, and with a deep breath, he addressed Gabe's tombstone.

"You probably know why I'm here. If you could hear me, talk to me, you'd probably ask me what the hell took me so long. Then you'd tell me what's been in my heart for months now. I know you'd want me to be happy, and I am. When you left, I thought you'd taken everything I had with you. Dex helped me see how wrong I was. You left everything there for me to give to someone else crazy enough to love me. I'll never forget you, Gabe." He reached into his pocket and pulled out a long chain, the small dog tags clinking together.

Sloane didn't bother to hide the tears in his eyes. He smiled and let out a shaky breath before placing the dog tags on the tombstone. He put his fingers to his lips for a kiss before moving them to the black marble. "Good-bye, sweetheart. Thank you for everything."

Sloane barely slept that night. He was too worried over whether he'd fucked things up with Dex for good. There was only so much someone could take before they walked out on you. At least that was Sloane's experience. The next morning at HQ after he'd showered, changed into his uniform, and hit the canteen for coffee, he'd been working up his courage to speak to Dex when a call came. Another dead body. The Coalition was at it bright and early, and this time it was really bad. Where Therians were concerned, dead wasn't the worst that could happen to a victim.

Initially Sloane had intended on talking to Dex last night, but he'd needed some time. Dex had given him his space. He hadn't called, but he'd sent Sloane a text telling him he was there if Sloane wanted to talk. Even with Sloane hurting him, Dex was still there to offer his support. He met the rest of his team in the armory as they geared up, and he headed for his locker beside Dex's.

"Hey." God, he sounded like such an idiot. He felt like an idiot. And a jackass.

Dex gave him a solemn smile. "Hey."

"Be careful." He always said that to Dex when they headed out. Usually Dex followed it with a joke or flirty remark. Now Sloane only received a nod. Sloane waited for their teammates to start for the corridor leading to the parking garage before he took Dex's arm. His partner stopped and patiently waited for him to say whatever he was going to say.

"I know we don't have time now, but can I come by tonight? Please."

There was a slight pause before Dex nodded. "Sure."

The fact Dex hadn't asked what it concerned didn't bode well. Dex hated waiting, especially when it was in regard to their relationship. There was so much Sloane wanted to say, but now was not the time. They headed out, most of the team chatting away in the BearCat. It was good to see Calvin and Hobbs talking again. Well, Calvin talked,

Hobbs mostly listened, but at least the two were communicating again, though there was still something missing. Calvin seemed to have lost some of his lightheartedness, and Sloane wondered what could have caused it. Cael was chatting with Rosa and Letty while Ash seemed to be lost in thought.

Sloane's own thoughts started edging toward Ash working with the Coalition. It wasn't that he didn't believe Dex, but something had to be going on there. There were a lot of things Ash could be accused of, but a traitor working for the Coalition? Whatever he was mixed up in, Sloane hoped they got to the bottom of it before Ash found himself so deep there was nothing Sloane could do for him.

The BearCat pulled up to a pizzeria at the intersection of Old Fulton Street and Front Street with the area having been secured by Recon before Defense agents arrived. There were tactical vehicles and flashing lights everywhere. Additional teams from Unit Alpha had their Defense agents posted around the taped-off area making sure no one got in. Just outside the restaurant was the forensics tent. That could only mean one thing. Sloane and Dex slipped inside the tent and found Hudson and Nina crouched over a zipped-up black body bag. There were bloodstains where all the blood had pooled covering the sidewalk.

Hudson took hold of the zipper, pausing to look from Sloane to Dex. "I hope you lads had a light breakfast." He unzipped the bag, and Dex turned away, his fist to his mouth to keep himself from throwing up.

"Jesus." Sloane nodded, and Hudson quickly zipped the bag back up. "Where's the rest of him?" Nina pointed over to a second black bag.

Fucking hell. The guy had been shredded beyond recognition with his lower body having been torn off. It was clearly the work of more than one feral Therian and, from the looks of it, two large Felids. His thoughts immediately went to the tiger Therian and cougar Therian hunting with the Coalition the day they'd found Cristo.

"Any ID?" Sloane asked.

"We'll have to wait for dental records to come in. There was no wallet or personal belongings found among the remains."

"Witnesses?"

Nina's frown deepened. "If there were, no one's come forward. Recon's working on it."

The CSAs mounted the body bags onto a gurney, and they all headed out of the tent. A familiar white-and-blue van rolled up to the scene, and Hudson groaned.

"Bloody hell. Here we go. Nina, let's get this body out of here right away."

"Got it."

"Fucking reporters." Sloane tapped his earpiece. "Sarge. Press is here."

"I'll handle it."

Sloane and Dex kept the area secure while they waited for Maddock to deal with the press. Of course, that didn't stop reporters from trying to get Sloane's attention. It's as if they knew of his aversion to them.

"Agent Brodie! Are the THIRDS even trying to catch the Coalition? Or are you glad they're doing your work for you?"

Sloane pressed his lips together to keep himself from telling the guy to fuck off.

"Do the THIRDS have any leads on the Coalition at all? Was the victim a member of the Order?"

Maddock pulled up in his black Suburban, and Sloane thanked his lucky stars. He headed for the BearCat with

Dex close behind. Sloane needed to get back to HQ to start piecing this mess together. Their first victim had been a member of the Order. The Coalition happened to show up chasing some other members of the Order, and Cristo ended up shot in the head. Now this victim had been shredded by two large Felids. He needed to know if the Coalition had been seen in the area. He also needed to know the identity of their victim. If he was a member of the Order as Sloane's gut was telling him, then there was more going on here than they thought.

The rest of the day was filled with reports and briefings. Maddock took Sloane's gut feelings very seriously, and Recon was working on gathering all the intel they could on their latest victim. If these two killings weren't coincidental, Sloane wanted to know what was so special about these men. Was the Coalition simply escalating the violence, or was it something else? If they were stepping things up, why bother making the first murder look like an accident?

TEN

"Hi."

"Hey." Dex stood to one side to let him in, then closed the door behind him. Walking into the living room, Sloane noticed the TV was off, which for anyone else wouldn't have been unusual, but not for Dex. The only time Dex ever turned his TV off was when he wasn't feeling well or when he was thinking. Sloane had a pretty good idea what Dex had been thinking about, especially since he could hear the drums and cymbals of a power ballad floating up from the speakers. His stomach flip-flopped, and he figured the sooner he got it out the better it would be for both of them.

"Dex, what you said in the office—"

"It's fine. Forget it." Dex headed for the kitchen, and Sloane followed, gently touching Dex's arm in case his partner wanted to pull away from him. He didn't. With a sigh, Dex turned, folded his arms over his chest, and leaned against the counter. Waiting. Was he expecting more excuses from Sloane? An apology that would inevitably lead to yet another apology? A vicious circle of Dex putting his heart out there for Sloane to crush before disappearing and crawling back?

"I don't want to forget it. I know things between us would be a lot easier if I wasn't so fucked-up—"

"You're not," Dex stated firmly. "You've been through a lot, and I understand that. I don't expect you to feel the same, and I don't want you to say something you don't mean. Hell, even I know it's too soon, but..." Dex shrugged and shoved his hands into his pockets. "I can't help it. You made it easy."

"Easy? I've made it anything but easy for you." Sloane stepped up to him, his hands slipping around Dex's waist to hold him. How could he need someone so badly yet be so terrified of getting close to him?

"You don't get it." Dex looked up at him, his eyes filled with so many promises, and unlike Sloane, Dex would never let him down, never run from him or from them. "I know this is going to sound cheesy, but the moment you showed up on my doorstep, drunk off your ass and in so much pain, I was gone, man. I'd like to say I don't know what it is about you that had me taking a swan dive into an empty pool, but I do know."

"Tell me," Sloane said quietly, not merely wanting to know, but *needing* to know. His fingers stroked Dex's jaw, feeling the stubble growing in. Scruffy looked good on Dex.

"The way you fight with everything you've got, even when it's against yourself. Doesn't matter how much pain you're in, you keep fighting. I admire that."

"Feels like I've been fighting my whole life."

"No matter how many times you walk away, you keep coming back. To me. And don't get me wrong, I hold on to that, but I have to tell you it hurts like fuck when you do that."

"I know."

"Do you?"

"I don't want to hurt you, Dex, and I hate how this is going to sound like an excuse, but it's not. I want you to understand."

"I'm listening."

"All my life, whenever something or someone good came along, I couldn't let myself get too close, because I truly believed nothing good could ever last. Even with Ash, it took me a long time to accept he was going to stick by me as long as it was in his power to do so. At the end of a good day, I'd be too scared to go to sleep, thinking everything would fall apart come morning. I've never been in this position before."

"Neither have I."

"What about Lou? You two were together for four years."

"I know. And I cared about him. A lot. Really cared about him. But I wasn't in love with him. He never gave me butterflies in my stomach just from him looking at me. Never made me feel like a horny teenager itching to touch him every time I saw him. He'd go on trips, and yeah, I'd miss him, but I never felt like he'd taken a part of me with him."

Sloane swallowed hard at the last part. Did Dex really feel as if a piece of him was missing when Sloane was away from him?

"After Lou broke up with me, my dad told me he wasn't the one. I'd gotten defensive at the time and asked him why he thought that. He said because when I love something, I throw myself into it completely." The flush on Dex's cheeks warmed Sloane's heart. "And he was right. Being with Lou was easy. It was comfortable. With you..." He averted his gaze and shook his head at himself. "I could have held back, but I didn't want to. The more time I spent with you, the more I knew there was no use fighting it."

The eighties power ballad switched to a modern love song, quiet and lulling. Dex started to sway, and Sloane followed his lead. He wrapped his arms around Dex's waist, and they rested their heads together. Sloane closed his eyes, smiling when he heard Dex's soft voice singing to him about being there and patiently waiting.

"I know I don't deserve it." Sloane put his fingers to Dex's lips to stop the protest he was certain would come. "I don't. But can you say it anyway?" Dex nodded, and Sloane moved his fingers away.

"I love you."

It was the shy smile afterward that broke Sloane. Cupping Dex's face, Sloane kissed him with all the hunger and tenderness he possessed. He might not be able to define what he was feeling, to make sense of the overwhelming emotions Dex brought out in him, or to explain the hope that flowed through his veins telling him that maybe he wasn't as fucked-up as he believed, but he could show Dex that whatever was inside him was fierce and threatening to tear him apart. All for the man in his arms. Because of him. He'd been honest with Dex, telling him he'd never been in this position before, but damn, he was glad he was here.

Dex kissed him just as passionately in return and pressed his body to Sloane's, silently pleading. Fire raged inside Sloane, and he couldn't get close enough to Dex. He wanted to feel Dex inside him. Wanted to be consumed by him. He pulled back, his chest rising and falling rapidly as he tried to catch his breath. With a smile, he took Dex's hand and rushed to the stairs with him. They ran up to the bedroom and tore at each other's clothes, leaving a trail of shoes, jeans, and shirts on the way to the bed before they dropped down onto it.

Sloane rolled over Dex, his fingers in Dex's hair as he did his damnedest to devour Dex. He trailed kisses over Dex's face, down his jaw to his neck where Sloane closed his mouth around Dex's collar bone and sucked. He wanted to mark Dex. Even if no one else could see, Sloane would know the mark was there. That Dex was his. Dex trembled beneath him as if he was privy to Sloane's thoughts. He tilted his head back, exposing his neck further to Sloane. To a Felid, the neck was the most vulnerable part of the body. Sloane's hand slid up Dex's smooth, tan skin to his neck, and his fingers wrapped around it. Dex moaned. Did he know how he was exposing himself? The Felid inside Sloane stirred. At that moment Dex's eyes opened, and he looked right into Sloane's eyes.

"I'd put my neck in your jaws without a second thought," Dex said hoarsely, his eyes reflecting fire and a trust the likes of which Sloane had never seen. Without hesitation, Sloane reached over to the nightstand, dug in the top drawer and came back with the bottle of lube. He handed it to Dex.

"Fuck me."

Dex stared at him. He took the bottle from Sloane and nodded.

Sloane had never bottomed before. Not because he had any kind of hang-up about it. He'd simply never felt comfortable enough with someone to let his guard fully down. To trust someone so completely he'd give himself over to them. Now he did. He trusted Dex completely. Sloane changed his position. He grabbed a pillow and shoved it under his hips, hearing Dex's soft curses behind him, followed by a sharp intake of breath when Sloane lowered himself to his stomach and spread his legs.

The mattress shifted as Dex positioned himself between Sloane's legs. Sloane concentrated on steadying his breathing and relaxing the tension in his muscles. He heard the pop of the lube's cap, heard the liquid being squeezed out and the cap clicking closed. The mattress shifted again, and he felt Dex's lips press to his searing skin. Sloane groaned and squirmed as Dex left kisses on his neck, shoulders, down his back, his tongue poking out to trace a line down Sloane's spine to his ass. A slick finger pressed into him, and Sloane bucked.

"Dex, please."

"Relax. It's okay. I've got you."

It was an odd sensation, feeling Dex's fingers inside him, but Sloane relaxed just as Dex asked because he believed Dex. The sound of Dex moaning as he spread the lube over his dick had Sloane painfully hard, and he thrust against the pillow. Soon, a warm hand pressed gently down on Sloane's lower back. A sharp sting that had Sloane hissing followed it. He gritted his teeth at the pain of being penetrated. Dex moved slowly, taking care with him, murmuring soft words of encouragement as he pushed in inch by excruciating inch. Sloane sucked in a breath, and Dex paused.

"Don't stop," Sloane pleaded and was relieved when he felt Dex once again pushing in until his partner was buried to the root, stretching and filling him. The pain soon gave way, and Sloane pushed his ass up and back, hissing at the delicious friction. "Oh God. Dex..."

On his cue, Dex moved his hips, sliding in and out until he had built a steady rhythm. His hands caressed Sloane as he moved against him. He draped himself over Sloane's back.

"You don't have to run anymore," Dex murmured, his fingers lacing with Sloane's. "Stay. Right here with me." He gave Sloane's fingers a gentle squeeze before letting go to move down Sloane's body. Dex pressed his lips to the back of Sloane's neck again, his kisses sending a shiver through him. His skin beaded with sweat, and he felt as if he might melt through the mattress.

Their sex was usually heavy, hard, and fast. It was fun and hot as hell. This time was different. This time it shook Sloane down to his core. He felt every breath against his skin, every fiery caress. His muscles bunched and strained, his body felt as though it was about to shatter, his heart ready to break. For a slip of a moment, he almost panicked, afraid he couldn't take the intimacy or unspoken promises Dex offered. Just as the thought entered his mind, he felt Dex's weight once again, as if he'd known what Sloane was thinking. Kisses landed beneath his ear before Dex snapped his hips, and Sloane gasped.

"Again," Sloane pleaded, reaching underneath himself to wrap a hand around his painfully hard erection. Dex did as he asked, snapping his hips over and over, driving himself deep into Sloane with each thrust. Their breaths came out ragged, and Dex craned his neck to kiss Sloane, their lips delivering sloppy urgent kisses. The bed moved beneath them, and Dex's movements grew erratic.

"Sloane..."

"Yes. Fuck. Do it." Sloane was on the verge of coming himself, and he felt the pressure rising as Dex's hips lost all rhythm. Dex straightened, and his fingers grabbed Sloane's hips.

"Oh God," Dex moaned, the sounds of his heavy

breaths and moans sending Sloane over the edge. He came, his muscles tightening around Dex's cock. Dex let out a strangled cry as he came inside Sloane, the sensation drawing out Sloane's orgasm. He fell into his release, loving the feel of Dex coming inside him. Once Dex was spent, he draped himself over Sloane again. His fingers tenderly stroked Sloane's arms, his cheek nuzzling Sloane's back.

"We're definitely doing that again," Sloane said hoarsely.

Dex chuckled, the rumble felt against Sloane's back. "Any time."

"So what happens now?"

"What do you want to happen?" Dex asked softly. It tugged at Sloane's heart knowing Dex would do whatever Sloane needed. The only problem was, Sloane didn't know what he needed.

"Nothing. Everything. I don't know."

"How about we keep doing what we're doing and see where it goes?"

Sloane's heart swelled in his chest. How had he wound up with such an amazing guy? Dex rolled off him, and Sloane followed. "Okay." He reached behind him, took Dex's arm, and pulled him close. He laced their fingers together and kissed Dex's hand, smiling when Dex snuggled up close. As he closed his eyes and drifted off with Dex pressed up against his back and his arms around Sloane, he was reminded that not only did he trust Dex, but he was also coming to learn he could trust Dex to catch him when he fell. The thought wasn't frightening at all. It was comforting. It was time he learned how to do the same for Dex.

A sharp buzzing woke Sloane up in the middle of the night, and he reluctantly moved away from Dex to answer his phone. If it hadn't been his work ringtone, he would have been tempted to ignore it.

"Hello?"

There was a groan, sharp intake of breath, followed by a low plea. "Sloane..."

Sloane sat up, his pulse skyrocketing and his eyesight sharpening. "Austen? What's wrong? What happened?"

"I got too close. Can you... I think I might need some help. Lots of blood."

"Fuck. Okay. Where are you?" Sloane threw back the covers and jumped out of bed. He ran to the other side of the room to grab his clothes off the floor. "I'll be there as fast as I can. Why haven't you called an ambulance?"

"No. No hospitals."

"Austen—"

"No hospitals. Bring one of your sexy medics."

Sloane couldn't help his smile. "You got it. Hang in there." The moment he hung up with Austen he called Rosa. She answered with a groggy "*¿Qué pasó?*" but was instantly awake the moment Sloane relayed the information and Austen's location. Sloane finished zipping up his jeans just when Dex sat up with a fierce yawn.

"What's going on?"

"I have to go. Austen's hurt. I think those Coalition assholes got their hands on him."

"Shit." Dex shot out of bed and started getting dressed. "I'm coming with you."

It took a moment for Sloane to snap himself out of his flabbergasted state. He'd never seen Dex move so quickly after waking up, especially before he'd had coffee. Dex got dressed and cast him a shrewd smile.

"What? Adrenaline kicks caffeine in the ass."

They rushed out of the house and took Sloane's car,

making it from Dex's house to the Brooklyn address Austen had relayed over the phone in less than twenty minutes. Sloane parked on Sullivan Street outside a rundown house with boarded-up windows. Rusted burglar bars secured the basement and first-floor windows, and the door looked solid. But the lock was a piece of shit, and all it took was a good kick. The door slammed open, and they quickly closed it behind them before taking the stairs two at a time to the second floor. There were several doors in the house which had clearly once been converted to apartments. Dex grabbed Sloane's arm and whispered hoarsely. "There."

Sloane removed his Glock from his holster and signaled for Dex to get behind him. Dex nodded, drawing his own backup weapon, and the two of them slowly approached the only door with a glowing light coming from underneath it. As they got closer, Sloane could see the door was slightly ajar. He was about to reach for it when he heard Austen groan.

"Place is clear, Sloane."

Regardless, they walked in with caution. It wasn't that he couldn't trust Austen, but he sure as hell didn't trust the Coalition, and there was no telling what they'd do or if Austen was operating under duress. Once inside the apartment, Dex and Sloane split up. Sloane swiftly checked the tiny box of an apartment when he heard Dex call out.

"Over here! I found Austen."

Sloane followed Dex's voice to what he assumed was supposed to be a living room. It was the only room in the place that wasn't filthy. The floor had been swept, and there was a clean mattress in one corner, a crate with a battery-powered utility lamp, some books, a duffel bag, a backpack, a large cooler doubling as a table, and propped up against the far wall was Austen. He held a hand to his shoulder, blood soaking into his T-shirt underneath.

"Austen? Shit." Sloane hurried over to the cheetah Therian and knelt down beside him. He carefully lifted Austen's hand to assess the damage. "Take it easy." There were three fresh slashes on Austen's shoulder. A felid had taken a swipe at him and caught him. "It's not bad, but you'll need stitches." He returned Austen's hand back to his shoulder and pressed down. Austen sucked in a sharp breath. "Hold on. Help's on its way.

"I'm okay. Someone tried to give me some stripes. Don't they know cheetahs don't look good in stripes?" He looked down at his bloodied hand. "Coalition piece of shit. Cougar asshole came out of nowhere."

"So it *was* them?"

"Someone snitched on me. A snitch snitched on the snitch," Austen said with a laugh then groaned.

"You'll be okay," Sloane promised him. The cuts were deep enough for stitches but not enough for Austen to bleed out.

Austen nodded, his expression turning somber. "The last two random acts of violence weren't so random."

"What have you learned?"

"That dude who got caught in the crossfire over on Broome Street? He was murdered." Austen closed his eyes, and Sloane panicked.

"Austen!"

The young Therian gave a start, his eyes flying open so he could stare at Sloane. "Easy there, Broody Bear. What you yelling at?"

"Sorry, I thought..." Sloane felt embarrassed. A part of him felt responsible for Austen. It was because of Sloane that Austen was working for the THIRDS to begin with.

"Aw, look at you," Austen purred. "All worried about me. I've grown on you."

"Like a bad habit," Dex muttered. Austen chuckled and gave Dex a wink.

"You're all right, Daley. Though sexy pants here is in a whole other league."

Sloane was aware of Austen's crush. The kid had been infatuated with him for years. He'd tried his best to let Austen know nothing could ever happen between them. He just didn't see Austen that way. It was hard not seeing him as that scrappy little kid he'd met years ago. "Austen, I..."

"You got a guy. I get it. 'Course you do. Look at you." Austen let out a soft laugh, though it fell flat. "Besides, I'm just an upcycled thief."

"Hey, you're an agent, and a damned good one. Without your skills, the THIRDS wouldn't have the information it does. What you do matters, Austen. You help save lives."

Austen pursed his lips. "Yeah, I am pretty awesome, aren't I?"

Sloane chuckled, and Austen's expression grew hard once more. "The Coalition executed that guy. Made it look like he got caught in the crossfire. My guess is he was set up. Your second victim is Craig Martin. Run their names for known associates dating back to the riots, and I'm willing to bet you're going to get more than you bargained for. There's more going on here than we thought. I've heard the word *rogue* whispered around, and I don't mean the cheeky kind you find in romance novels. I think some of the Coalition members have secretly gone rogue."

It was as Sloane had suspected. Something else was going on, and it had nothing to do with rounding up members of the Order. "You've done an amazing job, Austen. I'm really proud of you." And he was. He meant everything he'd said to Austen. The young Therian was one hell of an asset. One of the good ones. Ballsy and determined to see justice prevail.

Austen beamed brightly at him. "Thanks, man. I also found something on the prick looking to take over the Order."

"You've been busy."

"Don't want to let you down." Austen shrugged, his gaze moving away from Sloane. Sloane took hold of Austen's face and turned him so he could meet Austen's gaze.

"You never do. I wish you'd listen when I ask you to be careful."

"Life in the fast lane, my man." Austen was smiling again, and Sloane was relieved. It took a lot to get Austen down. Sloane had always admired that about the guy. Austen shifted, letting out a low hiss before continuing. "The rumors about there being more than one Human looking to crown himself King of the Crazies is bullshit. There's just the one. This new guy. He's got a tattoo running down the side of his neck. Big one. I looked it up. It's the Hydra, a multiheaded serpent from Greek mythology."

"You did great, Austen." Sloane gave Austen a gentle pat on the arm. "You've given us our first major leads and confirmed my suspicions on the Coalition."

"Sloane?"

"Yeah?"

"I'm worried."

"Don't be. I promise you'll be taken care of. You trust me, right?"

"I wouldn't be here if I didn't."

"Good." Sloane's phone went off, and he saw on his

caller ID that it was Rosa. He quickly answered and gave her the apartment number. Moments later she was unpacking her first-aid response kit next to Austen. While Austen flirted and bantered with Rosa and Rosa patched him up, Sloane had a chat with Dex who looked concerned.

"Sloane, he's going to need someone to keep an eye on him and keep him safe in case the Coalition makes another attempt to shut him up. At least until he's gotten all his strength back."

"I know just the guy for the job." Sloane pulled out his phone and scrolled through his contacts. "Osmond Zachary." He tried his best not to laugh at Dex's jaw nearly becoming unhinged.

"As in the guy who hung me upside down from my ankles because he wanted my Cheesy Doodles?"

"Yes."

"Yogi will probably eat him!"

Sloane frowned at Dex. "Don't call him Yogi. He doesn't like it. Call him Zach."

"Seriously?"

"He owes me a favor."

"For what?" Dex whined.

Sloane wriggled his eyebrows. "For me giving him your Cheesy Doodles."

"Sadist," Dex gasped. "I don't think I like you anymore."

"Yes, you do."

Dex stuck his tongue out at him and walked off toward Rosa and Austen. It didn't take long to explain the situation to Zach's team leader in Unit Beta. The agent's workload would be passed onto someone else on Zach's team. They were mostly low-risk warrants other agents could handle. Zach was happy to help Sloane. The guy wasn't much of a talker, and he looked damn intimidating.

Scary as shit was more accurate. But he was a really sweet guy—unless someone tried to steal his snacks. It was a shame others often dismissed him as a brainless muscle-bound thug. Zach was well-spoken and much smarter than he was given credit for. As if somehow size and muscle mass equated to smaller brains. Idiots. Rosa had just finished patching Austen up when there was a knock on the door.

Zach stood on the other side looking uncertain. "Hey, Zach. Thank you for agreeing to help." Sloane led him into the living room where Rosa finished applying the last bandage to Austen's shoulder. When Austen saw Zach he nearly jumped out of his skin.

"Holy fuck!" Austen's eyes went wide as saucers as he gaped at Zach.

"Austen, this is Agent Osmond Zachary from Alpha Sleuth, Unit Beta. Agent Zachary, this is Austen."

"What happened to him?" Zach asked, his eyes taking in all the bloodied gauze pads scattered around Austen before his eyes moved up to Austen's shirt. A deep frown came onto Zach's face, making him look even more intimidating, if that was possible.

"The Coalition wasn't happy with Austen for helping us. I'm afraid they might try to hurt him again. I need you to protect him."

Zach gave him a stern nod. "I won't let anything happen to him."

"Good. Call me if you run into any trouble." Sloane patted Zach on the shoulder and thanked Rosa for her assistance. He told Austen to behave himself. There was no snappy comeback or flirtatious quip from Austen who was eyeing Zach with uncertainty. Sloane put it down to Austen's skittish nature. Cheetah Therians didn't give their trust easily. It had to be earned. They were too vulnerable in the Therian scheme of things.

On the way to the car, Sloane asked Dex if he wanted to get some breakfast close to home. It was five in the morning. There was no point in going back to bed just to get an hour of sleep, if that. He found them a café a couple of blocks from Dex's house, and they sat across from each other in a booth and ordered coffee and breakfast. Well, Sloane ordered breakfast. Dex ordered a banquet. Where did his partner store all that food? Anyone who saw him eat would think he was a Therian with how he put food away.

"You really care about Austen, don't you?" Dex asked, after swallowing a mouthful of scrambled eggs, sausage, and pancake.

"I might have been the youngest agent to join the THIRDS, but Austen was even younger when he joined as an SSA. He was fourteen. That was almost ten years ago. The kid's had a tough life, and yeah, he was a thief, but he's always kept his nose clean. His parents kicked him out after his first shift. He was eight. State tried to find him a new home, but he kept running away. He has a hard time trusting people. And if he doesn't trust you, good luck keeping up with him."

"And then he met you?"

"Little prick tried to steal my wallet." Sloane chuckled at the memory. "I chased him all through Central Park. Lost him a few times, but I outmaneuvered him. He was really good, but his true potential was going untapped. With the right training, who knew what he could do? I told him who I worked for. There was a chance he'd bolt, but he didn't. He asked me to buy him a slice of pizza and a soda."

Dex gaped at him. "He stole your wallet, found out you

were the law, and then asked you to buy him a slice of pizza?"

"And a soda," Sloane reminded him. "He was very serious about the soda. Kid's addicted to sugar." He smiled slyly. "Sounds like someone else I know."

Dex actually looked insulted. "I'm not addicted to sugar."

"The first step to recovery is admitting you have a problem."

"Screw you. I don't have a problem," Dex grumbled.

"That's denial talking right there. Tell me," Sloane said, leaning back against the booth's seat. "What did you have for breakfast yesterday?"

"Leftover pancakes with fruit in them from the morning before last. Which *you* made. I've never had fruit in my pancakes before. It's weird."

"It's not weird. And if you will recall, I made very healthy pancakes with fruit, which *you* then drowned in maple syrup. Full calorie. High fructose."

Dex rolled his eyes. "I didn't drown them."

"They were floating."

"Back to Austen."

Sloane held back a smile. King of Evasive Tactics. "Like I said, I thought he was going to run. I bought him the pizza and soda—an extra-large slice mind you—and we got to talking. He asked me dozens of questions about the THIRDS and was so excited he could barely sit still. As it happened, there was a robbery while we were in the pizzeria. A tiger Therian came in with a knife and started threatening everyone. I told Austen to get under the table and not come out until I said so. Then I got up and tried to talk the guy into putting the knife down. The guy didn't take it well and came at me."

"Shit. What did you do?"

Sloane shrugged. "I did what I had to. I took him down. Body slammed him into the linoleum."

"You took down a tiger Therian?"

"I've had practice."

"Hobbs?"

Sloane nodded. "The bigger they are, the harder they fall. And while in their Human form, they don't always land on their feet. Anyway, the THIRDS came and took the guy away. I told Austen to come out and introduced him to the team. You should have seen his face. It was as if I'd introduced him to the Justice League or something."

Dex gave him a wicked grin. "Your geek is showing."

"Shut it."

Dex cackled and sat back. His expression softened. "I can't say I blame him. I would have been pretty starstruck too. Big sexy badass."

Sloane chuckled. "Well, I don't know about badass, but after that, Austen kept showing up everywhere I went. My biggest worry was when he showed up on calls. I was afraid he'd get hurt. I knew he wouldn't quit just because I asked him to. Stubborn little shit. So I started giving him small jobs with no risk involved. He loved it, and he was good at it. I spoke to Lieutenant Sparks, introduced them, and next thing I know, she's giving him a job. He's been working with us since."

"Do you think what Austen says is true? Do you think some of the Coalition members have gone rogue?" Dex finished his coffee, and Sloane paid the tab, ignoring Dex's grousing on having Sloane pay for his jumbo breakfast.

"If Austen says that's what he heard, I believe him. First thing, we're getting on this lead. We need to let Cael know so he can get the algorithm set up. I want to know why these particular Order members. What is the Coalition up to?"

They got into Sloane's car and headed for HQ. They'd shower and change there. Sloane had to fill Maddock in on what was going on. Something was about to give in this case. He could feel it.

ELEVEN

The next morning, they finally lucked out.

"We got something." Cael came rushing into their office and hurried over to Sloane's desk. He entered his code into the security panel on the right-hand side, and Cael's desk interface replaced Sloane's. A few taps later, and Cael was bringing up several windows.

"We ran Craig Martin's and Alberto Cristo's names through Themis like Austen suggested. At first, the only hit we got on them were some minor assault charges when they were teens. Then I ran their names through Themis for known associates, as you said, and I got a shitload of hits. Not only were they both members of the Order, but get this, during the riots in '85, a gang of Human youths calling themselves the Westward Creed went on a spree, assaulting Therian citizens left and right. The assaults were random and small-scale, but they soon escalated the violence until the gang members were arrested for causing the deaths of several Therians."

"Martin and Cristo were members of the Westward Creed?" Sloane asked.

"Yeah, but Cristo got out before anyone died. As for his friends, the charges were dropped due to missing evidence —or more likely due to the corrupt Human judge given the case. The judge was forced into retirement once the new Therian laws were passed." Cael tapped Sloane's desktop, and it split into eight screens with pictures and arrest records of the gang. The first one was of a young Craig Martin. Another photo jumped out at Sloane, and he sat forward.

"Hold on a second. That guy there." Sloane pointed to one of the mug shots. An eighteen-year-old punk named Angel Reyes. "Look at his tattoo. It matches Austen's description of the one he saw."

Dex came to stand beside Sloane. "Shit. You think that's the guy trying to take over the Order?"

"How many guys in New York have a tattoo of a multi-headed mythological Greek serpent over their face and neck?"

"True."

Cael slid his hands across Reyes's file, and it expanded, taking up the length of the desk. Several additional files popped up. He opened a side panel and ran a current search for Angel Reyes. "Dude lives in the Bronx."

Sloane tapped the address, and once the information menu popped up, he had Themis send it to his tablet. "Cael, can you bring up the list of victims from the riots?"

"Sure."

"Martin's and Cristo's deaths weren't an accident, and I'm willing to bet they won't be the last. I think these victims are connected to members of the Coalition, and someone's decided to take advantage of this war against the Order to get revenge. That would explain the rumors Austen's been hearing about members of the Coalition going rogue. Somewhere along the way on their little vigilante crusade, something changed. The only problem is, we don't know the identities of any of the Coalition members. No faces, names, or info we can run through Themis and cross-reference with the list of victims."

Sloane's phone went off, and he quickly answered, listening to Austen ramble off his latest intel. "Austen, you are fucking amazing. I'm going to make sure you get a raise. What? No, I won't go out on a date with you. Don't push your luck. Yes, I'm sure Zach isn't going to shift and eat you. Stop being such a scaredy-cat."

Dex chuckled. "I'm starting to like that guy."

Sloane hung up and got to his feet. "He reminds me of you."

"Two of them?" Cael shuddered.

"Thanks, bro." Dex turned his frown on Sloane. "I'm not sure I like the sound of that."

Sloane leaned over Dex and gave his cheek a pinch, throwing Dex's words back at him. "Aw, has anyone told you how cute your jealous-boyfriend face is?"

"Oh. You are good, sir." Dex wagged a finger at him. "I approve."

Sloane chuckled. "Come on. We've got a lead. Austen got a tip on Reyes. I need to inform Maddock." He turned for the door when Cael stepped in front of him. He rubbed a hand over his hair, his eyes on his boots as he looked embarrassed.

"I'm glad you guys made up. I'm sorry if I've been acting like a jerk." He lifted his face and gave his brother a pout. Where did these two learn to do that pouty-lipped thing? It was devious and highly effective. "I'm sorry, Dex."

"It's okay." Dex threw his arms around his brother and hugged him tightly. "You know I can't stay mad at you." He took hold of Cael's cheeks and squeezed them. "Look at that face. How can I stay mad at that?"

"You done?" Cael asked through squeezed cheeks, looking most unimpressed.

"I am." Dex smiled wickedly, and Sloane braced himself. "Chirpy." He released his brother and bolted from the room.

"You colossal jerk!" Cael chased after Dex, and Sloane couldn't keep himself from shaking his head at the two as he followed them out into the bullpen. Sloane left the brothers to their shenanigans while he headed for Maddock's office. Finally, they were getting somewhere. Sloane had gotten pretty sick and tired of always being one step behind these bastards. It was time for the tide to change.

Maddock stood at the podium at the front of the briefing room, addressing the three Defense teams. Sloane's meeting with his sergeant had been brief, but together they'd quickly devised a strategy—one that would hopefully give them the advantage they needed. The end was near. Sloane could feel it.

"Listen up. We've received a tip regarding the location of Angel Reyes, a Human we believe to be associated with the Order and possibly looking to assume leadership. If we can bring Reyes in, we might be able to get the locations of the remaining members of the Order and any bases of operation that may be left. This is the biggest lead we've had. Reyes has been sighted at the Baptist church on Hertz Street in Brownsville. I've already sent the location to your tablets. I want Reyes alive. We also need to get there before the Coalition, so everyone gear up and move out."

Everyone in the room dispersed, including Destructive Delta. As they headed for the armory, Dex edged up to Sloane and discreetly checked to make sure no one was within hearing distance. "How do you know the information won't get out?"

"Doesn't matter if it does. If the Coalition shows up at the church, they won't find Reyes."

Dex gave him a puzzled frown. "Reyes wasn't sighted at the church?"

"Reyes does attend the Baptist church on Hertz Street," Sloane replied before giving his partner a sly smile. "Just not the Baptist church on Hertz Street Maddock gave out."

"You've got a plan, don't you?"

"Maddock and I talked it over, and he agreed if we give out Reyes's location, the Coalition is bound to get there before we do. This way, we'll get there first. If we need backup, the teams will be just down the street."

"What about Ash?"

"Don't worry about Ash. I've got that covered."

Once everyone was geared up and in their trucks, Maddock instructed Hobbs to hang back and let Beta Pride and Beta Ambush take the lead. Destructive Delta took up the rear. Everyone was quiet as they rode toward Hertz Street, the anticipation palpable. They all knew how important the success of this mission was. The moment they drove onto Hertz Street, Sloane checked his watch. In four... three... two...

A delivery truck should be cutting them off and stopping in front of them with hazard lights flashing in...

One.

Calvin called out from the front cabin. "Sarge, we've got a problem."

Maddock told Hobbs to back up and go around before

tapping his earpiece. "Agent Stone, Agent Taylor, we're going to have to go around. Some jackass delivery van blocked our route."

Sloane heard a "copy that" from both team leaders, and shortly after, Sloane's phone rang. He held back a smile as he answered. "Good job, Austen, but I'm still not going out on a date with you." He chuckled at Austen's whine before the young Therian cursed under his breath and told Sloane that Agent Zachary was a card shark. Sloane hung up and turned to give Dex a wink. It was time to put the ball back in their court.

Hobbs parked a few doors down from the Peoples Baptist Church on Riverdale Avenue just off Hertz Street. Sloane knew for a fact Reyes wasn't at church. He was in the sub-basement of the boarded up, supposed-to-be-abandoned apartment building across the street. Destructive Delta climbed out of the BearCat with Cael and Maddock staying behind to manage surveillance on the area. Sloane signaled to his team, and they all fell into formation behind him. They quietly made for the back of the apartment building, rifles at the ready. Sloane reached behind him and signaled Dex. His partner removed his backpack and produced a set of bolt cutters. In seconds, Dex was cutting the thick chain securing the gate of the white iron fence. He returned the cutters to his backpack before tapping Sloane on the flank.

Sloane entered first, moving through the yard of the building. It was nothing but cracked concrete slabs, weeds, and dry leaves. He held out three fingers, and Ash appeared beside him.

"I thought we were going to pick up, Reyes?"

"We are. Find us a way in."

Ash quickly surveyed the area before pointing up to the

second floor. "Fire escape. Sliding-glass doors. No bars." Sloane gave him a curt nod and motioned for Hobbs to come over. He pointed to the fire escape's ladder.

"Grab that, will you?"

Hobbs reached up without any effort and carefully pulled down the ladder. With thanks, Sloane gave the signal, and Dex went up to breach. He kept an eye on his partner along with the surrounding area for any signs of movement. The neighborhood was quiet at this time of day. Dex leaned over the rail and held a thumb up. He'd gotten through the lock. Sloane went up next to watch his partner's back. Seconds later, his team was inside the empty room. The boarded-up sliding-glass door was closed behind them. Sloane gathered his team close.

"Calvin and Hobbs, you're team one. Rosa and Letty, you're team two. Ash and Dex, you're with me. According to our SSA, there are only a few members of the Order left here since Reyes has been moving everything to a new location. If anyone calls asking about Reyes or our location, you tell them we're working on it and will get back to them. I want to be notified of everyone who mentions his name. Watch your backs."

The three teams split up with Ash and Dex, sticking close to Sloane. Once the rest of the team had left the room, Sloane turned to Ash. "I want your com off. Leave only the emergency line open." If Ash turned it back on, Sloane would know.

Ash arched an eyebrow at him. "So much for the benefit of the doubt."

"Sorry, buddy, but I can't take any chances on this."

With a nod, Ash tapped his earpiece, and the tiny blue light turned amber. With a pat on Ash's shoulder, Sloane resumed his formation with Dex at his back and Ash bringing up the rear. They checked the hall before making their way down through the three-story building, leaving the rooms to the rest of the team. Sloane wanted the sub-basement. They found the stairwell down without any trouble and in minutes were at a large steel door. Dex stepped around Sloane and took hold of the handle, pulling slowly. The door was unlocked. His partner pulled the door open and assessed the area. He held a hand up, signaling the stairs were clear. Sloane once again took the lead, and they made their way down the grimy, stone staircase. At the bottom, they faced a set of double steel doors. Sloane turned to Ash. "Ready?" They both knew what he was implying.

Ash put his hand on Sloane's shoulder, his amber gaze unwavering. "I know I've disappointed you, but believe me when I say I'll always have your back."

"That's all I need to know." Sloane grabbed the back of Ash's collar and they bumped their heads together. "Let's do this." He took the position to the left of the doors while Ash took the right. Sloane gave Dex a nod, and his partner took hold of one of the door handles. He opened it slowly and just enough to sneak a quick glance. With a nod, he opened it wider and went in, his rifle aimed ahead of him. Sloane and Ash were at his back ready to neutralize any and all threats. Rosa's voice came in over Sloane's earpiece.

"We're heading your way. The first, second, and third floors are clear. Negative on suspects."

"Copy that." Sloane signaled forward, and they continued down the wide concrete corridor. It was empty except for Order propaganda posters littering the walls and a few empty tin drums lined up against one side. They followed the thick cables attached to the walls, which appeared to supply the place with lighting and possibly electricity. It smelled of damp and dirt. Ahead of them was a set of doors with small windows. Sloane held a hand up behind him, bringing them to a stop. He turned to Dex and drew a square in the air. With a nod, Dex crouched low and approached the doors with caution. He carefully rose and glanced through one of the windows. Dropping back down, he held his hand up, his thumb holding down his middle finger. Eight perps. A handgun sign followed.

Sloane's earpiece beeped, and once again Rosa's voice came over the line. "Sloane, we see you. We're coming in behind you."

"Copy that. We're going in. Eight armed Humans."

"Copy that."

Sloane and Ash approached the doors, making sure to stay away from the windows. On his signal, Dex swung open one of the doors, and Destructive Delta charged in.

"Hands in the air!" Sloane demanded. "Put down your weapons, or we *will* open fire!"

Three of the men immediately dropped their guns while the others scrambled. Ash and Hobbs moved in, and Calvin shot a tranq into one man stupid enough to raise his gun at Calvin. The guy fell to the floor instantly. The team rounded everyone up, pushing them to the ground and securing them with Therian grade zip ties just in case. A half dozen steel tables laid out with firearms and lethal weapons along with materials for explosives lined the room. Sloane was about to notify Maddock when a door slammed open at the far side of the room.

"What the fuck is going—" Reyes took one look at them and bolted. Sloane gave chase through the door and down another corridor. Either Reyes wasn't as smart as he thought he was, or he hadn't expected an infiltration. He ran right into a room with no windows, doors, or way out. As if realizing he was trapped, Reyes whipped out his sidearm and spun, pointing it at Sloane. Ash and Dex were soon at his side, their rifles aimed at the tattooed man.

"Put it down, Reyes," Sloane advised him. He needed Reyes alive, but Reyes didn't know that. "You might get one shot off, but there are three of us. Think carefully."

Reyes gritted his teeth. His dark eyes filled with hate and anger. He spit at Sloane's feet, muttering something about Sloane being nothing but a filthy animal. Then he slowly lowered his gun and placed it on the floor. Sloane moved in and forced him onto the concrete. He held Reyes's arms behind his back while Dex drew a zip tie over his wrists.

"Sergeant, we've got him. As soon as we get him in the BearCat, have Beta Pride and Beta Ambush pick up the others." Sloane dragged Reyes to his feet and pulled him along, Dex and Ash following. On the way out, Sloane instructed the rest of his team to stay with their suspects. They quickly got Reyes into the back of the BearCat where Maddock and Ash cuffed Reyes's wrists and legs with chains and secured them to the iron hook in the floor. Seconds later, Beta Ambush and Beta Pride rolled up. The two team leaders came running, both looking mighty pissed off.

Taylor reached Sloane first. "What the fuck happened?"

"There was a miscommunication in the location," Sloane replied. "When we took the detour, we came up on this church. We didn't know there were two Baptist churches on the same street."

"A miscommunication?" Taylor craned his neck to peer around Sloane, his eyes going wide when he saw the chained-up perp. "Is that Reyes?"

"Yes." Sloane could see Taylor bristle.

"A miscommunication and then you happened to find Reyes? That's pretty fucking convenient, Brodie."

Sloane narrowed his eyes. "Is there a problem, Agent Taylor?"

"Yeah, I like knowing when someone's trying to make an asshole out of me," Taylor snarled.

"Like I said. Miscommunication. My team has eight suspects detained in the sub-basement of the building behind us. Your teams can transport them back to HQ. Get them processed and ready for questioning."

Levi gave him a stern nod and walked off. Taylor hesitated. He started to turn, stopped, and met Sloane's gaze. "This is bullshit, and you know it." He thundered off toward his team, ordering them to move in.

Dex appeared beside Sloane. "I think he took it rather well."

"Yeah" was all Sloane said. As soon as the rest of Destructive Delta returned and climbed into the BearCat, they headed back to HQ. There was something bugging Sloane, he just couldn't figure out what.

It wasn't long before Sloane sat in the padded interrogation room across from Reyes. The guy was once again cuffed and chained to the floor, but he was lounging in his chair as if he didn't give a shit. He was cocky, a borderline sociopath, and fearless. Well, they'd see about the last one. Sloane had every intention of putting the fear in him.

Finished with his assessment of Reyes, Sloane laced his fingers on the table in front of him, his gaze never leaving that of the Human before him. "We believe members of the Order are being murdered by the Coalition and made to look like casualties of war. They've got a shit list and guess what? You're on it."

Reyes let out a snort. "What can I say? I'm a popular guy."

"A charmer like you? How can you not be? You seem to be able to get away with anything. Even murder."

Reyes leaned forward, his eyes narrowed. "I don't think I like what you're implying."

"Let me rephrase that. You got away with murder, and now you have to answer for what you did. There are no corrupt judges to bail you out of this one. The evidence isn't going to magically disappear. Did you really think it wouldn't catch up to you? That you wouldn't have to answer for what you did?" He watched Reyes. The guy was guilty as sin, but he felt no remorse for the crimes he'd committed because in his eyes, they weren't crimes, they were good deeds. He was answering the call of a higher power. Now he was about to answer to a different power.

"You can't pin that on me. You've got nothing."

"Oh, I'm sorry. Did you think you were with the HPF? This is the THIRDS. Things work a little differently here. You're going to tell me where the remaining branches of the Order are located and list the names of every member you know."

Reyes sneered at him. "And why the hell would I do that?"

"Because if not, I'm going to let you walk out that door."

Reyes frowned at him. "How's that make any fucking sense?"

With a grin, Sloane tapped the desk's surface. Photos of Martin—or what was left of him—from the crime scene, along with those taken of the guy at the morgue, spread out across the screen.

"Jesus." Reyes swallowed visibly, his eyes darting from image to image.

"Remember your old pal Craig Martin? Of course you do. He was on that shit list too. This is what's left of him." Sloane tapped the screen again, and photos of Alberto Cristo joined Martin's. "And that's your friend Alberto Cristo. Also on the list. You walk out that door, and you'll be lucky if all you get is a bullet to the head. It might take them a week, a month, maybe a year. But they'll hunt you down."

"But it's your job to catch these animals!"

"Really, Angel?"

Reyes sat back, fidgeting in his seat. "I mean, it's your job to stop them, isn't it?"

"It is. It's also our job to stop the Order. Then there are all the other crimes going on at this very moment. Come on. You know what it's like out there. We're government funded. How many agents do you think we have? We can't be everywhere at once. What if we're in the middle of a call when the Coalition tracks you down? Did you know they have members in their Therian form hunting alongside them at all times? You ever faced a jaguar Therian in his Therian form, Angel?"

Reyes shook his head. With a smile, Sloane turned his neck so Reyes could see his mark. The man's eyes widened.

"Do you know what my bite can do? It can pierce your skull in one motion. I can hunt at night, and you'll never see me coming. I can climb and swim better than you. My claws can rip your throat out in one swipe. Now, imagine the Coalition. A group of Therians. Let's say lions, tigers, cougars, and jaguars all looking for you. You think they won't find you? Would you like to meet a tiger Therian up close?" Before Reyes could answer, Sloane tapped his earpiece. "Cael, could you come in here. And bring Seb with you."

Seconds later, and the door opened. Cael walked in, and Reyes let out a bark of laughter. "That's your fierce tiger Therian?"

"Don't be rude, Angel. This is Agent Maddock. He's a cheetah Therian. Don't let his size fool you. His job is to chase you down and trip you up. He can go zero to sixty in three seconds. Once he catches you, he'll bite down on your throat until Agent Sebastian Hobbs gets there."

Seb padded into the room, his striped coat shifting and moving against his powerful muscles as he came to sit beside the table, his tail thumping heavily against the carpeted floor.

"This is Agent Sebastian Hobbs. Seb, meet Mr. Reyes."

Seb let out a fierce roar that made Reyes scramble to his feet so fast, his chair toppled over behind him. He tried to move away, but the chains kept him from getting far.

Sloane turned his attention to Cael, who stood by the door. "Would you bring in Hobbs and Ash?"

Cael returned shortly after with Hobbs and an agent who was a lion Therian but not Ash. While Seb continued to scare the pants off Reyes, Sloane approached Cael. The concerned look on the young agent's face was worrisome. "Where's Ash?"

"I don't know. I haven't seen him since we left the BearCat. He returned his equipment to the armory, but he wasn't in there when we arrived, so he must have gone ahead. This is Agent Ford from Beta Ambush."

Damn it. This wasn't looking good. Sloane prayed Ash wasn't doing what he thought he was. He had to hurry this along. He thanked Cael and resumed his seat. He smiled at Reyes who crawled onto the table when Hobbs and Ford joined Seb. Ford's roar had Reyes frantically clawing the table in his attempt to get away.

"Okay, Angel. Here we have two tiger Therians, a lion Therian and," he pointed to himself, "a jaguar Therian. Now, imagine we're hunting you with the intent of not letting you live." Seb, Hobbs, and Ford crowded Reyes who looked like he was about to shit a brick. Ford roared and Seb hissed. They both pawed at the table. Hobbs jumped up onto the table with ease, and Reyes let out a shriek. With a snarl, Hobbs lay down and simply stared at Reyes.

"This is intimidation," Reyes whispered hoarsely, sweat dripping down his face.

"No, this is a glimpse at your near and not so distant future. Except when that happens, you won't stay alive as long. The Coalition wants justice for what you did, Angel, and they're going to do everything they can to get it. There is nowhere you can hide." Sloane sat back and scratched his nose. On his signal, Hobbs rose. He lowered his head slightly, his tail swinging, and his pupils going wide.

"Oh, looks like he's going to pounce. I think he wants to play."

Reyes whimpered and curled up on himself. It was obvious when the guy decided to take over the Order he hadn't known what he was getting into. Sloane had no doubt Reyes intended on sitting in his cushy digs giving orders. It was all very well to start a war when you never planned on joining your men on the frontlines. "All right! I'll do it! Just get them to back the fuck off. Please!"

Sloane nodded, and the door opened. Hobbs jumped off the table and hurried out of the room. Seb and Ford followed. Once the door closed, Reyes gingerly slipped off the table. A few taps later, and Sloane brought up the documentation necessary for Reyes's statement along with a clean document. He handed Reyes a stylus.

"Take your time. We want to make sure you don't leave anyone out."

Reyes cast him a daggered look but swiped the stylus from him. He put his chair to rights, sat down, and started writing. As Sloane watched Reyes give up his organization, he told himself this was just the beginning. With the Order permanently disbanded, the Coalition would be next.

The moment Reyes had finished scribbling the final name, Sloane swiped the list, took a look at it, and sent it to Lieutenant Sparks and Sergeant Maddock. Almost as soon as he'd sent it, the table flashed red, and a band scrolled across the top with an APB for each member on the list. Sloane thanked Reyes and told him to hang tight before slipping out of the room. Maddock was waiting for him outside.

"Good job, son."

"Thank you. I'm concerned about where we should hold him. I'm certain the Coalition knows we have him in custody." And if they didn't, something told him they'd know soon enough.

"You're right. Keep him in the interrogation room until I can speak to Lieutenant Sparks. Right now, she's holding an emergency briefing." Maddock met Sloane's gaze. "Whatever it is. It's not good."

Dex sat at the conference table in the briefing room facing the front where his dad and Lieutenant Sparks stood talking quietly. The large screen on the wall behind them flickered to life but remained blank. Whatever was going on, it couldn't be good. If the lieutenant was holding the briefing, it was usually serious business, and her grave expression didn't bode well. Tony looked momentarily stunned by something the lieutenant said, and Dex knew it was bad. Sparks took the podium and held a hand up. The room immediately plunged into silence.

"What I'm about to show you will be difficult for you, but I ask that you remain calm until I've explained the situation."

An image flickered to life on the screen, and the room erupted into gasps and murmurs. Dex stared at the bound-and-gagged agent in disbelief. Sloane was on his feet instantly and in front of Dex, Cael gasped, "Oh my God. Ash."

"What the hell is this?" Sloane demanded.

Lieutenant Sparks patiently addressed Sloane. "I will explain, Agent Brodie. Please, have a seat."

Dex couldn't tear his gaze away from the screen where he saw Ash bound and gagged. The most unsettling part was how they had beaten the shit out of the fierce Therian agent. His face was swollen, his lip split, a cut trickled blood from his nose. He was bruised and covered in blood and sweat. His head hung low, and he looked as if he was out cold.

"Agent Keeler is a member of the Coalition."

Something about the statement and the matter-of-fact way the lieutenant said it struck Dex as odd. The room once again erupted into murmurs.

"Ash is the mole?" Cael asked, his voice barely rising above those around him but loud enough for the lieutenant to hear.

"Not the one we've been looking for," Sparks replied. "Agent Keeler is the mole we planted. He's been working undercover. The objective was to send an agent to infiltrate the Coalition, discover the mole from the inside out. Keeler's combat skills, field experience, and brash character made him the perfect candidate for the assignment. We knew the Coalition would jump at the chance to recruit him if they believed he could be swayed to fight for their cause.

"I instructed Keeler to play sympathetic to the Coalition's purpose. It didn't take long for our mole to make contact. Keeler received an anonymous text giving him a date, time, and place. He showed, spoke to someone who wasn't the mole but had contact with him or her. Keeler negotiated the terms. He would join their ranks and provide intel so long as Coalition members kept their distance from THIRDS agents, specifically his team. To maintain the illusion he'd gone rogue, it was necessary for Destructive Delta to be kept in the dark. I then fed Keeler inside information to pass along."

All this time, Ash had been working undercover? Everything suddenly started to make sense. The absences, the attitude, the constant justification of the Coalition's actions. The way he pushed Cael away. Dex had gotten it all wrong. Damn it. He should have trusted his gut. Ash had never been a traitor. In fact, he was the complete opposite. He knew what this kind of assignment would entail. How it would affect his relationship with those he cared about. But he'd gone out and done his job anyway because that's what a THIRDS agent who believed in what he was doing did. He put the safety of the city's citizens before all else.

"It was imperative Agent Keeler maintain his cover until the identity of our mole was discovered. Unfortunately, it looks like his position has been compromised. I received a digital ransom note from the Coalition twenty minutes ago. They want to do a trade. Agent Keeler for Mr. Reyes."

Agent Taylor shook his head. "How do we know they

won't kill Ash anyway?"

"They won't," Cael snapped. "We won't let that happen."

"Agent Brodie." Lieutenant Sparks laced her fingers over the podium. "Suggestions?"

Dex turned in his seat to watch his partner. He'd come to know that look. Sloane was running all the options through his head, the different scenarios and possible outcomes. He would be searching for a way that would result in recovering Ash, not losing Reyes, and possibly getting their hands on the Coalition once and for all. Sloane shifted his gaze to Sparks. "We give them Reyes."

Sparks studied him. There was something in her gaze. "What do you need?"

"For the Coalition to allow us to choose the location, since they have the upper hand."

"I'll get it done." She turned off the screen and turned to speak with Tony while Sloane addressed the room.

"Everyone, let's suit up and head out. You'll receive my instructions on the way."

Sloane wasn't taking any chances, and Dex didn't blame him. If they wanted to get Ash back in one piece, they'd have to tread carefully. The tension was palpable, and everyone looked grim and determined. Sloane informed Destructive Delta that they were going in heavily armed. One of their own was in trouble, and they would be retrieving him using any means necessary. Once they'd geared up, they waited in the BearCat until Reyes was escorted in. His hands were cuffed, but his legs were free. He was also wearing a tactical vest and helmet.

Tony secured their prisoner, and the BearCat headed off with Beta Pride and Beta Ambush keeping their distance. Sloane had relayed the location where he wanted them to stand by. He withheld the location of the tradeoff, instructing the two team leaders he'd give them the address when it was time to move in. Taylor had been livid. Sloane didn't care. Right now, Destructive Delta only trusted each other.

The BearCat drove up West Street and made a left on Oak Street, which was barely wide enough for the truck to fit through. The road abruptly turned to dirt and gravel. To each side of their truck was a long chain-link fence. Their left was pretty much clear with nothing but an empty lot. But ahead of them and to their right it was a mess. There were train compartments and storage units stacked all over the place in varying heights. There were piles of wooden pallets, bundles of rusted metal fencing, trucks, cranes, slabs of concrete, cinder blocks, and a whole lot of shadows. It was a tactical nightmare, but for some reason, it was what Sloane wanted.

Hobbs slowed the truck, and Calvin came out from the front. A black wool beanie covered his blond hair, and he was dressed in a black uniform rather than their standard charcoal gray. He looked like he was about to burgle someone, except the black tac vest and large, elongated black bag in his gloved hand stated otherwise. Calvin gave Sloane a nod, before silently slipping out the back of the truck.

Calvin was a quiet guy, but Dex was coming to learn the quiet ones were the ones you had to look out for. His teammate might not be a military sniper, but that didn't make him any less skilled or dangerous. Dex could see it in the guy's face. Something in his deep-blue eyes clouded over when he was about to take position for a hit. He never discussed how he felt about what he did or when he had to take someone out. That's what the THIRDS appointed psychologists were for.

With Calvin gone, the truck continued down the dirt road and pulled off to the right. The place was brightly lit in some areas from the floodlights while other areas were cast in shadows. Unless he was wearing his night-vision goggles, there was no way Dex would know what was stalking around in the darkness. It would be up to his Therian teammates to have those areas covered.

Sloane was out of the truck first, and the rest of the team followed. Maddock and Hobbs got Reyes out of the truck. The rest of the team got into formation, and they escorted Reyes into one of the brightly lit areas in the center of the yard. Showtime.

There were containers in front of them and behind, as well as to their sides. They stood in a neat little row, geared in their tac vests and ballistic helmets. They had enough firepower to take down a small army and were prepared to do so if the Coalition gave them any trouble. This would be the first time they'd be facing the group. They heard the sound of multiple footsteps on gravel and watched the masked members of the Coalition emerge one by one from behind one of the rusted steel containers. They were all dressed in black-and-gray camouflaged uniforms, black masks covering their faces, bulletproof vests, ballistic helmets and carried plenty of firearms. Bringing up the rear were two large Therians dragging Ash between them. They kept their distance, Ash held up between them.

Cael took a step forward, and Dex discreetly held a hand out to stop him. They couldn't give the Coalition any more power over them. Now that the bastards knew Ash hadn't really betrayed his team, they could use him against Destructive Delta.

"We have Reyes," Sloane announced. "Let's do this." He turned to Hobbs. "Hobbs—"

"I'm going," Cael said, his expression uncompromising.

Sloane shook his head. "Cael, Ash can barely stand on his own. His weight is too much for you."

"Then Dex will help me."

Sloane looked to Dex who nodded. If it's what Cael wanted, Dex wasn't going to deny his brother. Dex would have demanded the same if it had been Sloane. It was obvious Sloane wasn't happy about it, but he gave in.

"All right. Be careful. We'll watch your backs." Sloane gave a nod and stood to one side as Tony and Hobbs handed Reyes over. Dex could tell his dad was unhappy about the decision, but all he did was ask them to be careful. Dex had every intention of protecting his little brother.

They each took Reyes by an arm and walked him toward the members of the Coalition holding Ash. Dex felt the hairs on the back of his neck stand on end. He didn't like this. He knew Sloane had a plan, and his trust in Sloane was the only thing keeping him grounded right now. As they slowly made their way over, he quietly addressed his brother.

"You okay?"

"I've been better," Reyes muttered.

"I wasn't talking to you, asswipe."

Cael's gaze remained straight ahead of them. "I'm fine."

"I appreciate your concern, agents."

"You're wearing protection, aren't you?" Dex grunted. "So shut up."

"Yeah, because that's going to keep me from bleeding to death when I get shot full of holes everywhere else."

Dex smiled wickedly. "Don't be silly. They're not going to kill you here. They want to make you suffer." They stopped a few feet away from the two large Therians and Ash. The moment they released Reyes, Ash was shoved forward. Dex and Cael rushed over, catching Ash before he could crumple to the ground. Fuck, he was heavy.

"Ready?" Cael asked Ash softly.

"Cael?" Ash's voice was so low and weak, Dex barely heard him.

"Yeah, it's me. I'm here, big guy."

"I'm sorry," Ash said, his words coming out slurred as he hung his head. Dex felt for him and Cael. He could see how hard this was on his brother.

"We'll talk later. First, let's get you out of here."

Dex slipped his arm around Ash's waist and gritted his teeth. Even with Cael sharing the weight, it was difficult moving Ash and very slow going. He could feel Ash making the effort, hear him groaning painfully as he put one foot in front of the other. Those assholes had really done a number on him. Dex discreetly leaned into Ash.

"Who's our target?"

"Preston Merritt," Ash murmured. "He'll give himself away."

Dex discreetly tapped the communicator button on his vest. "Did you get that, Sloane?"

"Loud and clear."

Just as Sloane said the words, one of the Coalition members behind them called out after Ash.

"Hey, Keeler! We'll be seeing each other again soon, I promise you. I might just pay your twink boyfriend a visit."

Dex had no idea what the hell happened. One second they were holding onto Ash who could barely keep his own head up, the next thing he knew, Ash had let out a fierce roar to rival his lion Therian one and was heading for Merritt one faltering step at a time. Merritt raised his gun at Ash, and everything went to hell. Sloane yelled for Merritt to put his weapon down, and the guy did. Only to take aim at Cael.

"TARE!" Sloane's authorization for Calvin to take the kill shot echoed in Dex's ear, and he saw the visor of Merritt's helmet splinter before his body crumpled to the ground. Cael ran after Ash, and a Coalition member took aim at him.

"Cael!" Dex bolted toward his brother who was drawing his weapon as the shot rang out. The bullet never made it to Cael.

Ash made sure of it.

Destructive Delta opened fire as Merritt's gang scattered like roaches with Reyes running back toward Destructive Delta. First time Dex had ever seen a member of the Order running *toward* the THIRDS. The Coalition members went down one by one as they were shot with tranqs to keep them from escaping. Around them gunfire erupted, agents shouted as Beta Pride and Beta Ambush's agents flooded onto the scene. Dex could hear the chaos, but he was too busy dropping to his knees beside Ash, his gloved hands pressing down on the blood hemorrhaging from his body. "Agent down! We've got an agent down!"

"No. No, no, no." Cael shook his head and cupped Ash's face. "Why did you do that?"

Ash smiled at Cael, nudging his cheek playfully like he always did before he started gasping, coughing, and sputtering blood.

"Hold on, Ash," Dex demanded, as Rosa and the EMTs rushed over and got to work on him. There was blood everywhere, and Ash was coughing and gasping for air. Cael was growing frantic, panicking as Ash's eyes rolled back. "Sloane, get Cael out of here!"

Sloane grabbed hold of Cael who struggled against him

until the larger Felid was forced to lift him off his feet. "No! Don't you dare fucking die on me! You hear me, Ash? You asshole, you don't get to die on me like this! Ash!"

Dex stripped off his gloves as the EMTs peeled Ash's uniform off. He looked up at Rosa who'd gone pale. "Rosa?"

"I don't know..." Tears filled her eyes, and she gave a sniff, wiping at her cheek with the back of a gloved hand.

"Fuck." Dex left the medical team to do their job, watching as they prepped Ash for transport. He was covered in blood, had an oxygen mask over his nose and mouth, and IVs sticking out all over. Cael was too distraught to realize the ambulance had whisked Ash away. Rosa was attempting to comfort him when Sloane stepped up next to Dex.

"You okay?" Dex asked him, knowing this couldn't be easy for him either.

"No, but I'll manage. Right now, I think you should take Cael home to your place. He's going to need you. He'll want to go to the hospital once the shock wears off."

"What about you?"

Sloane gave him a small smile. "I always need you." He gave Dex a pat on the arm, giving it a gentle squeeze before walking off toward Tony and the mess in need of cleanup.

Dex put his arm around his brother and led him away from the noise and blood. "Come on, bro. Let's go home."

Cael nodded, though it was pretty clear his brother was elsewhere. As they walked, Dex did his best to comfort his brother, praying Ash would make it through this. Throughout this whole ordeal, Cael had never questioned or lost faith in Ash. Dex shouldn't have dismissed his brother's feelings or Ash's behavior. He promised himself if Ash made it out of this alive, he'd try harder to get along with the burly agent. Ash deserved that much.

TWELVE

Dex handed his brother a cup of hot chocolate piled high with mini marshmallows like their dad used to make them when they were feeling under the weather. Cael sat up and took the mug from him, the first movement he'd made in what felt like hours.

After getting to Dex's apartment, Cael had made straight for the couch, leaving equipment and clothing on the floor in his wake until he'd finally reached it wearing nothing but his boxers, undershirt, and socks. It had broken Dex's heart to watch his little brother curl up on his side, his head on the armrest and a throw pillow hugged tight to his chest. It was obvious then that Cael didn't just have a thing for Ash. He was in love with him. Must have been for some time.

Dex took a seat beside his brother, offering what comfort he could. Rosa had dropped by with an overnight bag she'd put together for Cael after stopping by his apartment. Cael had given his partner a key in case of an emergency. It was the first time Rosa had had to use it. Dex had managed to get his brother to the bathroom upstairs, and

Cael had numbly gone in for a long shower. When he was dressed and out, Cael wanted to go back downstairs to the couch, which is where he'd been since Dex had showered and changed. The whole incident had left Cael shocked. It was most likely the only reason his little brother wasn't fighting to get to the hospital.

"Why would he do that, Dex?"

Whatever Dex's feelings on Ash, they didn't matter now. What mattered was being there for Cael. "He cares about you."

"The things he said." Cael took a sip of his hot chocolate. He sucked in a few marshmallows—which made Dex smile—before putting the cup down on the small coffee table beside the couch. "I thought maybe..."

"He was protecting you. I realize that now. I should have known then. Sloane told me Ash asked him to keep us away from him." Dex pulled his brother in to his arms and held him tight. "I've always believed he was such an asshole, and he is, but so am I. I shouldn't have been so quick to judge him. You were right." It was hard for him not to feel protective over Cael. Dex had always been the outspoken one, the funny kid, the one getting into some kind of mischief or other. He'd been sent to the principal's office more times than he cared to remember, and that had carried over from high school through to the dean's office in college.

Tony was always teasing Dex, saying he was the cause of his gray hairs. It was most likely the truth. Cael had been the quiet one. The well-behaved one. The sweet, smart kid. Any mischief or trouble Cael got into was a result of following along with whatever harebrained scheme Dex's wacky little brain had come up with because Cael wanted to be like his big brother. He'd follow Dex around, trying to imitate him and do what he did. At least until he was old enough to know better. Holding Cael like this reminded Dex of all the other times some bastard had stomped all over his little brother's heart. Dex sure as hell hoped this wasn't going to be another one of those times.

"Dex, what if Ash doesn't make it?" Cael's voice was quiet, as if saying the words aloud might make it so.

"Ash is a fighter. You know if death comes knocking, he will beat the shit out of it." And Dex believed that. Ash was the hardest, toughest, meanest son of a bitch Dex knew. The guy wouldn't go down without a fight.

"What if he can't?" Cael pulled away, his eyes puffy and red. "I need to be there with him. I need him to know I'm not pissed off at him. That I understand why he did what he did."

Just as Dex opened his mouth to reply, his phone buzzed. Removing it from his pocket, he saw it was Sloane. He answered with his heart in his throat. "Hey. I hope you have good news."

Cael stiffened. "Is that Sloane? Is Ash okay?"

"Yeah? Awesome. We'll be right over. Thanks."

"What is it?"

"Ash is out of surgery. He has a shit-ton of recovery to do, but he's going to live to roar another day."

Cael threw his arms around Dex and squeezed him tight. Dex chuckled and hugged him back. "Okay, Chirpy. Let's go." His brother pulled back and wiped a tear away.

"I'm sorry I was such a dick to you," Cael muttered dejectedly.

"No, you were right. Sometimes I need reminding that you're not a little kid anymore. Being older doesn't always mean being wiser."

"You are wise. And I'll always be your little brother. But sometimes you do deserve a good kick in the ass."

Dex chuckled and helped his brother to his feet. "Come on, get dressed. You can't go in your boxers and..." He peered at Cael's feet and his blue-striped socks. "Are those koala bears wearing glasses on your socks?"

Cael smiled, his cheeks flushed in embarrassment. "Yeah. Ash got me them for Christmas."

"That's..." Dex searched his colorful vocabulary for the appropriate term, aware of his brother's wary expression. "Pretty damn adorable."

Cael beamed at him, and Dex told him to move his ass. His brother hopped to it and got dressed in jeans, a T-shirt, and sneakers. Less than half an hour later, they were at the hospital. They found Ash's room and Sloane sitting outside it in his uniform half-asleep. Dex couldn't wait to get him home. The poor guy looked exhausted. When Sloane saw Dex, he smiled the most beautiful smile Dex had ever seen, and Dex's heart did a happy dance.

"How is he?" Cael asked, and Sloane's smile fell away.

"The bullet didn't hit any vital organs, but he lost a lot of blood. Plus they'd worked him over pretty good, which didn't help. He's going to be okay, but he'll be on leave for a while."

"Can I go in?" Cael asked hopefully.

"Yeah. Doctor says it's okay for him to have visitors, but we need to make sure he's not overwhelmed by it. I've asked anyone outside Destructive Delta who wants to visit to come in starting tomorrow. Give him time to rest." He turned to Dex. "Your dad's waiting for me to finish debriefing. You mind keeping watch for a few hours?"

"No, of course not."

Sloane worried his bottom lip before turning Dex away from Cael who was watching Ash through the blinds in the window. "Dex, we need to watch our backs. When Ash woke up, he gave me a name. Beck Hogan. He's the head of the Coalition, and he's still out there. We killed his guy, arrested his men, and recovered Ash. I have no doubt he never intended to let Ash walk away. He's not going to take this lying down."

"He also knows Ash would take a bullet for Cael." Dex ran a hand through his hair. "Not to mention we still don't know who the mole is. Fuck."

"Yeah. Sparks is concerned, which means this is serious shit. Destructive Delta could be his next target. She's considering giving us all offsite assignments."

"Offsite assignments? What's that mean?"

"It's all up in the air right now. But it means we'd operate from an undisclosed location on undercover jobs until the risk at HQ is contained. Either way, Sparks will be holding a briefing with Destructive Delta before the end of the week."

Dex nodded. "Okay. Stay safe."

"You too." Sloane leaned into him, his fingers subtly taking hold of Dex's and giving them a squeeze. "I'll try to get back as soon as I can. I want some time with you." With that, he went off, and Dex stepped up to his brother who was still standing at Ash's window looking in.

"You ready?" Dex asked. "I'll be out here—"

"No." Cael turned to Dex, his eyes glassy. "Come in with me?"

"Anything you want." Dex followed his brother into the private room, closing the door behind them. As Cael approached Ash's bedside, Dex took a seat on the blue couch next to it. How many times would he be visiting this hospital this year? This time he wasn't a patient, though his injuries at the time couldn't compare to Ash's. The huge Therian looked almost average-sized in the Therian-sized bed. He was pale, his hair was a mess, and he sported an array of ugly bruises. One eye was purple and swollen, and he was hooked up to an IV among other things.

Cael approached Ash's bed with such care, it was heartbreaking. He reached out tentatively and put his hand to Ash's brow. The agent's eyes fluttered open, and he looked up at Cael. A slow smile crept onto his face.

"I can't believe you," Cael said quietly, taking in Ash's bruised and battered state.

"I'm sorry," Ash replied hoarsely. "I figured out the mole was someone who interacted with our team on a regular basis which meant they'd know... I couldn't let them know the truth about you."

"And what's that?" Cael asked softly.

"That you mean more to me than anything. I couldn't let them use you against me."

Cael sucked in a sharp breath. "What you said—"

"Was all bullshit to keep you away."

Cael nodded. "Good to know. But that's not what I was referring to. I meant I can't believe you took a bullet for me."

Ash's next words took Dex aback.

"I'd die for you."

"I noticed," Cael replied angrily. "Asshole."

"Don't do that." Ash frowned, casting Dex an accusing glare. "You look like your brother when you do that."

Dex didn't get offended. Ash had every right to be pissed at him. Dex hadn't exactly made his assignment any easier. Ash's frown fell by the wayside when he turned his head back to Cael.

"Please don't." Ash raised a hand to Cael's cheek and wiped a tear away. "I hate to see you like this."

"You almost got yourself killed. Why? Because I'm your teammate? Your friend? Because I'm the little brother you never had? What exactly am I to you, Ash? Every time I get my hopes up that you might... You pull away or do something to make me think I'm wrong."

"You're not wrong."

Cael took hold of Ash's hand. "Then why can't we—"

"No." Ash pulled his hand away, and Dex saw his brother's heart split in two. Dex would have been royally pissed off at Ash for breaking his brother's heart like this if it weren't for the fact the guy looked equally devastated. What Dex couldn't understand was why? Ash obviously felt something more for Cael than friendship. Dex could see how much he wanted to be with Cael. So why wasn't he?

"I'm sorry, Cael. I can't."

"Because you're not gay? Bi? Whatever you want to call the fact you feel something for me? For fuck's sake, Ash. You're lying in a hospital bed after surgery for taking a bullet for me. How can that be harder than telling me the truth? I love you."

Ash closed his eyes. "Why did you say that?"

"Because it's true. I've been in love with you for a while. I kept hoping you would realize it. I just don't understand. Can't you at least tell me why?" Cael waited, the room uncomfortably silent. Ash looked up at Cael, the pain evident in his eyes.

"Cael, I don't want to lose you. But I've got a lot of shit to work out. You deserve to be happy, and right now, I just don't think I'd make you happy."

Cael deflated before them. He nodded quietly and seemed to get lost in thought. Dex knew his brother well. There were two possible outcomes to this, neither of which would be easy on any of them. His brother would either slink off to lick his wounds and spend the next few months sulking, or he would do what Dex expected was happening now when Cael looked up at Ash. His pale gray eyes clouded over, and his jaw clenched. He straightened and held his head high.

"If that's what you want. Fine. Thank you for saving my life. I don't take such an act lightly."

"Cael..." Ash pleaded.

"It's fine, Ash. Just get better. Our team needs you."

There was no point in saying anything else. Dex knew it, and it looked like Ash did too. He nodded and watched Cael leave the room, closing the door firmly behind him. More silence followed. After what seemed like forever, Ash spoke up, his voice quiet.

"He hates me."

"He doesn't hate you. He's protecting himself. When something really bad happens, he shuts down." Dex had seen it happen plenty of times. He didn't envy Ash's position. Cael was sweet and kind, but when he was truly fucked off, his claws came out. And no one wanted to be at the end of a cheetah Therian's temper.

"I never meant for him to end up hurt. I just... I couldn't help it. Wherever he was, I needed to be there too. I was weak."

Dex felt for Ash. He didn't know the reasons behind his gruff teammate turning Cael away, but he hoped it was worth the personal hell he'd just unleashed.

"Ash, I'm sorry about all the shit I gave you. What you did was impressive and admirable. I shouldn't have been such a judgmental prick." The words didn't come easy, but Dex wasn't afraid to admit when he was wrong. Ash stared at him. He looked like he didn't know what to make of Dex. Not exactly a surprise considering their less than friendly relationship.

"Thanks, Daley." He turned his gaze toward the ceiling. "So, what am I in for with your brother?"

Dex cringed. "I'm not going to lie to you. He will fucking shred you like string cheese if he gets the opportunity. The only thing worse than him miserable is him fucked off and hurt when he doesn't know why. He'll hurt you, Ash. He might not mean to deep down, but he's in serious pain, and the only way he knows how to deal with it is to lash out at whoever caused it." Dex expected Ash to growl about it or get annoyed. Instead he closed his eyes.

"Whatever he does, I deserve it."

Damn. He never thought he'd feel worse for Ash than his brother. As much as he hated that Ash had broken his brother's heart, as Dex had feared he would, whatever was going on with Ash had to be just as difficult. Why else would he push away someone he clearly wanted to be with so badly? Dex didn't know what else he could do other than say, "I'm sorry."

Ash turned his face away and nodded. He muttered, "Thanks," before Dex saw the steady rise and fall of his chest. Ash was asleep, and all Dex could do was sit back and hope Ash knew what he was doing.

IT WASN'T until the next morning that Sloane managed to get away from work. HQ was buzzing with activity. The remaining members of the Order were being rounded up and brought in by the truckloads. Reyes was behind bars, his sentence reduced for having cooperated with the THIRDS. Preston Merritt was dead, and his groggy teammates were under interrogation, though as of recently refusing to talk about Beck Hogan who was still out there with a small number of operatives. Sloane had been right about the Coalition looking to get revenge. Beck Hogan's sister and mother had been killed by the Westward Creed during the riots. Themis was in the process of matching up victims from the Westward Creed murders to the Therians in their custody. Sloane needed to speak with Ash to find out if his friend had managed to glean any information on their mole.

Sloane had found Dex napping along with Ash. He'd stood there for a second watching his partner. His arms were folded over his chest; his hand rested on the Glock in the holster under his arm. Sloane made certain to let the door *click* when he shut it, and as expected, it roused his partner who quickly sat up. When Dex saw it was him, he relaxed and gave Sloane a smile, followed by a sleepy yawn.

"Thanks for staying," Sloane said quietly, taking a seat beside Dex and leaning in for a kiss. It was silly, but he'd missed Dex in the short period they'd been apart.

"No problem. He's been asleep for hours. Calvin and Hobbs dropped by earlier to see him." Dex's concerned expression wasn't lost on Sloane, and he took Dex's hand in his.

"What's wrong?"

"I should go check on Cael. He was upset when he left."

"Oh. Okay." Sloane wasn't exactly sure what Dex wasn't telling him, but he was sure it had something to do with Ash. "Go home, get some sleep, and be careful."

"I'll drop by later and bring you guys some lunch." Dex leaned in and kissed Sloane. It was a soft, slow kiss that left Sloane wanting more. A small moan escaped him, and he heard Ash's sleepy growl.

"You two are disgusting."

Sloane chuckled and pulled back. He gave Dex a wink. "I'll see you later."

As soon as Dex left the room and closed the door behind him, Sloane stood and went to Ash's bedside, nudging his friend's hip. Ash huffed but shimmied over so Sloane could sit beside him.

"Look at you," Ash said, a deep frown on his face. "All smiley and glowing like some teen who's just popped his cherry."

"Glad you're feeling better," Sloane replied cheerfully.

"I feel like shit."

Sloane recognized that tone, and it had to do with more than physical pain. "What happened?" His friend pressed his lips together, his gaze somewhere across the room. "Hey, it's me. You know you can tell me anything."

Ash seemed to consider that for a moment before he told Sloane everything that had happened with Cael. What surprised Sloane the most was the sheer pain in his friend's eyes. He thought back to Bar Dekatria and Ash's rambles about Cael after he'd had one too many. He recalled Ash's behavior toward Cael over the years. The way his friend had taken a bullet for the young Therian.

"You're in love with him?"

Ash didn't say a word, but he didn't have to. He closed his eyes and let out a heart-wrenching sigh.

"Ash, I don't understand. If you love him, why not be with him? You have to know Dex and I would never tell a soul. We'd find a way to make it work within the team."

"I can't, all right? Not right now," Ash said. Tears pooled in his eyes. "Every time I think about something happening between me and Cael, I remember *him*."

"Who?"

"Arlo." The crushed look on Ash's face pained Sloane.

He was one of the very few who knew about Arlo. It was something that had affected Ash deeply, and he refused to talk about it to anyone. Not even Sloane knew what had happened to Ash's Therian twin brother, other than the fact he'd been killed during the riots in the late eighties.

"I don't understand," Sloane said quietly.

"It's my fault he died, Sloane. If I'd done what my parents asked me to do... If I'd been more concerned with looking after him than following my dick, he'd still be alive. I abandoned him for some perky-assed twink who made out with me behind the bleachers at school. Arlo and I were supposed to go straight home after school because the streets were too dangerous. It was my job to protect him." A tear rolled down Ash's cheek, and he quickly brushed it away.

"But instead, I sent Arlo home without me because I was more concerned with shoving my tongue inside Davie Miller's mouth and my hand down his pants. I was just a stupid kid trying to figure himself out. When I got home, the police were there. Arlo never made it home. He got beat to shit on his way home by some Human assholes. When my parents found out what I'd done..." Ash shook his head, his lips trembling as he tried to regain control, but it was far too late. "They said Arlo was dead because of me. Because I was a degenerate piece of filth. Then to make things worse, I shifted for the first time. Right on the same fucking day Arlo died. It was too much for them. They called animal control. I was locked in a dog cage, and I wished so goddamn bad that they'd put me to sleep like a dog. Instead, Shultzon showed up and took me away. The rest you know."

"Jesus, Ash." Sloane was still trying to take everything in when Ash spoke up quietly.

"You know why I wasn't scared when they took me away for the tests?"

Sloane felt his throat thicken, wishing he could take away his friend's pain. "Why?"

"Because I believed with every fiber of my being that I deserved to be in pain for what I'd done to Arlo. I told myself what happened with Davie Miller was a one off. That I wasn't gay. And then I met Cael. My first thought was, 'I'm fucked.' because no one I'd ever met made me feel the way he did when he smiled at me. I wanted so hard to keep him at a distance, but I couldn't."

"So you're going to punish yourself for the rest of your life?" Sloane couldn't believe what he was hearing. "I know what happened was tragic, Ash, but you have to forgive yourself and move on. Do you really think Arlo would want you to live like this?"

"I don't know what Arlo would want because he's fucking dead, Sloane! And it's *my* fault. He wasn't just my brother, he was my twin. When he died, so did a part of me. It left a void that will never be filled. For years I felt guilty for having been the one who lived."

"So you won't be with Cael because he makes you happy, and you don't deserve that?" Sloane felt himself growing angry. If anyone knew how it felt to lose someone he loved, it was him. He couldn't pretend he understood what it was like to lose a twin, but he understood guilt. He didn't know if he'd ever not feel guilty over his mother's death, but to think he didn't deserve to lead a happy life because of it? Worse, to live a life of punishment? "Ash—"

"I won't be with Cael because I'm still fucked-up over what happened with Arlo, and I won't let that ruin whatever future we could have together. I can deal with all that other shit from the facility, with being the miserable fuck I am, because with Cael... Nothing will be the same again. But he deserves to be happy, Sloane, and right now, I can't give him that. I love you like a brother, but I'll deal with it myself. And keep this to yourself. Cael's hurt and pissed. Eventually, he'll calm down. When I'm ready, I'll talk to him about it. Right now, this is the way it has to be. Now do you want to hear about the Coalition or what?"

Sloane cursed under his breath. Sometimes he wanted to strangle his friend. He'd never known anyone so goddamn stubborn. "Fine," he replied through his teeth. He went to his backpack on the couch and pulled out his tablet. A few taps, and he logged into Themis. "Go for it."

"The numbers were codes for our initials. Each number represented a letter's location on the alphabet. So A.K. was one-eleven. The guy we offed was Preston Merritt, Beck Hogan's best friend and second-in-command. You can bet your ass Hogan's gonna want blood. Merritt hated me from the start. Whoever our mole is, he or she convinced Hogan to bring me on board. The longer I hung around them, the more I realized the mole was someone we worked closely with. That's why I volunteered to have Dex's party at my place. I threw a few lines to see if anyone would bite. I was given locations and times through text using a burner phone. I showed up and did what I was told."

Sloane entered all the information into his tablet exactly as Ash told it. "What about our victims from the Order. Can you confirm they're connected to Reyes and the Westward Creed?"

"Yes. Hogan set up the Coalition as a way to fight fire with fire. At first all he wanted was to stop the Order, but during one skirmish, he recognized one of the members of the Order. It was Cristo. That's when the plan changed. I overheard him and Merritt talking. The Westward Creed gang had killed Merritt's cousin. They decided to use the escalating violence as a way to pick off the gang."

There was a knock on the door, and Sloane logged off Themis before telling their guest to enter. It was Levi and Taylor.

"Hey, Keeler. Looking mighty fine in your hospital duds. You commando under there?" Taylor teased.

Ash gave a snort. "Wouldn't you like to know."

"I would." Taylor blinked at him. "That's why I asked."

"Dick." Ash chuckled, and the team leaders approached Ash's bed, chatting to him about what happened and how glad they were he was alive. The whole office was talking about Ash and what he'd done, infiltrating the Coalition, then taking a bullet for his teammate. Taylor teased Ash on his ego and how he was going to be more unbearable than ever. The three of them laughed, and Sloane observed his teammates, glad to see how pleased they were to see Ash.

"I'm glad you're okay," Levi said.

"Yeah," Taylor added somberly. "For a minute there, we thought we'd never see you again."

Levi waved a hand in dismissal. "Are you kidding? Ash is like a bad penny. He always turns up."

Sloane froze, his gaze darting to Ash. His friend was still smiling, his gaze on Levi. "Say, that's one hell of an expression," Ash said. "Where'd you hear it?" A dangerous leer quickly replaced his smile. "Wait, that's right. You heard it from me."

"What are you talking about?" Levi frowned, looking puzzled.

"There are five people who've heard me say that. One's dead, one's behind bars, one's Dex, the other's my best friend. And the fifth is the masked Therian who was there when I said it."

Sloane sprang to action, but Levi had already grabbed a stunned Taylor and in a heartbeat had his sidearm to Taylor's head. "Back off, Sloane," Levi snarled. "It wasn't supposed to be this way."

"What way was it supposed to be, Levi?" Sloane held his hands up, his tone calm.

"Don't fucking use that tone with me. I'm a team leader. I know all the tricks. The Westward Creed should have been dead long before you figured it all out. That piece of shit Reyes should be dead!"

"You lost someone close. I understand." It was the only explanation. The look of pain and anger on Levi's face was a familiar one.

"Fuck you. All those assholes got away with murder. Hogan had the right idea. If the law wouldn't give us justice, we'd just have to take care of it ourselves. I knew you wouldn't make the connection. When they put Carolyn's name in the system, they put her under our mom's maiden name. Unless someone dug deeper and cross-referenced her name specifically with mine, no one would know." Levi took a step away from Sloane, and Taylor slowly lowered his arm. Levi was onto him, wrapping his arm tighter around Taylor's neck. "Just try it you little shit, and I'll blow your brains all over the eggshell-blue walls."

Taylor held his hands up. "Okay. Take it easy, man."

"Don't fucking tell me to take it easy." Levi continued to back toward the open door with Taylor in his grip. "Do you know what that son of a bitch Reyes did to my sister? He fucking raped her and then passed her off to his friends. After they had their fun, Reyes slit her throat. She was sixteen! Then that piece of shit judge lets him go? Tell me, Sloane. Where's the justice in that?"

"Is that why you joined the THIRDS? Because of your sister?"

"I joined so scum like Reyes would pay for their crimes. So Therians like my sister would get justice. When I found out Reyes was going to head up the Order, I knew this was my chance. He wasn't going to escape justice this time."

"And he hasn't," Sloane said, slowly edging toward Levi as he continued to move out of the room and into the hall. There was a shriek from somewhere nearby, but Levi ignored it. His fiery eyes on Sloane.

"Prison is too good for him. He deserves to be mauled by the very animals he despises. Ground into pet food and fed to the wolves."

"So what's your plan now? Even if you leave this hospital, you won't be able to get to Reyes."

"That's what you think," Levi sneered. "If I can work with the Coalition right under your noses, I can get to Reyes. You think I'm the only agent willing to turn for the right reason? You can't be that naïve, Sloane."

"Levi, please, think about what you're doing."

"Shut up! I'm tired of talking!" Levi moved the gun away from Taylor to aim at Sloane when the agent's body started to convulse, the gun going off in his hand and a shot hitting the wall to Sloane's left. Both Levi and Taylor fell to the floor, the electric shock of Dex's Taser going through both agents. His partner's timing had been impeccable. Not just in showing up when he did, but in calculating the exact moment to stun Levi so no one was in the line of fire.

Sloane rushed over and waited for the discharge to complete before he grabbed Levi and turned him onto his stomach. He took the Therian zip tie Dex held out to him and secured it over Levi's wrists. Dex held Taylor as the agent recovered and Sloane called Maddock. Backup arrived shortly after Sloane explained everything to his sergeant, and they carried Levi away. The team was stunned, though not as much as Levi's team would be once they discovered their team leader was the mole.

"He was the mole this whole time," Dex said, helping Taylor sit on one of the chairs lined up against the wall before turning his attention back to Sloane. "I never would have guessed."

"Yeah." Sloane felt for the guy and he understood. Was he a hypocrite? Sloane had wanted Isaac dead for killing Gabe. How did it make him different from Levi?

"I take it there's someone on that list of Therian victims connected to Levi?"

Sloane nodded. "His sister. It was fucked-up what they did to her."

"I'm sure I wouldn't disagree. But he took part in the murder of two Humans."

"Humans who raped and murdered his sister in cold blood," Sloane replied angrily.

"So it's okay for him to go around executing people. Where would it stop?"

"I wanted Isaac dead."

Dex blinked at him. "It's not the same. You killed him because you had no choice."

Sloane met Dex's gaze. "Didn't I?" He watched his partner swallow visibly. "How was what I did different than what Levi did?"

"For one, you didn't hunt down Isaac for revenge. You killed him because my life and Shultzon's life were in danger. I'm not saying he didn't deserve it or that Reyes and his band of assholes don't deserve it either, but you did what you had to do to keep us safe. Levi did what he did purely for revenge without regard for the innocent lives caught in the middle. He didn't care if his fellow agents were killed either. It wasn't the only way."

Sloane thought about that. He wasn't sure if he agreed, but he allowed himself to take comfort in his partner's words. It saddened him to know how far Levi had gone to get justice for his sister because the system had failed him. But then those had been lawless times, especially for Therians. The world was still coming to terms with their kind, and a good portion of the Human race wasn't happy they were there. First came the violence, then came the laws. For some, it came too late.

Taylor came to stand beside Dex with a dopey grin. "My prince to the rescue."

"Don't make me regret it," Dex muttered.

Taylor's smile fell as he gazed down the hall where they'd escorted Levi away only moments ago. For the first time since Sloane had known him, Sloane saw past the cocky team leader to the vulnerable Therian underneath. Taylor looked as if he was going to be sick.

"I can't believe he betrayed us."

"I'm sorry," Dex said, patting Taylor on the arm. There were no jokes, no teasing, no inappropriate comments. Taylor looked completely lost.

"You spend so much time around your teammates, you think you know them. Then it turns out, you don't know them at all." Taylor resumed his seat. "We used to hang out all the time at work. We were friends."

Dex closed his eyes, and Sloane knew his partner was summoning the courage to say something. "Hey, Taylor. I'm having my birthday party in a few weeks at Bar Dekatria. You're welcome to come."

Taylor looked up at Dex with wide eyes. "You're

inviting me to your party after everything that happened at the last one?"

"If you promise to come as a friend and not someone trying to get into my pants."

Taylor pursed his lips, then laughed at Dex's glower. "I'm kidding, man. Of course I'll come." He stood and held his hand out to Dex. "And I promise to behave myself. Thank you."

Dex gave him a smile, and Taylor headed off. Sloane took the seat Taylor had vacated, watching as Dex got up and sprinted to a gurney two doors down. He came back with a plastic bag and dropped down into the chair beside Sloane. A dopey grin stretched across his face.

"I brought lunch."

Sloane chuckled. Thank goodness for Dex's obsession with food. "Good timing." He stood and motioned to Ash's room. "Come on. Let's have some lunch." They walked in with Ash cursing them out for not letting him know sooner that they were okay. Sloane explained what happened as they ate lunch, and afterward Ash and Dex argued over what was the best sandwich in Manhattan. It almost felt like any other day, though Sloane knew better. Something had changed. His concern for his team was growing. What was going to happen between Cael and Ash? And how would it affect the rest of the team? More importantly, what would Lieutenant Sparks decide? With Hogan still out there, none of them were safe.

Whatever Sparks decided, Sloane would do whatever it took to protect his team.

To protect Dex.

THIRTEEN

"THIS WAS THE BEST IDEA *EVER*."

Dex was floating on a cloud of heavenly post-sex bliss. His body ached, his ass especially, but it was to be expected after Sloane finished pounding into him against the wall of the utility closet. Thanks to Bradley, Dex had his own personal key to the unused space in the quiet hall behind the bar. Now whenever he and Sloane visited Dekatria with the team, they could escape for some sexy-time. And a sexy time they'd had indeed.

Sloane set Dex back on his feet and pulled him close to nuzzle his temple, his lips brushing down his cheek, leaving kisses in their wake. "We should get back to your party," Sloane suggested. He delivered another heated kiss before pulling back and helping Dex right his clothes. "Besides, I don't want to leave Ash on his own for too long."

Dex actually agreed. Ash was on leave, recovering from his gunshot wound. It had only been a few weeks, and he had a lot of recovery to do. Sloane had suggested his friend sit this one out, but Ash had been adamant. As of two weeks ago, Ash had been staying with Dex, sleeping on his sofa bed. Sloane refused to leave Ash on his own, and although the stubborn Therian tried to decline—complaining he didn't need babysitting—Sloane put his foot down and refused to take no for an answer. Since Sloane spent most of his time at Dex's anyway, and it was easier for Ash to move around in Dex's house than Sloane's apartment, Ash had reluctantly given in. Dex put the surrender down to Ash's medication and need for recovery.

Sloane slipped out of the utility closet first, giving Dex the okay to follow. They carefully made their way back to the party where Dex had invited fewer people in order to have a more intimate get-together rather than a crazed drunk-fest. Bradley—the new owner of Bar Dekatria as of a week ago—was happy to offer Dekatria as a venue, and it was awesome.

There was music, food, drinks, karaoke, games, and folks dancing the Hustle while the disco ball above the dance floor leisurely spun, casting a blanket of glittering diamonds across the room. Rosa and Letty came running over to Dex and grabbed his hand, hauling him over to one of the tables where the biggest, most amazing pornographic cake ever was laid out. Dex doubled over laughing.

Before him was the biggest puckered ass he'd ever seen. It came complete with balls and cock. Across the ass in white squiggly frosting were the words "Happy Birthday, Dex! We know how much you love it."

"You guys are fucking awesome." Dex wriggled his eyebrows at Sloane and stuck his finger into the cake, defiling it while he made moaning noises. At least until Sloane shoved Dex's face into it. Dex came up gasping and sputtering chocolate cake and frosting. He stared, stunned at his partner who was laughing his sexy little butt off. The sneaky bastard!

Dex grabbed a piece of cake and smushed it in Sloane's face. Everyone laughed and teased Sloane, asking him if he enjoyed the taste of ass. Bradley brought them over some wet towels, and they cleaned themselves up. Sloane gave Dex a wink, and everyone broke out into a horrible rendition of "Happy Birthday." Dex blew out the candles and everyone cheered. He couldn't remember the last party he'd had where he'd been this happy or had this much fun. Everyone grabbed a piece of ass cake, avoiding the actual ass where Dex's face had been buried. After cake and more booze, everyone went off to the dance floor.

Dex had chosen a classic playlist with music from the seventies up to more modern tunes, which everyone seemed to be enjoying. Rosa and Letty were with their partners, and even Calvin and Hobbs were dancing. Well, Calvin was dancing, Hobbs was shyly moving along with him. Dex was glad to see Calvin smiling again. He didn't know if they'd worked things out, but Calvin seemed content for now. Maybe he got tired of moping and missed his best friend. Dex had invited his dad, and after the horrified look left Tony's face, his dad politely declined, saying he'd leave that sort of thing to the youngsters. Like he was old or something. It was just his way of excusing himself so he wouldn't be there to see what god-awful situations his sons got themselves into. He made a compromise, stating he'd take Dex and Cael out for a family dinner over the weekend.

Over at one of the tables, Ash sat on his own looking miserable. Dex felt bad for the poor guy. He took a seat across from Ash who was nursing a vodka and lemonade without the vodka thanks to his heavy-duty painkillers. Sloane took a seat beside Dex. He looked concerned for his friend.

"Hey, big guy." Dex smiled widely at Ash, receiving a grunt in return.

"Can't you two be around each other five minutes without needing to hump like bunnies?"

Dex held back a smile. "'Bunnies' sounds weird coming out of your mouth." Medicated Ash was more fun than unmedicated Ash. The guy had even had some cake. Of course, that had followed him telling Calvin to fuck off when Calvin asked him if he was going to sing along to "Happy Birthday."

"Your ex was looking for you," Ash grumbled before taking a sip of his lemonade.

"How is Lou?" Sloane asked Dex. "Did you tell him about Levi?"

"I told him enough," Dex replied. He was still trying to come to terms with Levi's betrayal. Although he could understand the reasons behind it, he stood by what he'd told Sloane. There were other ways. How many people would Levi have sacrificed to get his revenge? "Lou was shocked, but somehow I don't think he was all that interested in Levi to begin with."

Sloane looked surprised. "Really? He seemed interested at your party."

"He was being friendly. And I think he found Levi kind of hot. But he had his eye on someone else the whole time." Dex motioned over to the bar where Bradley was leaning against the outside of it, flirting and laughing with Lou. There was a lot of subtle touching going on, and the space between them appeared to be quickly evaporating.

"I think he was more interested in Bradley to be honest. He's been asking me about him since that night he first showed up here." Why Dex hadn't realized it was beyond him. Every time he'd spoken to Lou, Lou had asked if Dex had been to Dekatria. If he'd seen Bradley.

"Why didn't he introduce himself then or ask you to introduce him?" Sloane watched the two at the bar with interest.

"Lou's actually pretty shy when it comes to someone he likes. He told me it took him a month to gather up the nerve to ask me out. We'd been going to the same coffee shop, and if he hadn't said anything, I wouldn't even have guessed he was interested in me. The guy never even made eye contact."

"Wow."

"I know. Bradley seems pretty smitten."

A few minutes later, Bradley had one of his bartenders bring over a tray full of drinks with some snacks for Ash since he couldn't partake in the alcohol goodness. Cael came bounding over, and Dex wondered how many drinks his little brother had had. From his wide smile, glassy eyes, and flushed cheeks, Dex would say *a lot*. That worried him. Cael wasn't one to get drunk. Charmingly tipsy, yes. But not drunk.

"Hey, big bro!" Cael threw his arms around Dex's neck and gave him a squeeze. He looked over at the table and gasped. "Booze!" He grabbed one of Bradley's foggy "specials" and downed it in one gulp before wheezing and coughing. "That was good."

"Hey, trouble." Dex watched his brother jump up and plop himself down on the edge of the table, his feet not reaching the floor. He swung his legs back and forth and grabbed another drink.

"Your party is awesome, Dex. Not that I ever doubted you."

"I'm glad you're having fun," Dex replied, his gaze going

to Ash who was concentrating awfully hard on his lemonade.

"I am. I've been hanging out with Seb. The guy's a fucking riot. And so hot!"

Uh-oh. "Cael..." He didn't want to sound like a jerk, but he was really starting to worry about his brother. Cael had a bad habit of making rash decisions when he was hurting.

"What?" His brother frowned at him. "I can hang with whoever I want. It's not like I've got a boyfriend or anything."

Cael's harsh tone during the last part didn't get past Dex. Judging by the grimace Ash gave, it hadn't gotten past him either.

"Seb's a nice guy. I like talking to him. He respects me and doesn't treat me like I'm a stupid kid."

Ash's head snapped up. "I never treated you like you were a stupid kid, and I always respected you."

Dex braced himself. He felt Sloane's hand rest on his knee under the table. Apparently Dex wasn't the only one bracing himself.

Cael smiled sweetly. "I'm sorry, Ash. You're right. You've always treated me with respect. What I meant to say is that I like how Seb has the balls to go after what he wants."

Fucking hell. Sloane squeezed Dex's knee. What exactly did his partner think Dex could do? Cael was old enough to do what he wanted. Dex glanced at Ash, expecting the larger Therian to get angry or lash out. Instead, Ash went back to staring at his drink. Now what? Dex was about to make an attempt to diffuse the situation when Seb showed up.

"Hey, guys."

Everyone greeted him, some more enthusiastically than

others. Seb didn't seem to notice. He was too busy flirting with Cael. He poked Cael on his side, making Cael wriggle and laugh.

"Damn it, Seb. I told you I was ticklish there."

"That's why I do it," Seb teased, leaning into Cael. "I like to see you squirm."

Well wasn't this just craptastic. Not that Dex was against Seb flirting with Cael. In fact, Seb was a really good guy, aside from the fact he was still in love with Hudson. But then again, if Hudson wouldn't give Seb the time of day, the guy had every right to move on. Jesus Christ, MTV would make a mint with a reality TV show about their unit. The relationship drama alone would carry the ratings, forget the actual fieldwork. Dex hoped Cael didn't end up hurting Seb. The tiger Therian seemed genuinely interested in Cael. He took Cael's hand with the pretense of fiddling with the Pac-Man wristband Cael had on. His brother loved swiping Dex's stuff when he wasn't looking. "I was wondering if you wanted to get a drink sometime this weekend. Maybe grab a bite to eat?"

Dex and Sloane exchanged glances, and Dex noticed his brother's eyes dart to Ash, the gesture going unnoticed by Seb. This was Ash's chance. *Speak up, Ash.* Dex couldn't believe he was rooting for the guy. The muscles in Ash's jaw clenched, but he didn't say a word.

Hurt flashed through Cael's face before he smiled up at Seb. "Yeah, I'd like that."

"Great," Seb smiled brightly. "Let me give you my number."

Cael reached into his pocket and pulled out his smartphone, tapping the screen before handing it to Seb so he could input his number. Then he called Seb so the guy would have his.

"How about Friday after work?"

"That'd be perfect," Cael replied, his big smile not reaching his eyes.

"Great! Looking forward to it." Seb waved to the rest of them before cheerfully, and obliviously, walking off. The table was uncomfortably quiet before Ash cursed under his breath, grabbed his jacket and left.

Dex came to stand beside his brother. "Cael, are you sure that's a good idea?"

"I put myself out there, and he turned me down without so much as a reason why. I deserved that much. What am I supposed to do? Follow Ash around like some lovesick puppy, living off whatever scraps of affection he throws my way? It'd kill me, Dex." Cael jumped off the table, his silvery eyes cold. "You were right. I should've put a stop to it when I saw it coming."

Dex didn't have time to reply. Cael sprinted off to catch up with Seb. He said something, and Seb nodded. He took Cael's hand and led him to the dance floor.

"That went well," Sloane muttered.

"Do you want to go after Ash?"

Sloane shook his head. "He needs some time on his own. I'm sure we'll see him tonight at your place. You sure you don't mind giving him a key?"

"I trust him." Dex turned to Sloane with a smile. "Wanna dance?"

"After I give you your birthday present." Sloane wriggled his brows, and Dex couldn't help but laugh.

"You look like you're about to do a striptease." Dex gasped dramatically and clapped his hands, doing a little bounce. "Are you going to do a striptease? Please tell me you're going to do a striptease. I'd considered hiring strippers for tonight but then remembered this was a birthday party."

Sloane rolled his eyes. "No, I'm not going to do a striptease."

"Dang it." Dex smiled, watching Sloane become all bashful. *Ooh*, that meant it was going to be good. He did his best to rein in his excitement when Sloane reached into his pocket and pulled out a small velvet bag. Had Sloane gotten him jewelry? Dex was so excited he could barely contain it.

"I thought rather than some flashy gift, you might like this better." Sloane handed him the bag. It was incredibly light. And flat. He opened the bag and dropped the contents into his hand. It was a silver key and a folded-up piece of paper. Puzzled, Dex opened the piece of paper. It said, "Top right-hand drawer."

"Um... I don't get it. Is it like a scavenger hunt?" Dex cocked his head to one side and wondered why Sloane was getting all red in the face.

"That's a key to my apartment, and that's the drawer I emptied out so you can put your stuff in it. For when you stay over, which can be whenever you want. You don't even have to ask."

Dex's jaw almost hit the floor. "I have my own drawer?"

"Yeah." Sloane shrugged and shoved his hands into his pockets. "Is that okay?"

"Okay?" Dex shoved the key and note into his pocket and motioned toward the bar. "You better get your ass in that utility closet before I blow our cover."

A huge smile split Sloane's face, making his amber eyes sparkle. He gave a nod and quickly went off. Dex lingered a minute or two behind to make sure no one was watching. He headed off after Sloane unable to believe what his partner had done. It wasn't uncommon for agents to give their partners keys to their apartments in case of emergency, but the only one to have a key to Sloane's apartment was Ash. Not just that, but Sloane had given Dex his own drawer, which meant he not only liked having Dex around, he was thinking about their future. Dex had wanted to suggest keeping an overnight bag or something similar at Sloane's, but he hadn't wanted to push it. His partner had already agreed to no condoms during sex. He really needed to learn to restrain himself and not spring things on Sloane. Maybe if he could ease things in, Sloane wouldn't feel so jittery over them.

Like a schoolboy on prom night, Dex stood outside the utility room door and took a deep breath. He gave a knock, his heart skipping a beat when Sloane answered, a beautiful smile on his face. Sloane leaned against the doorframe, his arms folded over his chest.

"How can I help you?"

Dex squealed internally. "I'm sorry to bother you, sir. But my car broke down in front of your house. Can I borrow your phone?"

Sloane raked his gaze over Dex, his expression positively sinful. "Sure. You'll have to use the one in the bedroom. The one in the kitchen isn't working." He stepped aside and motioned for Dex to come in. As soon as Dex was inside the room, he heard the click and lock of the door. Sloane stepped up close behind him, practically pressed up against him. He bent his head close to Dex's.

"Let me show you where it is. It's a little hard"—Sloane grabbed Dex's hips and jerked him back so Dex could feel his erection—"to find."

Dex let out a gasp, his whole body shivering with anticipation. First a key to Sloane's apartment, then his own drawer. Now his own porno fantasy.

Best. Birthday. Ever.

"This is so wrong."

Dex took a sip of his coffee at the kitchen counter beside Sloane. "You have to do something."

"Like what?" Sloane asked, his gaze on Ash who was sitting on Dex's couch in the living room just a few feet away.

"I don't know, but I can't stand seeing him like this. I'd rather he be cursing at me, threatening to kill me, trying to kick my ass. Anything is better than this. It's... sad." Ash had been fast asleep by the time Dex and Sloane stumbled drunkenly into Dex's house. The sight of beer bottles on the floor around Ash had sobered them up really quick. Sloane had rushed to Ash's side to check his vitals, waking his friend up. Ash growled at him and told him to fuck off. The two had gotten into an argument with Sloane telling Ash off for drinking alcohol with his medication. Ash had sulked and apologized. This morning when Dex and Sloane had come down to make breakfast, they found Ash wide awake and watching TV. They had no idea how long the guy had been up, but he hadn't moved since. He refused any breakfast that wasn't beer.

"I don't know what you expect me to do," Sloane said quietly. "He's like this because of your brother."

"No, he's like this because my brother told him he was in love with him, and he couldn't deal with it. He's trapped himself in his fucked-up little closet."

"It's not that easy for him."

"Why? People don't give a shit anymore. Not like they used to back in the day."

"True. We Therians kinda stole the spotlight on the whole 'abomination' thing," Sloane replied dryly.

That much was true. Back before Therians, being gay was at the top of every bigot's and zealot's shit list. There had been riots and protests. Then Therians had come along, and suddenly the Human zealots were singing a different tune. At least most of them. There was a new threat. A new stronger, more resilient, faster, bigger, *different* race had emerged, knocking Humans off the top of the food chain. The Human race needed to reinforce their numbers, and the scriptures changed. Suddenly Therians were the real threat to morality and the destruction of mankind. Not that there still weren't some old-school homophobes around. Dex wondered if Humans would ever stop acting so damn self-righteous. He shook those thoughts from his head and concentrated on the huge, unshaven, scruffy, smelly lion Therian on his couch.

"Sloane. What aren't you telling me?"

"Look, we've all got our demons, and that includes Ash. It wouldn't be my place to tell you."

"Well he can't continue like this." Dex got up and walked over to the living room. He sat down on the coffee table in front of Ash, making sure not to block his view of the TV. "Hey, buddy. You, uh, you planning on putting on some pants today?"

Ash let out a grunt and took a sip of his beer.

"You realize it's not even ten a.m., and you've had..." Dex's gaze went to the three empty bottles on the floor. Fuck. Okay. Dex stood and swiped the bottle from Ash.

"What the fuck?" Ash got to his feet, looming over Dex who scrunched his nose and waved a hand in front of his face.

"You fucking reek." He handed the bottle to Sloane

who was looking on anxiously. "Okay, here's what's going to happen. You're going to get your stank ass off my couch, take a shower, put on pants that A, do not contain an elastic band, and B, are thick enough to hide the fact you go commando, because frankly, some of us don't want to know." Dex let out a shudder, then grabbed Ash's arm and started hauling him toward the stairs. "Come on. Don't do this to yourself. You know you can hang with us as long as you want, but you can't go all hobo on us. Cael's dealing with it. You need to do the same."

Ash stopped in his tracks but didn't turn around. "He's not dealing with it. He's pretending to."

"Well, you've not really given him much of a choice. How'd you feel if he was doing what you're doing? Drinking and wallowing in his own misery."

"Shitty," Ash muttered.

"That's right. So hit the showers."

With a heavy sigh, Ash headed upstairs.

Dex turned to find Sloane gaping at him. "What?"

"He didn't tell you to fuck off or threaten to punch you."

"I know!" Dex threw his arms up. "You see why I'm worried?" He never thought he'd see the day where he actually *wanted* Ash to be an asshole to him.

"You're right," Sloane sighed and pulled Dex into his arms. He let his head rest on Dex's. "But there's nothing we can do. The only one who can do anything about this is Ash."

Ash padded back down, a pathetic pout on his face. "My bag's in my truck."

"Relax, big guy." Dex headed for the front door. "I'll get it." Sloane caught up to him and swiped the keys from him. He gave Dex a kiss.

"I'll get it. I need to get my backpack from my car anyway." He ran a hand down Dex's back until he got to his ass and gave it a squeeze. "How about when I get back, we get into bed for a little post-birthday-party party?"

Dex moaned against Sloane's lips. God, he was such a lost cause. Sloane had him wrapped around his little finger, and Dex loved it. "Okay."

"You two make me sick," Ash called out, followed by, "The alarm's on."

Sloane held up Ash's keys. "Got it." He gave Dex a wink and headed outside, closing the door behind him.

Dex was feeling all swoony. He couldn't wait to get back into bed with Sloane. He picked the beer bottles off the living room floor and carried them into the kitchen. He had just dropped them into the recycling bin when an explosion rocked the foundation of Dex's house, causing the front window to shatter. Dex ducked behind the counter on instinct, for a moment thinking the place was going to come crashing down around him. He heard footsteps thudding down the stairs and stood to find Ash staring at him.

"What the fuck was that?"

"I don't know. Sounded like an explosion out—" Dex's world came crashing down around him. *No, please.* "Sloane!" He bolted for the front door, not caring what dangers might be on the other side. All he could think about was getting to Sloane. He had to make sure he was all right. He prayed with all his might. Sloane had to be okay.

"Dex, wait!"

Dex threw the door open and was met with clouds of thick black smoke. The sidewalk in front of his house looked like a war zone, littered with debris and pieces of mangled car parts. The leaves of the tree out front were ablaze, and Dex coughed as he ran down the steps into the smoke.

"Sloane!" Where the hell was he? Dex reached the sidewalk when Ash yelled from somewhere behind him.

"Dex, get down!"

Something hard slammed into Dex, the force knocking him to the ground and stealing the air from his lungs. His painful cry was drowned out by a harsh, agonized growl, and it took Dex a second to realize it had come from Ash. He didn't know why the hell Ash was on him, but he had to get himself free. Dex pushed against the cold pavement, but Ash's weight had him pinned. The familiar pings of bullets ricocheting around them echoed in Dex's ears. His eyes stung and his lungs burned. The smoke and dust swirling in the autumn breeze made it hard to see and breathe. He lifted his head and spotted a dark lump under a piece of mangled door.

"Sloane!" Dex pushed against the ground, screaming at Ash to get off. Tears sprang in his eyes and ran down his cheeks, blurring his vision. His chest hurt but no more than his heart. "Ash, get off! Sloane!" Why wouldn't Ash let him go? Dex was briefly aware of sparks bursting around them, and only then did it occur to him they were being shot at. Ash dragged Dex with him, succeeding despite Dex fighting him every step of the way. He clawed and struggled, but Ash's iron grip never faltered, and Dex found himself shoved up against a parked car with Ash huddled over him. Dex tried to push, but it was like trying to move a brick wall. His hand felt wet, and he stared dumbly at it. It was covered in blood. He dropped his gaze to find blood seeping from the gauze covering Ash's healing stitches.

The wailing of sirens intensified, and Dex watched in horror as a flurry of uniformed bodies rushed onto the scene. Firefighters assessed the situation before lifting the truck's door off Sloane. There was blood everywhere, and he wasn't moving. Dex could barely see through his tears as the EMTs turned Sloane over. His skin was smudged black and red from smoke and blood. Then Dex caught sight of the jagged piece of metal jutting out of Sloane's side. An anguished cry tore through Dex, and Ash pulled him hard against him, thick biceps smothering him while a hand went to the back of Dex's head to keep him from going anywhere.

EMTs cut through Sloane's shirt before starting CPR and chest compressions. An oxygen mask was applied to his face, and they swiftly lifted Sloane onto a gurney. They were taking him away. *No*. They couldn't take Sloane without him. Dex tried to push against Ash, but he was exhausted, his world darkening around him. He buried his face against Ash's chest and clung to him, his heart breaking in two as he surrendered to his grief. How could this be happening? Then it struck him.

"It should have been me."

Ash pulled him back enough to look into his eyes. "What?"

Somehow Dex found the strength to meet Ash's gaze, stunned by the guy's tearstained cheeks. Dex's voice was hoarse when he spoke, his throat feeling raw. "It should have been me." He was supposed to have gone out to the truck. It should have been him caught in the blast.

"No," Ash said through his teeth. "That bomb was in my truck. It was meant for me."

Dex stilled. Ash was right. Most of the mangled and crushed steel were the remains of Ash's truck. The pain in Ash's expression matched the one in Dex's chest. "Ash..."

Ash pulled him close against his chest and buried his face in Dex's hair, his words barely audible. "I know. I'm sorry, Dex. I'm so sorry."

Dex shook his head, but no words came out. All he

could do was hold on to Ash as he watched the world burning and crumbling around him. He could hear the EMTs calling out to them, feel their hands on him as they tried to help. Right now, all Dex wanted was to close his eyes and hide from everything and everyone. Beck Hogan had made a liar out of him. Violence was never the answer, but violence was the only thing that asshole seemed to understand. Dex opened his eyes and felt the darkness rising inside him. He told himself not to go there. He remembered the last time he'd felt this. He'd been five years old, and his parents had been taken from him. His anger, hatred, and confusion had threatened to take hold of him, but Tony had taken his hand and pulled him back.

Well Tony wasn't here right now, and Dex was no longer that frightened little kid. He was a trained Defense agent for the THIRDS. For Hogan's sake, Sloane better live through this.

Either way, Beck Hogan was going to pay.

What's next for Dex, Sloane, and the Destructive Delta crew? The adventure continues in *Rise & Fall*, the fourth book in the THIRDS series. Available on Amazon and KindleUnlimited.

A NOTE FROM THE AUTHOR

Thank you so much for reading *Rack & Ruin*, the third book in the THIRDS series. I hope you enjoyed Dex and crew's shenanigans, and if you did, please consider leaving a review on Amazon. Reviews can have a significant impact on a book's visibility, so any support you show these fellas would be amazing. The adventure continues in *Rise & Fall*, available from Amazon and KindleUnlimited.

Want to stay up-to-date on my releases and receive exclusive content? Sign up for my newsletter.

Follow me on Amazon to be notified of a new releases, and connect with me on social media, including my fun Facebook group, Donuts, Dog Tags, and Day Dreams, where we chat books, post pictures, have giveaways, and more!

Looking for inspirational photos of my books? Visit my book boards on Pinterest.

Thank you again for joining the THIRDS crew on their adventures. We hope to see you soon!

CAST MEMBERS

You'll find these cast members throughout the whole THIRDS series. This list will continue to grow.

DESTRUCTIVE DELTA

Sloane Brodie—Defense agent. Team leader. Jaguar Therian.

Dexter J. Daley "Dex"—Defense agent. Former homicide detective for the Human Police Force. Older brother of Cael Maddock. Adopted by Anthony Maddock. Human.

Ash Keeler—Defense agent. Entry tactics and close-quarter combat expert. Lion Therian.

Julietta Guerrera "Letty"—Defense agent. Weapons expert. Human.

Calvin Summers—Defense agent. Sniper. Human.

Ethan Hobbs—Defense agent. Demolitions expert and public safety bomb technician. Has two older brothers: Rafe and Sebastian Hobbs. Tabby Tiger Therian.

Cael Maddock—Recon agent. Tech expert. Dex's

younger brother. Adopted by Anthony Maddock. Cheetah Therian.

Rosa Santiago—Recon agent. Crisis negotiator and medic. Human.

COMMANDING OFFICERS

Lieutenant Sonya Sparks—Lieutenant for Unit Alpha. Cougar Therian.

Sergeant Anthony Maddock "Tony"—Sergeant for Destructive Delta. Dex and Cael's adoptive father. Human.

MEDICAL EXAMINERS

Dr. Hudson Colbourn—Chief medical examiner for Destructive Delta. Wolf Therian.

Dr. Nina Bishop—Medical examiner for Destructive Delta. Human.

AGENTS FROM OTHER SQUADS

Ellis Taylor—Team leader for Beta Ambush. Leopard Therian.

Levi Stone—Team leader for Beta Pride. White tiger Therian.

Rafe Hobbs—Team leader for Alpha Ambush. The oldest Hobbs brother. Tiger Therian.

Sebastian Hobbs "Seb"—Defense agent for Theta Destructive. Middle Hobbs brother. Tiger Therian.

Osmond Zachary "Zach"—Defense agent for Alpha Sleuth in Unit Beta. Has six brothers working for the THIRDS. Brown bear Therian.

OTHER IMPORTANT CAST MEMBERS

Gabe Pearce—Sloane's ex-partner on Destructive Delta. Killed on duty. Human.

Isaac Pearce—Gabe's older brother. Detective for the Human Police Force. Human. Former head of The Order of Adrasteia. Killed during a THIRDS op.

Louis Huerta "Lou"—Dex's ex-boyfriend. Human.

Bradley Darcy—Bartender and owner of Bar Dekatria. Jaguar Therian.

Austen Payne—Squadron Specialist agent (SSA) for Destructive Delta. Cheetah Therian.

Angel Reyes—Member of the Order. Former member of the gang Westward Creed.

EXTREMIST GROUPS AND GANGS

The Order of Adrasteia—Group of Humans against Therians. Has one primary leader.

The Ikelos Coalition—Vigilante group of Unregistered Therians fighting the Order. Has a leader and second in command.

Westward Creed—Gang of Human thugs who went around assaulting Therian citizens during the riots of 1985. Were arrested for causing the deaths of several Therians but released due to "missing" evidence. Eight members all together but only five became members of the Order: Angel Reyes, Alberto Cristo, Craig Martin, Toby Leith, Richard Esteban, Larry Berg, Ox Perry, Brick Jackson.

GLOSSARY

Therians—Shifters brought about through the mutation of Human DNA as a result of the Eppione.8 vaccine.

Post-shift Trauma Care (PSTC)—The effects of Therian post-shift trauma are similar to the aftereffects of an epileptic seizure, only on a smaller scale, including muscle soreness, bruising, brief disorientation, and hunger. Eating after a shift is extremely important as not eating could lead to the Therian collapsing and a host of other health issues. PSTC is the care given to Therians after they shift back to Human form.

THIRDS (Therian-Human Intelligence Recon Defense Squadron)—An elite, military funded agency comprised of an equal number of Human and Therian agents and intended to uphold the law for all its citizens without prejudice.

Themis—A powerful, multimillion-dollar government interface used by the THIRDS. It's linked to numerous intelligence agencies across the globe and runs a series of highly advanced algorithms to scan surveillance submitted by agents.

First Gen—First Generation of purebred Therians born with a perfected version of the mutation.

BearCat—THIRDS tactical vehicle.

Human Police Force (HPF)—A branch of law enforcement consisting of Humans officials dealing only with crimes committed by Humans.

ALSO BY CHARLIE COCHET

FOUR KINGS SECURITY

Love in Spades

Be Still My Heart

Join the Club

Diamond in the Rough

FOUR KINGS SECURITY UNIVERSE

Beware of Geeks Bearing Gifts

THE KINGS: WILD CARDS

Stacking the Deck

LOCKE AND KEYES AGENCY

Kept in the Dark

PARANORMAL PRINCES

The Prince and His Bedeviled Bodyguard

The Prince and His Captivating Carpenter

The King and His Vigilant Valet

THIRDS

Hell & High Water

Blood & Thunder

Rack & Ruin

Rise & Fall

Against the Grain

Catch a Tiger by the Tail

Smoke & Mirrors

Thick & Thin

Darkest Hour Before Dawn

Gummy Bears & Grenades

Tried & True

THIRDS BEYOND THE BOOKS

THIRDS Beyond the Books Volume 1

THIRDS Beyond the Books Volume 2

THIRDS UNIVERSE

Love and Payne

COMPROMISED

Center of Gravity

NORTH POLE CITY TALES

Mending Noel

The Heart of Frost

The Valor of Vixen

Loving Blitz

Disarming Donner

Courage and the King

North Pole City Tales Complete Series Paperback

SOLDATI HEARTS

The Soldati Prince

The Foxling Soldati

STANDALONE

Forgive and Forget

Love in Retrograde

AUDIOBOOKS

Check out the audio versions on Audible.

ABOUT THE AUTHOR

Charlie Cochet is the international bestselling author of the THIRDS series. Born in Cuba and raised in the US, Charlie enjoys the best of both worlds, from her daily Cuban latte to her passion for classic rock.

Currently residing in Central Florida, Charlie is at the beck and call of a rascally Doxiepoo bent on world domination. When she isn't writing, she can usually be found devouring a book, releasing her creativity through art, or binge watching a new TV series. She runs on coffee, thrives on music, and loves to hear from readers.

www.charliecochet.com

Sign up for Charlie's newsletter:
https://newsletter.charliecochet.com

facebook.com/charliecochet
twitter.com/charliecochet
instagram.com/charliecochet
bookbub.com/authors/charliecochet
goodreads.com/CharlieCochet
pinterest.com/charliecochet

Made in the USA
Middletown, DE
22 July 2022